PENGUIN

MONTER

Lindsay Hatton is a graduate of Wi
from the Creative Writing Program at New York University. She currently resides in Cambridge, Massachusetts, with her husband and two daughters, but was born and raised in Monterey, California, where she spent many summers working behind the scenes at the Monterey Bay Aquarium.

Praise for *Monterey Bay*

"*Monterey Bay* . . . deftly conjures up a Cannery Row that can still exist in fiction. . . . Hatton gives us plenty of memorable *Cannery Row*–like parties to revisit, and Steinbeck himself makes vivid and startling appearances. . . . With intelligent, painterly prose, Hatton adds the story of Margot to the cast of characters who inhabited Cannery Row, suggesting that it is love that ultimately best connects past to present. To read *Monterey Bay* is to be invited to go back in time, and to join the party."

—Marie Mutsuki Mockett, *San Francisco Chronicle*

"A tasty stew of people, fish, and romance . . . A strength of Hatton's approach is her delicate yet dramatic descriptions of sea creatures, most of which few readers will have encountered. . . . Local color bleeds through on every page. . . . Overall, a mood of thwarted love reigns. You feel she knows her stuff, and there's poetry in it."

—NPR.org

"Plunge right into 1940s Monterey, and the Cannery Row made famous by John Steinbeck, in this historical novel about famously charming biologist Ed Ricketts. In limpid prose and acutely captured sensual detail, Hatton tells the story of fifteen-year-old Margot Fiske, who arrives at Cannery Row with her entrepreneurial father, but snarls up his plans by getting mixed up with Ricketts—first as his sketch artist, then as his lover."

—*Huffington Post*'s Summer 2016 Books You Won't Want to Miss

"Hatton's first novel, *Monterey Bay*, is just so beautiful. . . . Her book is full of sentences I wish I had written, and it's such a bold act of imagination, unfolding across decades, mixing history and fiction with a confidence that's awe-inspiring. All novels suffer from pithy summary. *Monterey Bay* is about a young woman and some old men who end up creating an aquarium on the titular body of water. But really, it's a book about ambition, art, sex, obsession, and the devastation wrought on this planet by people—and the unsettling fact that no matter what we do to it, the planet will outlast us."

—Rumaan Alam, *The Millions*

"Intense . . . Margot Fiske [is] a lively . . . character."

—*The Dallas Morning News*

"[Hatton's] knowledge of the area and its history lend her novel an impressive richness of detail. . . . [Margot] is not a character to be trifled with, and the blunt ways she deals with obstacles in her path are what give *Monterey Bay* its narrative acceleration and emotional drive. . . . *Monterey Bay* gets to the heart of a remarkable place, a vanished time and a singular relationship."

—*The Portland Press Herald*

"This is not a timid text. . . . Margot is the fully fleshed out, unpickled woman Steinbeck might have written: moody, sensitive, entrepreneurial, introverted, crafty, sometimes cruel . . . Margot is the living organism. . . . Hatton handles her source material—Steinbeck's and Ricketts' work particularly—with the kind of deep admiration that breeds familiarity and contempt. This is the kind of rich engagement that decenters without anger, that recognizes Steinbeck's brilliance but unapologetically fills in his blind spots." —*The Week*

"[Hatton], who grew up in Monterey Bay herself, has written an impressively detailed and beautiful love story for her native home—but, like all complex love stories, there are myriad moments of darkness."

—*Refinery29*'s Books to Read in July

"The descriptions of marine life are sensuously precise. . . . Hatton shapes a jagged coming-of-age and growing-old story with fine vignettes held together by Margot's pluck and her commitment to feelings and memories that matter deeply. Along with creating a fully realized, realistic heroine seen across decades, Hatton is a writer of often exceptional prose." —*Kirkus Reviews* (starred review)

"An unforgettable debut." —*Library Journal*

MONTEREY BAY

LINDSAY HATTON

PENGUIN BOOKS

PENGUIN BOOKS
An imprint of Penguin Random House LLC
375 Hudson Street
New York, New York 10014
penguin.com

First published in the United States of America by Penguin Press,
an imprint of Penguin Random House LLC, 2016
Published in Penguin Books 2017

ISBN 9780143110484 (paperback)
ISBN 9781594206788 (hardcover)
ISBN 9780698407503 (ebook)

Printed in the United States of America
1 3 5 7 9 10 8 6 4 2

Designed by Meighan Cavanaugh

This is a work of fiction based on actual events.

For Geordie

This coast crying out for tragedy like all beautiful places:
    and like the passionate spirit of humanity
Pain for its bread: God's, many victims', the painful
    deaths, the horrible transfigurements: I said in my
    heart,
"Better invent than suffer: imagine victims
Lest your own flesh be chosen the agonist, or you
Martyr some creature to the beauty of the place."

—Robinson Jeffers, "Apology for Bad Dreams"

AUTHOR'S NOTE

Once upon a time, people made myths to explain things they didn't understand. Today, when so much can be understood by way of science and history, myths serve a slightly different purpose. They unearth emotional truths that the facts themselves can't explain. This book is, among other things, a creation myth for the Monterey Bay Aquarium. While most of the operational details and biological descriptions in the novel are factual, the founding impulse behind the aquarium is fictional. Most of the founding personalities are fictional, too. As for John Steinbeck and Ed Ricketts—two real people who appear in these pages as characters—I've tried to respect their legacy by remaining as close to the known historical truth as possible.

1

1998

WHEN HE'S FIFTY YEARS DEAD, SHE DREAMS SHE'S gone back. Back to the small white house in the neighborhood that splits the difference between Monterey and Pacific Grove, back to the streets where the cannery workers used to live. She dreams of rising from the horsehair sofa in that bruised hour when the sky is still dark and the bay is still black. She dreams of the place where the old Monterey still exists, or at least the Monterey that's found its way into stories: the last quarter mile of the bike trail—the one that starts in Seaside and then moves up slightly from the coastline before running parallel to Cannery Row—where there's an odd, untended bit of land marked with the broken shell of an old steel storage cylinder. And here, in the weeds and ice plants, in the rusty metal that smells salty in the sun and bloody in the fog, she dreams of everything that has slipped away, everything that will never come back.

Then she dreams of the descent. Like the cannery workers before her, she aims for the door of a cannery or, better yet, the door of his lab. Instead, she arrives at the aquarium. Inside, it is empty: the barometric dead zone before the rush of the coming crowds, the air abuzz with the clean, nervous smell of salt. She lets the kelp crabs pinch her on purpose. She siphons the pistol shrimp exhibit and leaves her lips on the tube for a second too long so that some of the ocean gets in her mouth. She picks parasites from the accordion folds of a leopard shark's gills and wonders, for what seems like the millionth time, if breathing water is better than breathing air. She feeds the sea nettles a cup of bright green rotifers and marvels at the orange embrace of the world's most elegant killer. She sees something hovering in the distance, huge and terrible and tentacled and white.

And, as she wakes, she remembers three things he once tried to teach her.

First, that human blood contains the exact same liquid-to-salt ratio as the ocean.

Second, that murder can be necessary.

Third, that living in a tank is exactly like being in love.

2

1940

HER BODY WAS EATING ITSELF.

That's what it felt like. Head, neck, arms, legs rushing toward a pit of internal gravity. Upon her descent from the train, the pit had been no larger than a seed. Now, however, it was the size of a billiard ball and growing quickly, which meant there was work to be done. Keep steady, keep calm, notice things beyond yourself and let them distract you, let them stretch you back into a workable shape. Notice the tide pools, notice the fog. Notice the biologist picking through the water. Notice how he swings the bucket as he walks, how he whistles out of the corner of his mouth, out of key. Notice the bucket in your own hand: its emptiness, its rusty handle. Her father had told her to assist the biologist in his collections, to scan the water for the sort of boneless, brainless creatures the biologist prized. Heroes advance when it makes sense to retreat, her father had reminded her when she protested, and cowards retreat regardless of what makes sense. But he was wrong. He was wrong to have brought her here, he was wrong to have dismissed her, and now she knew without shame or regret that she would rather be a coward.

So she began her calculations. The retreat's first phase would be the most difficult: jagged, weed slicked, a long stretch of water and rocks leading to a gray strip of sand in the distance. On the beach, she could start to run. The hotel lawn could be taken at a sprint, after which she'd have to improvise: hitching a ride in the gardener's truck, stealing a delivery boy's bicycle. At the train station, she could barter something for a ticket to San Francisco, and then she would be gone. Away from her father, away from this town, away from this dreary coast and the tides that rasped across it, away from the bleak half-moon of Monterey Bay.

The plan assembled, she put her bucket down and waited for the panic to loosen its grip. Escape was possible and, at fifteen, she was old enough. The hotel, however, seemed to be suggesting otherwise. From the water's edge, she could see both the building and the shadows of its history. Once a playground for the sporting elite, it was now a sad husk of another era's opulence, a grotesque hybrid of the Spanish Revival and the Carpenter Gothic, its grandeur eroded by diverse misfortune: arson, pine mistletoe, bark-boring beetles, a rash of unsolved murders and suicides, inklings of witchcraft on the polo grounds, a stench from the nearby canneries that was, on certain days in the high season, strong enough to be visible. If the hotel had endured, it was only in theory. Margot and her father were the establishment's first paying guests in well over a month, and although this didn't bother her in principle, it did in practice. The emptiness was like an accusation, the lobby and ballroom and dining room and hallways flaunting their vacancies as if delighted by the prospect of causing her personal offense.

In truth, she had sensed catastrophe from the outset. There had been the disaster in the Philippines, of course, and then two journeys of equal foreboding: the cargo ship from Manila to San Francisco and then the southbound train that had taken them the rest of the way down the coast. The drive to the hotel in the rented Packard had been no better, her forehead pressed to the window as she took inventory. Alvarado Street: Monterey's jittery, provincial downtown strip. The Coast Valleys gas holding tanks: two cylindrical metal landmarks of uneven height and identical ugliness. The Presidio: a pantomime of military preparation, canvas-roofed convoys trudging through the unlocked gates. Lake El Estero: a man-made ditch of brackish water, its redundant shores just a stone's throw from the bay itself. She waited for her father to echo her apprehension, to support it. But he remained silent as they reached the far side of town and came to a stop on the hotel's gravel drive, and now, ankle-deep in seawater, she knew. It wasn't just the fog, it wasn't just the smell. It wasn't just the fact that, after years of working at her father's side, she had been exiled. It was a bone-deep certainty that Monterey was out to destroy her in the same manner it had already destroyed itself.

The escape, then. The Philippines beckoned, but so did other places: Indonesia, the Channel Islands, Bolivia. In each locale, her apprenticeship to her father had taught her many skills, most of them in lucrative fields. She had a flair for languages and a talent for negotiation. She wasn't a beauty queen, but with the possible exception of her height, she wasn't a sideshow freak either. The one thing that stood in her way, logistically speaking, was the biologist. She had been forced into his company almost an hour earlier and since then had genuinely grown to hate him. Here was a case in which the hammer had already fallen, the wings had already been clipped, life's capacity for meaningful action obliterated. There were several dozen yards between them, the sound of his whistling obscured by the crashing surf, his shape like its own shadow moving across the bay, but even from a distance she could see it all quite clearly. The dullard's delight with which he allowed himself to be engulfed by the shoreline, the unnecessary reverence with which he plucked a specimen from the water, gave it an inexplicable sniff, and then added it to his bucket. When a sea lion belched, he paused and bowed his head like a penitent at the steps of an oracle. Then a furtive yet urgent search of his left trousers pocket. The withdrawal of a flask. A long, guilty chug.

Run, coward, she commanded herself. *Run.*

But her legs refused. They had already been eaten by the

black pit of panic. So she stumped along, slipping and hobbling over the rocks, until, just a few steps from the beach, the sound of laughter made her freeze. In spite of herself, she turned around. The biologist's mouth was emitting the sounds of mockery. His eyes, however, were flashing with mockery's opposite: a gentle sort of surprise that almost made her proud.

He frowned at her. She turned and ran.

And then it was over. She was on her stomach, limbs askew, eye to eye with something that could have belonged in her sketchbook: a small black snail, its dark foot sliding across what she knew to be a widening pool of her own blood.

She dreamed of the biologist: his hands gripping the wheel of an old Buick, his fingers pale beneath the strobe of the passing treetops, her breath emerging as a drowned man's gargle. The smell of fish. Heavy limbs, swollen head.

"We're almost there," he said. "Whatever you do, don't fall asleep."

When she awoke, she was being carried up a staircase.

Although the pain was exceptional, it was also bright and precise. Not, in other words, a dream. It was all actually happening: the sound of feet against wood, the sensation of being hoisted up and turned around, of being shoved through a curtain or a door, of being dropped into a nest of laughter. The high scratch of a phonograph needle.

Then the most disorienting thing yet. Silence. A wide berth of it, white and expectant, the pain brimming and stretching.

She grunted and writhed and tried to escape. The biologist tightened his grip.

"Wormy," he said. "Where's Wormy?"

"Dunno, Doc."

"For the last time. I'm not a doctor."

"What happened?"

"Smashed her head."

"She's so . . . tall."

"All of you. Go home. Now."

"I'll help."

"Ethanol ampoules. The box in the garage."

Silence again.

"Arthur! The garage!"

Another rattle of footsteps, voices retreating, smells of new and old milk, new and old smoke. A low ceiling and black walls, dented waves of yellow glass, small things watching her, bleached flesh and jellied eyes. An embryo in a glass jar, fingers on her head, pressing down, slipping on something wet that had been left there. And then a fierce tugging between her eyes, the suddenness of it wrenching her upright, and now it was only in the darkness behind her eyes that she could see what was happening. She was thrashing like an animal, but the fingers were strong, grabbing one of her wrists and then the other.

"Wormy. Hold her down. Tell her not to fight."

A woman's smell moving in close.

"Don't fight."

A vial nudging itself between her teeth.

"You can hate me for this later. Just lie still."

"Who is she, Doc?"

"The Fiske girl. I tried to warn her about those shoes."

"She isn't one of your sharks, Edward. Please tell me you haven't been drinking."

"Out! Both of you. Out!"

High heels, low murmurs.

And when the sounds had faded away, when she was alone with the biologist again, all that was left were the fingers on her head and a sick suspicion. The rubbing alcohol, the needle, the thread. A process no longer of sewing something together, she realized as the room turned black, but of sewing something on.

3

INSECTS ON HER FOREHEAD. BIG, TROPICAL ONES.

She lifted a hand. She found the brittle legs. She tried to yank them away but couldn't, and that's when she remembered. The hotel, the tide pools, the biologist, the fall. Eyes still closed, she released the trail of sutures and lowered her hand, trying one last time to summon it: the prismatic color of the Philippines, its heat and certainty. But when it wouldn't come, she opened her eyes. There was a sagging rope mattress beneath her, her feet dangling over its edge, and a moist woolen blanket atop her that felt as though it weighed several hundred pounds. The light was dim and bleary, a noon-hour dullness soaking its way through a green-curtained window above the bed and casting the room in a submarine gloss. And the biologist was sitting next to her on an upended wooden beer crate, gazing at her with a dark pair of eyes.

He blinked twice but otherwise remained perfectly motionless. His beard was thick and brown, his clothes tattered. A tin plate of steak and soft-fried eggs sat in his lap, the meat deconstructed into a pile of small, equal pieces, as parents do when feeding a child.

"You're awake," he said.

She stared at the steak.

"My God, you gave me a scare." He extended a beer bottle in her direction casually and without reserve, as if they were friends. "Turns out it's little more than a concussion, but you were so delirious for a while there that I almost considered tying you down."

She swatted at the bottle and looked away. She could recall everything now, and in near perfect detail—the blackness of the rocks, the way he had lifted his flask, the union of the snail and the blood—and she couldn't decide whether it made her want to scream or fall back asleep.

"All right," he said, nodding. "Something to eat, then."

He selected a fibrous morsel from the plate and smeared it into the yolk. He lifted the fork and moved it toward her face. She tried to close her eyes again, but the pressure between them was too intense.

"My father will kill you."

"I certainly hope not."

"He's done far worse. On account of far less."

"I'm sure he has. And I'm sure I'd enjoy the story. But for now . . ."

He put the plate on the floor and rose from the crate as if he were about to leave the room. Instead, he approached the bed, put a hand behind her neck, and slid a pillow into place. She flinched, and then allowed her head to drop, the pillow releasing a brief hiss of air that smelled like pickling brine.

"For now," he continued, "you should rest."

"Where is he? He should be here."

"I inquired at the hotel, but no one knew."

She gripped the sides of the mattress and tried to pull herself upright.

"Careful now."

"I'll find him myself."

"No, you won't."

"Yes, I will."

But the nausea pushed her back down. A galaxy of small orange sparks was sizzling in the corners of her eyes, and he was smiling again, cocking his head and peering at her as if her discomfort were something to be studied instead of something to be solved, the smell of the meat strong enough to make her gag.

"Please remove that steak."

"If you need to be sick . . ."

He indicated a metal bucket at his feet: one of the same ones he had carried through the tide pools. She retched. He held the bucket beneath her chin. She emptied herself into it. Then, with what seemed like the biggest and most concentrated effort she had ever expended, she wiped her mouth on the back of her hand, sank into the mattress, and let the universe knock her down.

When she woke again, it was dark.

Her vision was steadier, the pain in her head had softened and condensed, the sickness had abated. Dusk had made its blue black deposit, pale streetlamps shining beyond the window like lesser moons. On the small table next to the bed, she could see the satchel that contained her sketchbook, its leather water-stained from her fall. Outside, she could hear voices and cars, but not a lot of them. She could hear the ocean, too, and the biologist was still sitting on the crate next to the bed, exactly as before. The only difference was that the tin plate and the beer bottle were gone and in their place was a typewritten manuscript, which he was studying with a focus so complete, it was almost certainly fake, like how a sinner might pray. Before, in the tide pools, she had come to several conclusions, none of which had been proven wrong. Now, though, there was the question of setting. At the water's edge, he had appeared to her in blunt-chiseled relief. Here, however, surrounded by his own necessities, the ceiling low and the light dim, it was more like something rendered in oil instead of stone: his outlines definite yet malleable, the paint dry but not quite hard.

She coughed. He looked up from the manuscript and fixed

her with the same peculiar gaze as before. She shifted her limbs, testing them. He chewed on his beard with his upper teeth. The sparks returned to her periphery and fizzled away.

"Well, well, well." He smiled. "Up and at 'em, I see."

She looked away.

"Can I get you some water?"

She shook her head. He studied her for a moment longer and then returned his attention to the manuscript. She examined the room. Before, in the midst of her delirium, her only impressions had been those of danger and anarchy. Now only the anarchy remained. Rows of salt-stiff books, towers of warped glass jars, ragged undershorts and photographic negatives dangling side by side from a length of fishing line. A typewriter on a folding table, its keyboard a good deal larger than normal and outfitted with many foreign-looking keys. A collection of deer antlers in a hammered copper basin. Dozens of postcard-sized reproductions of famous works of art crookedly pinned to the wood-paneled walls.

"Where am I?"

He smiled again and tapped the papers against his knee. Then he rose from the beer crate and wedged the manuscript onto a crowded bookshelf across from the bed.

"My home," he answered genially, returning to his seat. "My lab."

"Lab?"

"Biological. I study things from the sea."

She leaned back, narrowed her eyes, and inspected the room again. *The biologist* was not a designation she had questioned when her father had first introduced them. Now, however, she was skeptical. There was nothing here that indicated the contemplation of science, much less its practice.

"I see," she replied.

"Skeptical, eh? Well, I don't blame you. Around here, I'm afraid I'm best known for embalming cats." A pause. "And then there are the tours of the tide pools, but I tend to reserve those for only the most oceanically inclined of the hotel's guests."

She slumped against the bed and pressed the heels of her hands against her temples.

"What's wrong? Should I get the bucket?"

"I'm not *inclined* toward the tide pools. Not one bit."

"That's funny. Your father said you were obsessed."

"He was trying to get rid of me."

"Now why would he want to do that?"

She shook her head, her hands still knitted around her skull as if holding her brains in place.

"I really think you should have some water."

"Fine."

"How about something to eat? Something that's not a steak?"

"Just the water."

His smile was so big that he almost appeared to be in pain.

When he stood, she anticipated the relief of being left alone. But he remained in the room, stopping in the doorway and craning his neck just slightly beyond it.

"Arthur? Some water, if you please."

In response, the drumming of fast footsteps, the squeak of a loosening tap, water splashing into a sink and continuing to splash for longer than it should have taken to fill a drinking glass. The biologist returned to her side.

"Sorry about the wait. It always takes a minute or two for it to run clear."

Another smile, another alarming inflation of his face. She looked away again, her eyes landing on the nearest wall. Out of all the oddities this room contained, the little postcard galleries were perhaps the oddest. They were arranged with no deference to style or period and were, for the most part, in exceptionally bad taste: three too many Renoirs, the most predictable Manet in existence, something that looked like a lesser Picasso but was probably a Braque. There was also, however, a work she admired: Caravaggio's rendering of Bacchus, his ruddy face and sunburned hands those of a cheerful outdoorsman, a torpor in his heavy-lidded stare that seemed both inept and threatening all at once.

"The god of wine," the biologist explained.

"I know." She looked down and straightened her blanket.

"Caravaggio."

"I know."

"A great artist, but an unpleasant man. Nervous, temperamental, violent. Kept bad company."

"I know."

"Art, then. Do you practice? Or do you just preach?"

She made fists, the blanket bunching between her fingers. "Neither."

"Don't lie."

"How dare—"

"Beg pardon." A voice from the doorway.

The biologist swiveled around and beckoned the interloper forward. She recognized this young man, but just barely: his hive of red hair, his stout limbs and blocky posture. He had been there postfall, amid the confusion and fear, but she couldn't remember what role he had played or if he had been as nervous as he was right now. His hands trembled as he approached the bed and offered her the cup. She took it, drank, and passed it back without comment.

"Thank you, Arthur," the biologist said. "She's quite grateful."

"Is there anything else?" Arthur murmured.

"You're sure you don't want that beer?" the biologist asked her.

"I'm sure."

"How about some oil? From a basking shark liver?"

"From a what?"

"Arthur. The oil, please."

"No, I—," she insisted.

"Arthur, there's a fresh box down in the garage."

"There's a fresher one at the market. I delivered it yesterday. I'll go back and—"

"I said no!" she barked.

The two men froze, eyes wide. The biologist cocked his head in the direction of the door. Arthur scurried out of it. Margot clenched her calf muscles until they cramped.

"Sounds strange, doesn't it?" The biologist's words were coming much slower now, and with a new undertone of caution. "But it's known in the East for its general tonic properties, especially for allergies and arthritis. It's chock-full of something akin to cortin, a substance used to keep cats alive after they've been adrenalectomized. Also something of an aphrodisiac, if John's Hollywood friends are to be believed."

"Keep treating your son like that and he'll revolt."

When he threw back his head and laughed, a strip of white skin flashed beneath the border of his beard.

"Oh, is that what's got you so worked up? Arthur's not my son, I'm afraid, not at all. He's an orphan of the classic type, dust bowl and whatnot, plucked straight from the pages of John's book. Came to town to make a living in the canneries but seems to spend most of his time here in the lab. Fixing the Buick, catching the cats, being generally underfoot."

She considered the Caravaggio again. Its initial appeal had faded a bit, its cheeks and lips now bordering on the feminine. Escape was pointless. Pointless then, pointless now.

"Funny," he said. "I think I've forgotten your name."

"Margot."

"You're French."

"And Swedish."

"Ah, yes. Form and function, all in one."

Her legs went stiff again, causing the blanket above them to shiver.

"Why don't you explain it, then?" he continued. "Tell me how wrong I am."

"I'm in business with my father. Or at least I used to be."

"They say he's got the sardine game in his sights. I hope he isn't too upset when he finds out most of them are already in cans."

"I don't know anything about that."

"A rift between you, then. Was it ugly?"

Too much talking, too many questions. He was her captor, she wanted to remind him, not her confidant.

"And does he see the value in your art?" he continued, undeterred. "Beyond the commercial, that is?"

"Excuse me?"

"The sketchbook. In the satchel. It fell out when you took your tumble, but I was too much of a gentleman to open it without asking permission first."

"I don't think—"

"If you're too shy, I understand completely." He gestured at his walls. "As you can see, I have some dreadfully high standards."

She retrieved the satchel from the bedside table, withdrew the sketchbook, and tossed it to him.

"Mine are higher."

"That's more like it!" he crowed.

And when he opened the book, she was surprised at her nervousness. *He's no one*, she told herself. *He likes Renoir.* But her pulse disagreed, her heart hammering as he thumbed the pages with the same intense, almost hyperactive concentration he had lavished on the typewritten manuscript, lingering on each image for several seconds longer than seemed necessary. Many of the earliest sketches didn't warrant the scrutiny: a fly-haloed bowl of *pancit*, the head and torso of an emaciated water buffalo, the bloodied corpse of a fighting cock. Then there were a handful of which she was actually proud: a shiny-skinned *lechón* spinning on its milk-doused spit, trash fires burning in the alleyways, their well-contained heaps dotting the city with distant flares of orange heat. Her best work, however, took the form of two recent portraits, both of which had been completed on her last day in the Philippines. There was her father standing alone within the loamy wasteland of what should have been his tobacco fields. Then, on the very next page, there was one of Luzon's millions of rural poor, a girl no older than herself, a newborn twin baby at each nipple, breasts swollen to the point of hard, shiny pain, the look on the young mother's face that of suffering and startled ecstasy.

She glanced up from the sketchbook. He was frowning at the

image, just as he had frowned at her in the seconds before her accident.

"I'm sorry if it's beneath your expectations," she muttered.

"Quite the contrary. It vastly exceeds them."

She didn't know what to say.

"After Sargent?" he asked.

"That was the idea. Yes."

"Can I have it?"

"What do you mean?"

"For my collection."

She looked at the wall. "I don't think there's room."

"Then we'll send one packing. Your choice."

"One of the Renoirs."

"Which one?"

She pointed.

"I thought you'd say that."

Smiling, he tore the page carefully from her sketchbook and stood. He unpinned the Renoir from the wall, shoved it in his pocket, and secured the nursing mother in its place, after which he didn't return to the crate. Instead, he sat alongside her on the bed, his hands behind his head, his legs just inches from hers. He was admiring the sketch as proudly as if he had drawn it himself.

"The Philippines?" he asked.

"Yes."

"Hmmm. A fellow from the bureau of fisheries was here a

few months ago, direct from Manila. The way he talked about it made me want to do something irresponsible. Close up the lab. Scare up the steamship fare. Go over there for a while to collect."

She nodded, lips between her teeth.

"Did you ever see one of those horse fights?" he asked, eyes sparkling. "Rumor has it they're downright ghastly."

"No." She thought he would accuse her of lying again, but he didn't.

"Well, I'm sure you—"

"Doc! *Doc!*" Arthur's voice, coming from somewhere beneath them.

"Oh, for God's sake . . ."

"Doc!"

"Coming!"

He swung himself off the bed, rope mattress whining. At the doorway, he stopped and looked over his shoulder.

"How much do you want to bet there's nothing actually the matter?"

She began to speak.

"No, no!" he interrupted. "You'll suggest something I won't be able to afford."

When he had gone, she watched the doorway and listened. This time, however, there were no hints—no footsteps, no running water—so she picked up the sketchbook, counted the remaining blank pages, and slapped it shut. Nine more drawings and then it would be over, at least temporarily, the book eased into a fire, rising into smoke, settling down into ash. She had done it twice now, and each time it had been an absolution born of pure, puzzling impulse: the blistering cardboard, the papers thin and orange. Now, however, she was reconsidering. His interest had been sudden and more than a little suspicious, but affirming nonetheless, which made her wonder. Had there been something in those first few books worth keeping?

She listened again. He was not someone who interested her, especially in an aesthetic sense. For some reason, though, a more definitive assessment now seemed long overdue, so she retrieved her pencil and began to draw. She worked for thirty minutes, maybe forty, and when she was done, she held the sketchbook out at arm's length, almost entirely certain of what she'd find. The image, however, shocked her: features as precise as they were handsome, a cool, cunning glint in the eyes, the subtle execution of which seemed far beyond what she had always assumed were the limitations of her talent.

A shadow across the page. She looked up. He was standing there, watching her. She closed the sketchbook and pushed it beneath the blanket.

"A bit too late for modesty, don't you think? I've already seen everything you've got."

Since he'd left the room, something about him had changed. His attention now seemed reluctant and divided, his tone blunt and low and almost suggestive. A large glass jug was in his hand, its label reading "FORMALDEHYDE" in unambiguous script. His face was nowhere near as open and flushed as before. Instead, a gloom had settled behind his eyes, which made his hair appear even darker, his skin paler, his body even more agile and kinetic. What's more, music had begun to play without her having realized it: a string quartet from the phonograph in the other room, its melody unrushed and familiar.

She looked out the window. Midnight. Or later.

"Shame is almost as useless as pride," he warned.

"I'm not ashamed."

"Then why did you hide your drawing?"

"Because you interrupted me. Before I could finish."

"Unfinished work makes you anxious?"

"Very."

"Toil away, then."

"Don't move."

"Not a muscle."

But it didn't matter if he moved or not, because she didn't even have to look at him. Everything she wanted to add to or subtract from the sketch was already outlined in her head, so she drew for a few minutes longer while he stood beside the bed, swaying and humming atonally to the music.

"I thought I told you to hold still," she said.

"You didn't tell me to be quiet, though."

"Be quiet."

"Fine. I'll try. But I'm afraid it's like the *Patiria miniata*. Cut off one arm at just the right angle to the central disk and two arms grow back in its place."

He took a long drink from the jug of formaldehyde. She looked down at her sketch. Yet again, the sight of it was alarming, transcendent. Her father always claimed that certain industries were built for his manipulations, even if they seemed nonmanipulable on the surface, and now, for the first time, she fully understood what he meant.

"What's wrong?" he asked. "Are you all right?"

"I changed my mind about the beer."

"Oh. It's too late, I'm afraid. The last bottle was dispensed with hours ago. But I can certainly offer you some of this."

He brandished the formaldehyde. She took it from him and put it to her lips. The liquid hissed down her throat like a snake.

"I could have sworn you had better sense." He laughed. "But then again, it's always the ones who look so well-adjusted . . ."

"What's in there?" she sputtered, wiping her eyes.

"Very expensive tequila. I keep it in the formaldehyde jug to fool the others."

The song ended, its final chord just a step shy of resolution. A brief pause. And then another song began, its tempo and motifs almost indistinguishable from the first. When he reclaimed his seat beside her on the bed, it was without permission.

"Much better," he said, indicating the sketchbook on her lap. "I look a bit less like General Sherman."

"You should be flattered. Sherman was ruthless."

"Come work for me." His voice was clear and even, totally absent of its earlier, sullen depth. "I need some drawings for my catalog."

She looked out the window at the deepening night.

"That's not the kind of work I do," she replied.

"Of course it is!"

"No, it's not. To call myself an artist would be like you calling yourself a . . ."

"A what?"

She felt a redness rising. She put her hands over her face.

"Quick! Have another drink!"

Her second taste was less like a snake and more like a trail of determined ants. This time, she didn't cough. Instead, she remained motionless as the tequila reached her belly, as the warmth erupted and then fizzled, a sorrow claiming her that had nothing to do with tears.

"I know that look," he said. "You're either homesick or in love."

"Wrong on both counts."

"Then what's this?"

When he picked up the sketchbook she was appalled, at first, to think he was referring to his own portrait. But then he flipped back to one of the earliest sketches: her and her father's former residence, all balustrades and terra-cotta, the Spaniards and their elaborate leavings.

"I had to practice on something," she grumbled. "Didn't matter what."

"What happened here? Not so very long ago, but so very far away?"

The phone rang. She looked at the empty beer crate and then at her sketch on the wall.

"Another drink for courage," he insisted.

She waited until the phone stopped ringing. Then she drank. To confess herself was not a possibility. Too pathetic. Too risky. Furthermore, there was no chance a man like this would understand the stakes, which was why, when she started talking, she knew the liquor had already done its work: summoning the words, doling them out with an almost magnanimous ease. She described their arrival in the Philippines, their occupation of a condemned colonial manor on Manila's outskirts. She outlined their newest and most ambitious project to date: the acquisition of nearly a thousand acres of mango orchards and their subsequent transformation into tobacco fields. She had been doing this sort of work, she assured the biologist, almost since birth. She knew exactly how to assist her father in his industrial transformations, which meant everything went precisely as it should have until the night he fell ill. At first, it didn't seem like much: just a moderate fever, an aching in the joints, chills that made his limbs tremble but not shake. By morning, however, his skin was blazing and his eyes were dull, his arms and legs thrashing, his mouth spouting foamy green bile, his slender torso coiled desperately around the expulsions.

Later that night, he slipped into a coma. The next day, she

took the helm. It wasn't something she had attempted before: this total assumption of responsibility, this mimicry of experience and knowledge. But she had been raised to believe she was not only capable of such things but destined for them, and in this moment of decision, belief seemed tantamount to proof. She paced the mango orchards with the tobacco farmers and considered their advice on fertilizing with wood ash versus powdered horse manure. She debated with the local politicians as to which nearby village should be used to obtain the children who would lay the screens of protective cheesecloth across the delicate seedlings. She traveled to the city by mule-drawn cart and answered the banker's questions with a succinct, merciless professionalism. For the next three months, she triumphed. The venture proceeded exactly as planned; success floated before her eyes like an opalescent sphere, a bubble that contained both the promise of the future and the substance of past. But then the bubble burst. Without warning or reason, the farmers began to mislead her. The children returned to their villages and wouldn't be coaxed back to the fields. The banker claimed she needed to refile forms she had already filed twice. No matter how hard she worked, she couldn't stem the tide. Each day seemed to drag her further down failure's depressive, unpaved spiral, until it was clear to her and everyone else that she couldn't manage it on her own.

On the day she finally gave up, she didn't tell her father. He had regained consciousness a week earlier, but he was still delirious with fever, and her shame was too great. So instead of confessing herself or trying to put things right, she roamed the manor that for the past several months they had called home. Since their arrival, she hadn't had either the time or the inclination to explore it fully. Now she made a point of examining every room. In most ways, she was unmoved. It was just like all the other residences her father tended to favor: intact enough to ensure basic human comforts, yet squalid enough to invoke a sort of ethical high ground. The rooms were large and humid, all of them frilled with elaborately carved teak and ravaged by the twin stresses of abandonment and equatorial proximity. The only thing that seemed unusual was the almost biblical sense of loss, one that went above and beyond human haunting. She didn't know why this was the case until she noticed the large, pale stamps on the walls where paintings had once hung, which led her, on instinct, to the root cellar. And there, stacked in the blue darkness among the piles of yucca and taro and sweet potatoes, she found the stash: hundreds of framed forgeries of well-known masterpieces. The sight was unexpectedly compelling, so she began to dig through the canvases. She didn't know what she was looking for. All she knew was that, as she searched and studied, she could forget her recent failure, she could forget her father moaning and perspiring upstairs, she could forget there were things in life that evaded direct translation. She worked quickly. With the help of some books in the mansion's library, she decided which artists were the most skilled and upsetting. She learned whom to emulate and whom to dismiss. When she had narrowed it down to a solid two dozen, she bought a sketchbook and charcoal pencil and a small leather satchel from a woman at the local market and allowed herself only an hour of immersion per day, two if she felt decadent, but it was among the most efficient and satisfactory learning she had ever done. She made copies of the copies, and then, when copying no longer seemed productive, she began to choose her own subject matter, her fingers clenched hard around the pencil as she made meticulous record of things she had witnessed both in the countryside and on the Manila streets. She tried out different styles, different methods of expression and organization: Fra Angelico, Holbein the Younger, Holbein the Elder, Rivera, Modigliani, Memling. The root cellar deepened itself: darker, wetter, colder, a realm of lawlessness and foreign language, much like being fathoms underwater. And it was in this way that a full six months passed, the Philippines taking on the characteristics of a place she loved, not because it felt comfortable, not because it felt safe, but because it showed the clearest and most direct route to what she had begun to believe was her destiny: a life of solitude, a life of work—hers, not her father's—rising up around her like walls.

But then her father recovered, his physical and mental health twice as robust as before.

"And you were found out?" There was an excitement in the biologist's eyes that, for the first time, actually reminded her of a biologist, of someone who was gathering data and imagining it being put to use.

"Yes. By that point, the fields were beyond salvaging."

"He blamed you."

"And rightfully so."

"And what about the sketchbook?"

"He didn't care."

"Maybe someday the two of you will go back. Fix things up."

She shook her head. "My father never returns to a place he's already been. What's more, the embassy had started to evacuate on account of the Japanese."

"And your mother?"

"What about her?"

"Mothers usually have opinions about things like this."

"Not mine."

"Why not?"

"She's dead."

"Oh no. I'm sorry."

The furrows in his brow were so dark and deep, they looked like tattoos. She shrugged and looked away.

"Just the two of you, then, and so late in the game," he continued. "No wonder you're unhappy."

"Not unhappy. Just unproductive."

"Fair enough."

Just then, the air began to shriek. Three deafening whistle blasts from the street outside: short, long, short.

"The Del Mar cannery," the biologist explained, hands shielding his ears. He was trying to look disappointed by the interruption, but he was clearly as thankful for it as she was. "Arthur will be crushed. The poor lamb's already worked four shifts this week."

"The canneries are open this late?"

"The canneries are open whenever there's something to can. The whistles blow, they open the throttles, and everything starts to shake."

She heard stairs being taken at a hurry, and then Arthur was in the doorway, panting. When he saw the two of them sitting together on the bed, his eyes widened.

"Some of the *Styela* are still in the m-menthol," he stuttered.

"It's all right. I'll finish up."

"And I'm afraid one or two of the *Okenia* got a bit . . . flattened."

"It's all right, Arthur."

"I'll be happy to stay if you need some—"

"No, no, no. We don't want you on the foreman's bad side. Again."

Arthur nodded at the biologist and then at Margot, a great seriousness on his face. For a moment, she felt serious, too, as if a piece of crucial information were about to be revealed, but then Arthur was gone and so was the feeling.

The biologist let out a long exhale, lips fluttering.

"My God, did you see that look he gave you? Someone needs

to inform him you're not a damsel. And you're certainly not in distress." He squinted at her forehead. "Or are you?"

"I've endured worse."

"You certainly have."

She held his gaze until the aforementioned shaking began, until the tension that had existed prior to the whistle blast re-knotted itself. Then she looked out the window. The green curtains were almost perfectly translucent now, the fabric dissolved by the streetlights, the canneries' rattling seeming to both solidify the enclosure and erode it.

"It's all my fault," he said.

"What is?"

"We were really starting to get along, but then I pushed too hard. And you told me too much."

"I don't require careful handling."

"But you do require something. A balancing of the confessional scales, I think."

He stood and scanned the room in what looked like desperation. Then he went over to the bookshelf, retrieved the manuscript, and dropped it onto her lap.

"I wrote it," he explained.

He sat down next to her again. She looked at the first page, which was blank except for a title. *Breaking Through.*

"You showed me yours," he continued. "And now I'm showing you mine."

She flipped to the second page, expecting to be disappointed.

But from the very first sentence, she couldn't look away. It was like reading the transcript of something she had dreamed and then lived and then dreamed all over again. There was almost nothing in the way of economy, even less in the way of design, the hand-scrawled edits in the margins nearly equal in volume to the typewritten text. The images created by his words, however, were indelible: the ghetto inferno, the split-open head, *the tragedy*, he wrote that someone else had written, *that breaks a man's face and a white fire flies out of it.* A trinity, but not necessarily the Christian one, opposing forces meeting in honesty and a new magic birthing itself in the juncture. Most of all, there was his description of the aftermath. She had felt it before, and in otherwise disparate parts of the world: how communities acquired harder outlines following near erasure; how individuals, in moments of shock, catapulted themselves into unearned clarity. She had felt it, but she had never voiced it, and seeing it on the page was like seeing her own reflection in the harshest possible light.

When there were just a few paragraphs left, most of which praised the trade unions in a way her father would have derided, she stopped reading.

"So?" he asked.

She returned the manuscript to him. Her brain didn't feel right anymore. The synapses were firing a bit too fast, the ideas too big and loud.

"You're wrong," she said.

"About what?"

"Tragedy doesn't always clarify. And pain doesn't always produce."

"You must have misread me, then, because I never said it did."

She took another swig from the jug. And because she was feeling particularly righteous, abnormally eloquent—the drink and his essay and their pulpy fusion making her tongue warmer and her mind looser than ever before—she supposed it wouldn't hurt to expand her argument. She supposed it wouldn't hurt to begin even earlier than the Philippines, even earlier than her own birth. Her grandfather's exodus from Sweden, his relocation to New York City's most squalid tenement, the amputation of his surname—*Filtzkog*—into the leaner, more American-sounding *Fiske.* Then, the birth of her father, Anders, and the onset of his precocious entrepreneurship, his knack for using known infrastructures to exploit unknown sources of income: mining zinc in the British uplands instead of copper, farming ostriches in South Africa instead of goats, distilling vodka in the Spey River Valley instead of Scotch. All of this emerged from her fluently and in a way that seemed to prove her point. It was only when she reached the part about her mother that her confidence flagged and another drink was taken. As for this tale, she had heard it only once, so it was easy to feel unsure. New Orleans, she told the biologist. The Babineaux family, Louisiana's most viciously aloof clan of French transplants, their longing for the homeland fierce enough to present itself as a genuine psychological disorder. Marcelle Babineaux, seventeen years old: a narrow waist, a substantial topknot of hair, a caustic temper. A hasty courtship, an even hastier marriage, and then a departure for Bolivia, where Anders purchased a coffee plant in the hope of switching it over to chocolate production. Work was not halted when the floods started or when Marcelle began to vomit all morning and sleep all afternoon. And so it was that Margot was born at 11:59 P.M. on February 13, the rain drumming away at the hut of the village midwife, Anders shivering beneath a leafy overhang outside, thrilling to the shrieks of his first and only child as she emerged into a wet and borderless world.

Here, she paused, waiting for the charm of her birth story to sink in. But instead of looking awed, the biologist looked impatient.

"What's your point?" he said.

The point, she replied, was that Marcelle would never actually meet her daughter. By the time Margot emerged, her mother was already dead, a victim of hemorrhaging and fever. Per local custom, the midwife let the body stay in the hut long enough for the baby to take a few fortifying suckles at the breast, long enough for Anders to kiss both mother and child on their sweaty brows, and then Marcelle was carried to the outskirts of the village and burned in a fire that, because of the rain, took nearly two days to adequately dispose of the corpse.

She stopped talking. The biologist was staring at her, unsmiling.

"A straight line, then," he said finally, taking the jug from her and drinking what seemed to her like slightly more than his share. "Between two fixed points."

"What do you mean?"

He waved at her drawing, at the babies and the breasts.

"A coincidence," she replied.

"And what about the fires? And what about the collections and the copies? All of them just as good as the real thing but also incalculably worse?"

"More coincidences."

"No! The fakes in the root cellar, the fakes on my walls. Circles are circles, Margot Fiske. That's why everything always comes back around."

"Circles? I thought you said it was a straight line."

"All right." He took a deep breath and retrenched, and she was surprised at how much it thrilled her. The man in the tide pools—the dull, pointless obstacle—was gone entirely, replaced by a bizarre yet compelling intellect, one that seemed to both reek and glow. "A personal example, then. When I was a boy, my uncle gave me a field catalog, a drawer full of dusty old animal corpses, and the very same magnifying glass I still keep chained to my belt loop. And now, here we are. As if not a moment has passed, much less thirty-odd years."

She had had beer and wine before, but never anything much

stronger. It was as if she could actually see and smell the corpses: their papery skin, their powdery hides.

"That's precisely what I don't understand, though," she protested. "How can anything in that essay be related to anything in the tide pools? How can any of it be connected, except by someone who's trying to make excuses for himself?"

He took the jug from her and put it on the windowsill. Then he hopped up from the bed, left the room, and returned after what seemed like only a few seconds.

"Here," he said when he was sitting beside her again. "I got you a live one."

He placed something yellow and cylindrical into her hand. There was the urge to flinch, to toss it across the room in disgust, but she kept her hand steady. She let it roll against her palm, light and wet, its ridges like worn-down tire treads. Then she picked it up by the small stem at its base and held it above her, as if peering into the speckled center of a foxglove.

"What are you doing?" he asked.

"Looking."

"Would you like to know what you're looking at?"

"If I must."

"It's a *Styela.* One of the animals you were supposed to be helping me collect. One of the animals Arthur failed to properly anesthetize. The tubular part is called a tunic. And the skinny part you're holding on to is called the stalk. Which explains its common name: stalked tunicate."

"Oh."

"Some people also call it a sea squirt."

"Why is that?"

"Give it a squeeze and see for yourself."

She held it over the edge of the bed and did as instructed. The result was precisely as he had described: a little bit of the sea squirting out onto the floor.

"Are people always so literal?"

He laughed. "For the most part, yes. But every once in a while you get a pleasant surprise. The sarcastic fringehead. The Portuguese man-of-war."

She pinched out the last of the seawater and put it in her lap.

"Go ahead," he said, picking up the sketchbook and pushing it at her. "I know you want to."

"No, I don't."

"Yes, you do."

"No, I don't."

"Why not?"

"I just don't."

"It has a heart, you know. It literally has a heart. The water came out of the atrial siphon."

"I don't care."

"And it may not look like it, but it's a closer relation to you and me than any other invertebrate. As larvae, they have backbones and spinal cords. Just like us."

"That's nonsense."

"It most certainly isn't."

"You're trying to trick me."

"Why on earth would I do something like that?"

Her father was never coming back, she told herself. And now everything was up to her, just as it had been in the tobacco fields.

"I'd like another drink," she said.

"Me too."

As he reached over to the windowsill to retrieve the jug, she could see the strip of skin above his belt. She would squeeze him around the waist just as she had squeezed the *Styela*; she would see the ocean coming out. He passed her the jug. Her mouth and throat were completely accustomed to the sensation now; it was only her belly that continued to respond. The fire flaring up, the fire cooling down.

"You know," he said, watching her closely, "last time I drank this stuff, some strangeness happened."

"What sort of strangeness?"

"Well, a slapping contest for one thing. Right on top of my desk. Joe and I sat there for hours and hit each other as hard as we could. Then John took a turn."

"Why?"

He smiled and looked sheepishly at his essay, which was still sitting on the bed. "We wanted to see if we could break through."

It was as if he were speaking in code. And the most puzzling thing was that she hadn't even earned it yet. It usually took so much more than this to be invited inside a stranger's world.

Money, connections, shows of good faith. But she had offered him none of this and yet, here she was.

"Let's do it," she said. The tequila was a sword in her brain: brave and shimmering. "Let's do another slapping contest."

"Absolutely not."

She raised a hand and tried to connect it to his face, but he grabbed her wrist and forced her arm back down. When he released her, she shifted onto her side and faced the wall. There was only one light source in the room—a rawhide-shaded lamp on the bedside table—and the shadow it cast of her body was huge against the expanse of paneled wood.

"Don't pout," he said after a moment. "It wouldn't have worked anyway."

Sleep was overtaking her now, quickly and violently, and she was glad of it.

"There's another technique, though." His voice cut through her drunken fatigue like scissors through wet silk. "One that's a bit less likely to leave a mark."

In response, she didn't flip all the way around to face him. Instead, she rolled onto her back and stared up at the ceiling.

"I'll need to look into your eyes," he said.

"Then look."

She kept her gaze fixed firmly upward. He snorted in either amusement or frustration. Then, suddenly, he was the only thing she could see: his body covering hers but not touching it, his legs spread wide, his torso held aloft on bent elbows.

"What am I supposed to do?" she asked.

"Nothing. Just stare at me. Stare the life right out of me."

The air was gray dust and her fingers were driftwood. She had been taken here against her will, just like the *Styela*, and she would end up like them, too: prodded and observed and put to death. Her earlier instincts had been right. Resist, retreat, run.

But then she met his eyes and a different set of concerns surged forth. Just a few hours earlier, she had been so proud of her portrait of him. Now she felt differently. It wasn't enough to represent something faithfully. The important thing was the order in which it all happened. Was she, in other words, taking something whole and breaking it apart? Or was she building up disparate elements until they formed a known shape? Her father always judged his success on the product, on the amount and quality of what came out. But what if it was actually about what went in? *You're getting somewhere*, she told herself. *You're finally getting somewhere.* But then all she could think about was her left shoulder. He was stroking it with his thumb, tracing the seam in her shirt.

"Explain it to me," she said. "Explain it like I'm the dumbest person in the world."

The thumb stopped. But then it resumed its tracing.

"You're not dumb at all. I'll bet you did marvelously in school."

"I've never gone to school. Just to work."

"Which I suppose explains the Surrey collar," he said, popping the fabric. "Very debonair."

"My father and I share a tailor."

"Of course you do."

"Please. Explain it."

He sighed. There was reticence in his expression and she knew why. She had never tried to justify her drawings to anyone because she knew it would sound complex, and complexity could easily be mistaken for weakness.

"Like I said before," he began carefully, "I collect specimens from the tide pools. Then I preserve them and sell them to universities. But I also do other things."

"The essay."

"Yes. And other essays much like it, none of which I can ever seem to get quite right. I like trying, though. I like to think about poets and composers and artists and their access to the divine. There's the shark oil situation, which I believe in fervently. I'm trying to get the real story from both the fisheries and the population scientists to determine just how many sardines are left in the bay and whether or not we should keep on canning them. In my more optimistic moments, I feel like I'm just one idea away from figuring out a whole new method of categorizing each and every living thing. And someday I'm hoping it will all come together in a clear and beautiful way. In a way that even the dumbest person in the world will understand."

From somewhere on the street outside, the sound of glass breaking, women howling in laughter. She had always thought her father was ambitious, but his goals were nothing compared with this. The biologist's fingers moved from her collar to the side of her face. She felt very ugly. Very young.

"Please," she said. "Don't."

"Oh," he said, pushing himself back onto his heels. "I thought you were—"

"I'm not," she replied, the words slightly emptier than she intended.

"I'm so sorry. I don't usually try that sort of thing unless I'm quite certain."

"Certain of what?"

At this, his eyes went blank. Then he stood from the bed and sat on the beer crate, the mattress shifting audibly beneath her as if dismayed by the sudden imbalance. She, too, felt dismayed. It hadn't necessarily been pleasant to have him above her, to have him touch her on purpose. *Pleasant*, however, no longer seemed to be the point.

She stood from the bed and moved to the doorway, toward the room from which, if she listened hard enough, the music still seemed to emanate, even though it had stopped hours ago.

"Where do you put them all?" she asked.

"All of what?" He was standing now, too, and watching her more intently than ever.

She cleared her throat. Something was blocking her voice.

"You should lie back down," he cautioned. "You might feel like you're ready, but you're not."

"You go out there and take things." He was right, she realized. Reclined on the bed, she had felt fine. But now that she was standing, the blood was plummeting from her head and the liquor was staking its belated claim. Within seconds, she would pass out and fall over. "You take things from the ocean and put them in here, so when do you know when it's enough?"

"Well . . ." He grinned. "That's the thing. It's never really *enough*."

When the next urge arose, she aimed herself in his direction and steeled herself for the impact.

"Whoa, there." He caught her by the waist and guided her onto the bed. Instead of returning to the crate, however, he remained upright, his thigh within easy swatting distance.

"I actually *am*," she said. The fabric of his trousers felt slightly damp beneath her fingers. She was finding a seam, too.

"Excuse me?"

"I actually am . . . interested." *What's the other word?* she asked herself. *The less ambiguous one?* "Available."

Ricketts grimaced and shook his head.

"Rumor has it your father's going to ride all over this town, guns blazing. Only an idiot would knowingly step into the crossfire."

"Good thing you're a first-rate idiot."

"Barely a day together," he said, smirking, "and it's like we've known each other a lifetime."

"Then what's the harm in getting to know each other even better?"

Whose words were these? she wondered. Whose desire?

"I don't want to hurt you," he said, a sparkle of sweat visible at his hairline.

"Too late," she replied.

She had heard him laugh before, but not like this.

"Some more music?"

"Please."

He ran from the room. She held her breath, expecting the return of that measured, careful polyphony. This time, however, the noise from the phonograph was something very different: a song that might have been popular during her father's boyhood, a tenor's excessively upbeat caterwauling.

"Not this," she said when he reappeared in the doorway. "I want what was playing earlier."

"Oh."

He excused himself and made the switch.

"You were right," he said upon his return. "Bach is a far better choice."

She scooted over to make some room for him on the bed. For several seconds, he didn't move. Then it was just as before: a resumption of his earlier position, all four of their legs stretched out in chaste, nonconjoined parallel. At one point he started swiping his feet back and forth to the beat. After a bar or two, she joined in, and so it went until he purposefully broke the rhythm in order for their toes to collide. *Negotiation,* she remarked to herself. *I know about this.* So she made what she hoped was a persuasive counteroffer: flinging her entire left calf over his right shin. An error, though. It was too much and he was retreating now, his joints stiff, so she responded with the only remaining maneuver in her arsenal: doubling down and then some, tilting herself over and slightly up until her mouth was touching his.

He let her remain there for several seconds and then gently pushed her away. She sank back against the pillow, jaw grinding.

"Maybe it's best to keep things simple," he said. "The world already has far too much trouble as it is."

"What makes you think I'm trouble?"

"Because I can't seem to resist that sort of thing."

She closed her eyes, certain it was all over. Whatever instinct had spurred her on was proving itself unreliable now, unsafe. But then she felt a hand on her leg—the same leg that was still crossed over his. Her eyes flew open.

"Margot Fiske," he mused. "Sounds like something that should be on the marquee of a Left Bank cabaret."

"I don't sing or dance. And certainly not for money."

"A woman of business. I know, I know."

The hand drew the leg even closer to him, even farther apart from its twin.

"I thought you didn't like trouble," she said.

"Oh, I don't know. Sometimes trouble is good. Sometimes trouble makes things show up."

With his index finger, he pressed down on her kneecap as if

pushing an elevator button. Then he was looming over her again. He looked at her for a while, appraising the stitches, savoring the sight of his own handiwork. Then his mouth was where his eyes had been, kissing the perimeter of the wound.

"Ouch," she whispered.

"Liar," he countered, moving his lips down the bridge of her nose and onto her mouth.

And this time, she realized, it was real. Earlier, when she had been in charge of the kiss, it hadn't quite taken shape. But now the imbalance was being righted: form and function, all in one, just as he had said. The form of his mouth, the function of his hands, everything moving slowly and with lethal purpose. Once or twice, she found herself distracted by the smell of his beard, but not in a bad way. After several minutes, he pulled back. He took off his shirt, unfastened his trousers.

"There is a final question, though," he said, head tilted, eyes downcast. "The question of . . . uhhhh . . . age."

She felt her face turn a color: white or red, she didn't know which.

"Not that I'm particularly hung up on that sort of thing. But in this case I feel like it might be best, you see . . . for all involved . . . just to be certain . . ."

"Guess."

"Excuse me?"

"Guess how old I am."

He brightened, visibly pleased by the challenge.

"You just turned twenty. This past spring."

"Spot-on."

He shucked his trousers to the floor and freed himself. She undid her own buttons as quickly as possible so that he wouldn't see her hands shaking. Then a moment of genuine uncertainty. When his face vanished, she felt disappointed. But then his mouth made itself known again—not on her mouth this time, but on a different place, equally eloquent, equally unstable—and when he crawled back up the length of the bed and entered her, there was almost nothing in the way of resistance or pain. Nothing was being broken. If anything, it felt like diving into very hot water. His lips pulled, his hands worked, a blade-sharp knowledge consuming her from the inside out, his convoluted philosophies suddenly crystal clear. Time was passing, but there was no telling how fast, and when she finally stiffened and cried out, she saw light in the darkness of his eyes, his face slack with an emptiness she hoped matched her own.

When it was over, they lay there for a long while, her head on his chest. She curled her arms and legs into balls; she tried to make herself as small as possible. Soon, the sun was rising, the gulls screeching at it, calling it forth or pushing it away. Sea lions, too, what seemed like hundreds of them, barking like hounds. Beneath the ruckus, his heartbeat: the sound coming at her through a fortress of tendon and flesh and bone. Put it in a bucket, put it in your hand, squeeze it, and make it soft. He knew her name, but she didn't know his. And the fact that this inequity barely troubled her was the first indication of something she hadn't even expected to consider: that failure, as she had always understood it, might be something else entirely.

Then, a duet of sounds that made her jump. Footsteps climbing the exterior stairs, a voice calling her name.

She jerked away from the biologist's body. He vaulted off the bed.

"You'll want to freshen up?" he asked, dressing himself with remarkable speed. Her clothes still lay in a pile next to the pillow.

"Please."

"I'll tell him you're in the bathroom."

He nodded vigorously, glanced over to where the jug and the sketchbook lay upended on the floor, and left the room.

When he was gone, she rose from the mattress, the pain in her head snarling instantly back to life. She didn't feel strong enough yet to put on her clothes, so she staggered to the bathroom naked. In the bathroom, it was very difficult to stand, so she gripped the edge of the sink and looked into its basin, the color of which seemed to be the same color as the throbbing between her eyes: a mottled white that wanted very much to be clean but wasn't. She could hear voices from the front room, the words obscured. There was fluid running down her thighs and she needed to wipe it away, but she was afraid to let go of the sink. So she tightened her grip and stared into the mirror. The wound looked precisely the way it felt, like something out of a comic strip: deep, diagonal, a battlefield gash running all the way from her hairline to the bridge of her nose, the broken skin sealed shut with thick and uneven stitches, a patch of lurid blackish purple marking the place where her forehead had hit the rocks.

"Margot!" her father called.

She bit her cheek and looked down.

"Margot!"

"One moment!"

She looked up again. And even more affirming and more cartoonish than her wound, somehow, was the rest of what she saw in the mirror: her face and body, yes, but also the bathtub behind her. Like the sink, the tub was stained and chipped and dirty white, but instead of being empty, it was filled with the pus-colored bodies of nearly a hundred tiny crabs, their small forms scampering over and under one another, clawing at the walls as if trying to escape a catastrophe only they could predict or understand.

4

1998

WHEN SHE ARRIVES AT THE AQUARIUM—FOR REAL this time, not in the prior night's dream—she receives his first message. A mass beaching of Humboldt squid on the same spot where, as a girl, she once read the morning paper.

It's upsetting on many levels, but mostly because it's a distraction. For weeks now, she's tried to whittle down her focus to a single point: to the release of the *Mola mola*, or ocean sunfish, a longtime aquarium resident that has grown far too big for both its tank and a conventional sort of extraction. She's sketched out some plans, she's consulted with her aquarists, but decisions like this are far easier discussed than made, so she rises from her desk in her office in the administrative wing, puts her work aside, and goes to the window. The first body—nearly four feet long and red as blood—has already rolled up with the surf, tentacles and mouth arms twisted like intestines. The second one appears moments later, bigger than the first, mostly white with some purple around the eyes, which are the size of bocce balls and just as blind looking. When the third body materializes, she knows it's only a matter of time. The institute scientists will show up, a jogger on the bike trail will get nosy, the tourists will descend and congratulate themselves on their discovery, so she postpones the task at hand. She takes her camera out of the filing cabinet, looks at it, and then puts it back in. Then she hurries outside: past the food room, past quarantine, through the employee parking lot, through the automatic gate in the security fence, and down onto the sand that, in the minutes since she's left her office, has welcomed an additional five corpses.

At first she just stands there, the toe of her black rubber boot touching the smallest one's soft, blotchy flank. In truth, she's been expecting something like this for a while now, but she didn't expect it to look so inconclusive. For one thing, they've assembled themselves wrong: some of them stranded high up on the beach, some of them logjammed horizontal to the surf line, all of them indicating different compass points, different ways to explain and excuse the same human life. Disappointed, she reaches down to take a quick feel, the flesh slick and taut and familiar. With the same hand, she rubs the scar on her forehead. She looks behind her. The TV news crews are parking their vans on the street above. Soon, they'll be stringing their paraphernalia all the way from the bike trail to the water's edge, a net of cameras and microphones and excellent teeth ready to exhort and ensnare. The onlookers will layer themselves like sedimentary rock, several strata deep and stiff with geologic certainty.

Fine, she tells him. *Fine.*

And because she can't go back to his lab, she does the next best thing. She goes back to the aquarium. Specifically, to the food room. Everything here emits light, everything echoes loudly. There's a metal scale hanging from the ceiling like a huge, hard piece of mechanical fruit. The walls and floor are covered in large, white, hose-downable tiles; the radio on the windowsill is tuned just a few millimeters shy of the ideal frequency. When she opens the walk-in freezer, it belches white mist: a transient fog that surrounds her as she retrieves a cardboard box and wrestles it to the countertop. She removes a knife from the magnetic strip above the sink and cuts the box open. The squid inside are long dead, long cold, and only a fraction of the size of the ones on the beach. But they'll do just fine.

And as she begins, it's like listening to music she once knew by heart but hasn't heard in ages. The head comes off with a quick, easy tug. Then she jabs her finger into the notch below the neck and sweeps side to side, separating the respiratory tract from the internal walls of the mantle, and then—*pop!*—those two dark, squishy eyes, a pseudoskull the size of a hazelnut, the whole thing coming free with an explosion of lace and slime, the squid's guts trailing behind the head like the veil on a demented bride. The dull, satisfying snap of severed connective tissue, a vibration in her fingertips. Then a bulge beneath the skin as the livers rise and emerge at the busted lip of the body cavity: two mercury-dipped ovals, their silverness so dirty and organic that it takes her breath away to see the reflection of her own fingers on their surface. This silverness, she knows, will break. It will break and stain the cutting board with something that approximates the color and texture of old menstrual blood. First, however, there's a brief and wondrous pause, the fluid inside held back by the temporary inertia of its own viscosity, and then a small tear in the silver, and then a tiny hole, and then there she is. Younger, angrier, smarter. Nothing in front, nothing behind, and for the first time in her life since before his death, she's balanced on the edge of his fast-melting world.

5

1940

THEY CHECKED OUT OF THE HOTEL DEL MONTE WITHout delay, their belongings loaded once more into the rented Packard, their departure just as unexplained and unheralded as their arrival.

To be honest, she had hoped for more of a scene. She had hoped her father would dole out a shard or two of his icy wrath, berating the hotel staff as to their many recent shortcomings: their failure to protect her, to retrieve him, to delegate her medical care to someone other than a man who mummified sharks for what barely passed as a living. But just as on the ride from the train station, just as on the preceding transpacific crossing, he said nothing as they drove away from the hotel and toward the property he had spent the prior day evaluating and acquiring: a small white house on a hill that overlooked Ocean View Avenue, a street the locals referred to as Cannery Row.

As was their custom, they brought in their trunks first. Then they assessed the structure, studying the place from the outside in, Anders nodding with the dour, crisp satisfaction he offered in lieu of compliments. It was, without question, a perfect fit: as decrepit as the place in Manila but without the extraneous square footage. In fact, it was little more than a shack, the external walls pale and flaking, the windows on either side of the front door looking blankly onto the street like a simpleton's pair of wide-set eyes. The gable roof was yellow black with lichen and rot. Inside, there were four squalid, diminutive, half-furnished living spaces—a sitting room, a bedroom, a bathroom, and a kitchen—all of which featured the same faded botanical-print wallpaper, the same forest of black green mildew unfurling from each damp corner. The house's only favorable characteristic, to her mind at least, was the large bougainvillea bush to the left of the front stoop: a knotty, dark-leaved, pink-flowered behemoth that looked outstandingly capable of annexing not only the house itself, but the entire street on which it sat.

When his evaluation was complete, her father returned to the kitchen. She followed and watched from the doorway as he removed a coffee mug from the cabinet and attempted to fill it with water.

"You have to wait a minute for it to run clear," she said.

He stepped away from the sink, brown water still flowing, and continued to take inventory of everything except her. Linoleum flooring, ornately dimpled and green with grime. A can of hardened bacon grease on the windowsill above the sink, the delights of which had not escaped the notice of nearly a hundred swarming ants. She had seen this type of behavior before: his impenetrable remoteness that stretched and lingered, his victim twisting in the wind. The difference now was that the victim was her.

"There's only one bedroom," he announced. "You'll sleep on a straw pallet in the sitting room. Like you did in Indonesia."

"The straw pallet gave me a backache."

"We'll get a sofa, then."

She knit her brows, which made the stitches pull and burn. She touched her forehead and winced, but his disinterest remained immaculate.

"I need to know why we've come here," she said finally.

When their eyes met, it was like a match striking.

"Then do something to earn it."

He turned away from her and toward the open tap. He squinted at the water, filled his mug, and then emptied it in one noiseless, perfectly efficient swallow. She went outside and sat down on the porch next to the bougainvillea. Her earlier show of discomfort hadn't been entirely feigned. Her skull ached, her eye sockets throbbed. She hadn't eaten in well over a day, and her gut felt like the sort of hole in which one could find dinosaur bones or Roman ruins. Worst of all, she could sense the prelude to her body's monthly rebellion, a riot of pinches and aches echoing in her lower abdomen: a feeling that reminded her of the Philippines, but not the good parts.

When she looked down the hill, however, the feeling disappeared. From this house, she couldn't quite see the same tide pools in which she had taken her fall, but she could see the bay that had facilitated it. She could see how its blue black water became blue green in certain pockets close to shore. Most of all, she could see the shore itself, the rocks like scar tissue from the most violent meetings of ocean and land, the juncture crowded with human designs and animal ones: canneries, cottages, cormorants' rookeries, rats' nests. The biologist was out there, somewhere in or near the water, somewhere on the lip of that infinite black meniscus, and for the first time since leaving the lab, she allowed herself to remember it in detail. It was getting late, but she wasn't sleepy. So she waited on the porch until the kitchen light had been turned off and her father had gone to bed. Inside, she unrolled her pallet, her body abuzz, her underclothes lined with folded sheets of cotton wool in preparation for blood. And when she awoke to find the cotton wool unstained, she read it as a sign from the universe that even though her father was determined to exclude her, he was too late. She had already been let in.

For the next week, mornings and afternoons that were unremarkable and long, a bit of wind in the evenings and then a silence so deep she could hear the advance and retreat of each individual wave.

To her father, it must have seemed like inertia, inexcusable and indulgent, but she knew she was doing important work, almost as important as the work she had once done at his side. She had been considering it obsessively, and had come to the following conclusions. Her time with the biologist had been more than just a drunken tryst, but that didn't mean she could act on it. For one thing, there was no strategy in place. For another, she knew it looked hackneyed and girlish—the accident, the forced rehabilitation, the unlikely romance—even though it felt unique and vital, and she wasn't sure how to manage the resulting dissonance. So she did the only thing she could do while conditions were still unstable: mimicking Anders's stoicism and using it to silently engineer her return to the lab. The landscape seemed important in this regard, so she studied it closely. Soon she could recognize the trees by their shadows alone: Monterey oaks with their thuggish forearms; Monterey pines with needles she preferred to think of as syringes on account of how long and meaningful they looked once they fell to the ground. Off-black trees against an off-white sky, the crookedness of the cypresses, the vertiginous intensity of the redwoods. Occasionally, the head wound would reassert itself and she would feel a bit ill, as if she had eaten something on the verge of rotting; but she endured without complaint, watching her father descend the hill at sunrise and climb it at dusk.

The only interruption to this stasis was when the cannery whistles blew. For some reason, the sound allowed her to relax a bit, to unclench her jaw. From her perch on the hill, it could all be witnessed from above: the sardine boats skirting the land, the gulls descending, her neighbors spilling onto the streets as if spit out by their own homes. At first, she expected all of them to look like Arthur, but they didn't. The cannery workers in her neighborhood were entirely Italian, almost entirely women, denizens of that peculiar socioeconomic territory of the ascendant middle class. The husbands, she soon learned, had jobs on the boats, catching the fish the wives put into cans, and the circularity of this arrangement fascinated her. What was it like, she wondered, when both husband and wife came together at nightfall and began to move behind their windows? Was it clean inside their houses? Did they eat their dinners together? Did they share the same beds? Did the beds smell ineradicably of fish? When they had their festivals—processions that guided life-size plaster saints through the streets—did they feel better in the aftermath, did they feel as if something had been addressed or solved? Or did they feel the way she always did during moments of supposed import: holidays, birthdays, anniversaries, none of them signifying anything except the unfortunate human desire to kick the can of meaning further and further down an endless road?

The most important ideas, though, didn't come to her on the porch. They arrived at night and they had nothing to do with the cannery workers or her father. Stretched out on the straw pallet, she would indulge in the gory, exhilarating specifics. She would stare at the walls, using their pocks and fissures to map out what had been taken from her, what had been given, the biologist's body on top of hers, her mouth on his neck, her freedom so complete that she felt as though, if he moved aside, she would float up to the ceiling and stay there until someone found a gun and shot her down. She could no longer be patient, she told herself, she could no longer wait. But then the sun would rise and her father would remind her—not in words, of course, but in actions—that she would get what she wanted only by pretending not to want it. Keep calm, keep watchful, keep ready for the proper moment to take her aim and tighten her grip.

Then, one day, the moment was at hand. At first, the signs were subtle. In the morning, a doctor came to remove her stitches, utter a few stock phrases of reassurance, and then leave her with nothing but an aching head and a vial of disinfectant. Around lunchtime, someone from the rental company reclaimed the Packard, which had been sitting unused on the street since their departure from the hotel. That afternoon, the arrival of the promised sofa: a claw-footed, button-tufted, horsehair monstrosity. That night, when the water grew black against the sky, her father's shape appeared at the base of the hill a few minutes later than usual. He looked the same as ever, at least in terms of attire: the three-piece cheviot suit, the striped necktie, the polished brogues, the same Surrey collar that she, too, had long favored. In his hands, however, was a bag of groceries and on his face an almost theatrical contentment.

When he reached the house, she stood and followed him inside.

"Get out the good china," he said, placing the groceries on the kitchen counter.

"We have good china?"

"We do indeed. It came with the sofa." The broadness of his smile shocked her.

"Why?"

"Because I just bought the largest cannery in town."

As they prepared dinner, he was unusually animated, as lively as the night was still.

"And the biggest question of all is how anyone fails to see it!" He stopped midchop and looked up at her with big, sharp eyes, the diameters of which were increased nearly twofold as a result of his eyeglasses. "Time was, you could sell one otter pelt—just one—to a member of the Chinese aristocracy and earn enough to buy a house. So they all swooped in: Spaniards, Russians,

Bostonians, all of them convinced the supply would never dwindle, which of course it did. But did they turn their sights in a new direction? Seek out an alternative to self-inflicted feast and famine? No! No, indeed! When the otters were gone, they went for the whales: a man named Davenport blazing the trail, only to be throttled at his own game by the Portuguese, who ran the show until—in a surprise to end all surprises—the whales disappeared, too. And we could talk about the abalones, but I'd hate to sound tiresome."

Here, he fell silent, but not peacefully so. There was effort involved in this version of muteness, and he was taking it out on the squid: the beheading, the disembowelment, the slicing into rings. He enjoyed kitchen work, butchery in particular, viscerally and without any shame regarding the perceived gender reversal, and tonight it seemed especially significant. The resumption of a ritual. A possible sign that their mutual antipathy was at an end.

She scooped up the squid rings, dumped them into the hot skillet, and waited for the white flesh to start popping.

"The abalones," she prompted after the proper interval had passed. "What about them?"

His knife was working again, ripping through a foreign cluster of herbs, rocking and flashing against the wooden board. "It was the local Chinese who reaped the rewards first, who created the overseas market. Then, before they knew it, their big-city cousins had come to town: thousands of San Franciscans with better fishing methods and bigger boats and more secure connections to the homeland. When the abalones were gone, the visitors from the north ended up rich. The locals, needless to say, did not. They had to start fishing for squid instead."

He smiled at the squid in the skillet as if they had done him a personal favor, then smothered them with a handful of minced greenery. She hadn't expected it to feel this good—this return to business as usual—but it did. Her father's sudden enthusiasm was sweeping away any former notions of patience, payback, or restraint. *Just like the burned sketchbooks,* she thought with a shiver: the catharses that were always so final until, at a certain point, they weren't.

"And what about the squid? Did they disappear, too?"

"No. The bay is still full of them, but that's not the point. The point is that, for centuries now, people have been doing the same damn thing. Breaking the bay, waiting for it to fix itself, and then breaking it again. And I'm certain there's a better way."

He reached across her to give the skillet a little shake.

"And what way is that?"

Instead of answering, he took a tiny jar from his vest pocket, opened it, and dosed its contents into his palm.

"Smell," he said.

She paused. This was the most conciliatory gesture he had made in months, and something about it worried her. But then she bent over his hand and inhaled. Hot, musky, semisweet. As specific and strange as the unknown herbs.

"What is it?"

"Chinese five-spice powder. Try to guess all five."

Guess, she remembered telling the biologist. *Guess how old.* She closed her eyes and took another sniff.

"One: cinnamon. Two: cloves . . ."

"Star anise, fennel seed, and Szechuan pepper."

"I was just about to say that."

"No," he teased. "You weren't."

The powder hit the pan, its smells unifying and then exploding.

"Quick," he said. "The plates."

She opened the nearest cabinet and withdrew two pieces of the good china, which had been placed there without her knowledge, as if in deliberate secret.

"Cook it for too long," he said, easing the squid out of the skillet, "and it turns to rubber."

"I know."

And then the rebirth of another tradition: dinner on foot. For as long as she could remember, they had eaten like this, as if in readiness for fight or flight, their legs shifting beneath them as they chewed, her father's enjoyment of the meal's creation vastly exceeding his enjoyment of the meal itself. When they were done, she put down her fork and looked at him. He didn't resemble the biologist, not one bit. But in a moment like this, when the turmoil within him had been temporarily silenced, when something had been successfully planned, executed, and consumed, the similarity was both unsettling and undeniable.

"So," she said. "Have I earned it?"

He folded his napkin into quarters and placed it neatly on the countertop.

"Earned what?"

"An explanation."

"A lucrative opportunity. Nothing more."

"From what I've heard, the sardine game isn't so lucrative these days." In her mouth, the biologist's words seemed precious and oddly shaped. "Most of them are already in cans."

"For one thing, it's not a *game*. For another, it's not the sardines that interest me."

"Then what does?"

He lifted his chin, the tendons in his neck jutting forth like buttresses. So it wasn't over, she told herself. Not yet.

"I thought you were no longer interested in my affairs," he protested, head tilted in reclamation of his earlier disdain.

"I thought you had deemed me unworthy," she replied, mirroring his stance.

"Not unworthy. Just in profound need of correction."

"Correction made."

"In that case, fire away."

Her pulse skipped. This *was* a game: one they had played countless times before.

"The sellers?" she asked.

"The Agnellis. Monterey's most powerful family." He was enjoying this, too, but pretending he wasn't. "They know which way the winds are blowing. Or at least they think they do."

"The price?"

"Far less than my nearest competitor offered, which ruffled some feathers, to be sure."

"Location?"

"Just down the hill, at the intersection of Cannery Row and David Avenue. A few doors down from the place where that Ed Ricketts fellow tended to your wound."

She put one hand on her stomach, one hand on the countertop. Ed Ricketts: a name she hadn't known until just now, a name that brought her back to the strange, isometric desperation of the past seven days. Thinking back on it, she realized it hadn't been calmness, not at all. It had been a million forces converging down on her all at once, slyly yet firmly freezing her in place.

"A lab," she said. "His place is actually a lab."

"I know. I've been there several times this week."

She kept her face flat, her breath even. There were scratches on the kitchen table that looked like handwriting. Stains on the linoleum that looked like train tracks.

"And while he hasn't exactly blessed my ambitions," he continued, "he hasn't cursed them either."

"Why would he?"

"Because he's the town's self-proclaimed expert on everything fish related. Which is tiring in person, but useful in practice."

And there it was: fate.

"So I'll accompany you to the cannery tomorrow," she replied. "Seven A.M. Just like always."

He shook his head. Her chest tightened. Whenever they cooked, she wanted to tell him, he never let her use the knife, only the blunt things. The rolling pin. The wooden spoon. The pan.

"I want to work," she said.

"And work you shall." The light was catching his white hair and making it glow. "But not necessarily in the cannery. And not necessarily with me."

"Then where? And with whom?"

He squared his shoulders and grinned; a stray green fleck stuck to his lower lip.

"With Ed Ricketts. In his lab."

That night, she didn't sleep.

For a while, she sat on the porch, a buzzing sensation in her belly and groin, the stink of the canneries fighting against other stinks: iodine, mulch, mildew.

At around three in the morning, she returned to the sofa,

where she watched the walls wash themselves lighter and lighter, the daylight swinging across the land and water. Part of her was amazed at how well everything had turned out, her father's schemes coming into miraculous alignment with her own. He had explained it to her succinctly and without room for dispute: how the lab's finances were a disaster and how she was more than qualified to set things straight. Her real purpose, however, would be not that of the accountant, but that of the spy. She would eavesdrop on conversations, memorize statistics, and then report back to Anders. Even more important, she would curry favor with Ricketts himself: an element of the plan that, according to her father, was indispensable to victory.

So it was a simple arrangement and one that promised dual satisfactions. Ample reason to be optimistic, perhaps even joyful. But she wasn't. Ricketts's appeal, she remembered now, hadn't exactly been benign, and his ambitions hadn't exactly been straightforward. At times, he had watched her a little too closely. He had laughed at her terror and had offered her a beer, and now when she tried to summon the image of them sitting side by side on the bed, she saw not only their bodies and faces and her drawing on the wall, but also the green-curtained window. In her mind's eye, she looked through it, hoping to see nothing more than the fog moving beneath the beams of the streetlights like the sorts of vapors some mistake for ghosts. Instead, she saw a face looking in at them, a pair of eyes assessing them with curiosity and envy.

She sat up. The daylight was growing stronger, the cushions seeming to actively repel her weight. A train whistle blew in the distance, a gull screamed. She stood and tiptoed over to the clock on the mantel—a German timepiece with a loud, bossy tick—and saw herself reflected in its glass face. She looked the same as she had yesterday: pale, scarred, perched at that odd inflection point between youth and adulthood. But there was also something else. A new severity, a new definition, almost as if her features were too sharp to belong to a child.

When she heard her father waking, she turned from the clock and listened. The rush of running water in the bathroom sink. The hollow plunk of one of his shoes and then the other. The rustle of his files and papers as they were swept into his valise. His suit, she knew, would be pressed and spotless. His thick, colorless hair would be neatly pomaded and parted down the middle. Their descent would be wordless, dignified, her father humming a little as he walked, chin raised and arms rigid. In these ways and more, she knew what to expect. What she didn't expect, however, was how tall he would look when he finally emerged from his bedroom. As they left the house and proceeded down the hill to Cannery Row, his six feet and five inches seemed as distant and immovable as a cathedral ceiling, and she felt very small in comparison: as close to the ground as a dog, unusually aware of smells and the transitions between them.

When they were just a step or two from their destination, the sidewalks dense with cannery workers, the street loud with trucks, he stopped and searched her face and must have been troubled by what he found there, because what came next were the type of words that, in the wake of last night's détente, shouldn't have been necessary: instructions that assumed the worst about her instead of the best.

"You're not to roam the streets. You're not to come here after dark," he said. "Other than that, all I ask is that you behave in a manner that is least likely to tarnish the simple dignity of your family name. Is that something you can manage?"

"I believe so."

And moments later, there they were: shoulder to shoulder in front of the dark, salt-swollen door of Ed Ricketts's lab.

6

THE MAN WHO ANSWERED THE DOOR WAS NOT ED Ricketts. Not in the least.

"John," Anders said. "I was under the impression you had already left for Baja."

"Not yet," the man replied, shaking her father's hand and then returning both long arms awkwardly to his sides. "Still trying to talk some sense into Ed, and that could take months."

The man produced a labored smile, a horse's set of big, yellow teeth layered across his gums like roof tiles. He was shorter than her father but looked as though he should have been taller on account of his coarse, oversize features. His brow was broad and bunioned, his nose a weighty bulb at the base of a funnel-like bridge, his ears those not of a human being but of some sort of huge nocturnal mammal. She stuck out her hand and tried not to startle when her fingers were engulfed by his.

"John Steinbeck," he said.

"Margot Fiske."

"I know. You couldn't look more like your father if you tried," he answered morosely, squinting at the scar on her forehead. "Plus, I can see the telltale damage. The sign of the beast."

She met his gaze evenly. "That's not the proper usage of the phrase."

"Margot," her father cautioned.

Steinbeck turned away without a word. Anders and Margot followed him inside. She scanned the front room anxiously. It was quiet and bright. The contents were much the same as before—the cluttered desk, the overburdened bookcases, the ancient phonograph, the Coast Guard buoy with a fern planted inside of it, the file cabinet in which there sat a half-empty bag of flour, the same wooden beer crate that had served as Ricketts's bedside chair. The only change was an odd and obvious one: a ring of unlit tallow candles in the middle of the floor.

"Take my eye off him for one second . . ." Steinbeck grumbled, kicking a candle onto its side.

"We can wait." Anders tapped a foot in impatience.

"Please do."

Steinbeck trudged out the rear door. Her father deposited his valise and hat onto the desk and surveyed the room, his upper lip wrinkled in distaste.

"Good Lord," he said. "He's worse at housekeeping than we are."

And then a voice from behind.

"The Fiske family. A delightful surprise!"

She paused before turning to face him, taking care to keep her expression neutral. He was wearing an ankle-length oilskin apron, a stained undershirt, and the sort of green visor favored by gamblers. Arthur was at his side again, as was a woman—below average height, above average looks—who seemed familiar, but in a way she couldn't quite place.

Ricketts walked briskly up to her father and extended a hand.

"It wasn't meant to be a surprise," her father said, completing the handshake, taking a small step back, and reexamining the candles' broken circle. "I sent word we'd be here at ten past, but—"

"You did? To whom did you speak?"

"I think he called himself . . . Bucky."

"Ah yes! Bucky. Lives across the way in one of those big storage cylinders. Answers my phone sometimes, but he's usually too drunk to write anything down. If I had known you were coming, I would have made things a bit more presentable. Or at least cleared away some of the evidence."

Her father lifted an eyebrow.

"In case you're interested," Ricketts continued, "tallow beats beeswax. Almost always."

"For what purpose?" her father asked warily.

"For the purpose of the séance. I think we might have actually broken through for once, although I'm not sure it was worth the trouble. I always get so nervous in the presence of the supernatural."

At this, he looked directly at her for the first time since entering the room, his examination prolonged yet buoyant, as if the two of them were in on a joke the others were too slow to understand. She looked at his hands. They were nimble and callused and held a bucket each, just as they had that morning in the tide pools, and at the sight there was a surge of interest strong enough to make her stumble. Whose ghost had he summoned last night? And why?

"Can I offer any of you a beer?" Ricketts asked. "Or a steak?"

She tried to answer but couldn't.

"She's shy." The woman smiled.

"I can assure you she's anything but," her father replied.

"Wormy, Arthur." Ricketts handed the buckets to his companions. "If you please."

"Doc, perhaps she'd like to—"

"Arthur. Downstairs."

"They're just *Styela*. I don't have to—"

"Arthur!"

Arthur scowled and followed Wormy through a small door at the far end of the room. Ricketts turned back to Margot and her father.

"Oh, *Styela*." He grinned. "Don't know why I even bother anymore, to be honest with you. Can't get the boys to bring me much else, so why should I be out there getting them myself?"

In reply, Anders studied Ricketts and then helped himself to the seat behind Ricketts's desk. Ricketts settled himself contentedly on the beer crate. Margot remained standing and watched as her father began eyeing the papers on the desktop. To anyone else, it might have looked like an idle perusal, but she could see its underlying intensity, assimilative and scathing.

"Any new orders since last we spoke?"

"A few," Ricketts replied, stretching his legs out in front of him. His pants were rolled up to his knees and his shins were hairier than she remembered. The green visor made him look a little seasick. "But most of the universities ordered their supplies for the spring term in the fall. Which means I have more than a couple dogfish out back just begging for someone to buy them and slice them in two."

When he turned to smile at her, he looked like a clown, but not the funny kind.

"A challenging business model, isn't it?" Her father found a document that interested him and inspected it carefully, blinking as if his eyelids were camera shutters. "Flush one minute, broke the next. I don't know how you manage."

"Not very well, I'm afraid. If it weren't for my illustrious benefactor, I don't know where I'd be."

"Don't be so modest. I'm sure John knows a bargain when he sees it."

"John knows a story when he sees it. And I usually deliver on that front, I'm sorry to say."

"Yes. His latest book was . . . unusual. Those peach farmers really had the worst of it."

"Funny. Most people sympathize with the pickers."

Her father raised his hands in the air. "A heartless capitalist! Guilty as charged!"

"Making something from nothing is what our society values, I'll grant you that. Making nothing from something, though . . ." He gestured around at the lab. "Well, that's the real trick."

"Sadly enough, most people in this town seem to agree."

"Well, I suppose you're as much of an expert as anyone," Ricketts said amiably. "All those Methodists living in tents beneath the butterfly trees, singing the praises of the immaterial. It must have been extraordinary back then."

When her father looked away from the desk and toward Ricketts, it was with an almost audible snap.

"I've overcome my youthful follies and I'm thankful for it," Anders said, his voice controlled and toneless. "Some men aren't so lucky."

"Are you talking about the Renoirs? Because your daughter hated them, too."

She flinched. This time, Ricketts had certainly gone too far. But there was something in his delivery—a self-deprecating, peaceable sort of humor—that seemed to neutralize the comment even as he voiced it. Her father, too, had been disarmed. She could tell by the way he smiled, shook his head, and reached down to straighten a stack of errant papers.

"I enjoy our banter, Edward." He sighed. "I truly do."

"The feeling is more than mutual. Entertaining the Fiske family gives me great pleasure indeed."

"In that case, I'll be back for her at five. She gets Sundays off. Not on account of religious superstition, but on account of labor laws."

"Of course, of course." Ricketts nodded and looked at Margot. "I'm not sure what I'll be able to pay her, but once she familiarizes herself with the way everything operates she can decide what seems appropriate and then—"

"No payment is required," Anders huffed. "Consider her services a much belated act of gratitude. For the kindness you showed her after the accident."

She heard a chuckle from the corner of the room. During Ricketts and her father's conversation, Steinbeck had somehow rematerialized unnoticed. He was settled deeply now into a low-slung rocking chair in the corner, knees hitched up to chest height, a large notebook open on his lap, looking for all the world as though he had been there for a century or more and had been disappointed by every second of it.

"If I were you," Steinbeck suggested, "I'd consider the debt already repaid. In full."

Her father gave Steinbeck a bemused look and then turned back to Ricketts.

"Five, then?"

"Whenever you like," Ricketts replied.

"Make sure you knock first," Steinbeck added. "Or else you might interrupt some . . . how did you put it, Anders? Some 'youthful follies'?"

"John . . ." Ricketts laughed nervously.

"Yes, yes," Steinbeck continued, undeterred. "I'm quite the comic. Have you heard the one about the sea otters, Anders? When the male otter takes a mate, he sinks his teeth right into the female's face and holds on until he's done!"

She raised an inadvertent hand to her wound and then quickly lowered it. Her father's left eye twitched.

"I don't concern myself with lesser mammals," he sniffed.

"If only your daughter shared your aversions."

"John." Ricketts's voice was solemn now, completely absent of its earlier mirth. "I'm sure you don't know what you're saying."

"And I'm sure he didn't mean to insult my book."

"Your book was sentimental," Anders replied. "And unclear."

"Unclear? How's this for clarity? Ed fucked your daughter."

Her father's face sank and then reacquired a terrifying blankness. He turned to Ricketts.

"Edward?"

"Anders, there was nothing—"

Steinbeck leapt to his feet, the chair rocking violently in response.

"One more lie from you and I swear! I swear I'll break every jar, Ed. I'll release every shark. I'll burn this stinkhole to the ground."

"You'll have to excuse him," Ricketts explained frantically, his underarms dark with sweat. "He's under quite a lot of stress. He's been getting death threats from the agricultural associations, the movie studios won't leave him alone, his wife has started raising rabbits and—"

"Margot?" Her father was standing very close to her now, his smell an ancient indictment.

She shook her head.

"Say it," Anders insisted, grabbing her shoulders and shaking them. "Say it in words."

"You have no right," Ricketts yelped, as if it were his body under assault, not hers. "She's a human being. Of age."

"Of age?" He released Margot and strode across the room in Ricketts's direction, toppling the remaining candles. "What monster considers fifteen years old *of age*?"

Ricketts blanched. Margot stopped breathing.

"Fifteen?" Ricketts coughed, slinking back in the direction of the beer crate. "I must say, Anders. One could be forgiven . . . on account of her height, you see . . . for thinking she was a good deal . . . ahem . . . older."

"My God," her father whispered.

An interval of hellish silence, Steinbeck's chair squeaking as its empty form continued to rock. In the distance, she thought she could hear the voices of the woman and the boy, Wormy and Arthur, laughing at something in the water.

Her father put on his hat and made for the door.

"Anders, I certainly hope—"

"Oh, let him go, Ed," Steinbeck said. "He's no friend of ours. And neither is the girl."

On the street, Anders plowed ahead and Margot did her best to keep up.

Earlier, as they had made their way downhill, she had been too distracted to take in the detail of her surroundings, but now she seemed capable of nothing but, the entire landscape suddenly revealing itself as the sort of omen only a fool would misinterpret. There had been a half-dozen whistle blasts in the past twelve hours, so the canneries were full even though the high season was still months away. The buildings convulsed, some of them howling with the expulsion of cooking steam, some of them leaking gray smoke from tube-shaped stacks. The street itself, however, was strangely empty, a shallow, uneasy stillness in the air that made it feel like the moment before the revelation of some very bad or very meaningful piece of news. There were conclusions to arrive at, she told herself, new tactics to consider, second chances upon which to insist. She couldn't, though. For now, all she could do was try to guess at her father's next steps.

When they reached the Row's terminus, she expected him to turn left on David Avenue, to begin the uphill climb. Instead, he stopped in front of the last building on the street. Unlike some of the neighboring canneries, which featured architectural nods to the Spanish-built missions that dotted the length of the state, this one was a blank white box, a message in its austerity that, more than anything that had just been said inside the lab, made her dizzy with panic.

"If you'll just—"

"I trust you can manage dinner on your own," he said.

"Nothing needs to change. You've never cared about—"

"It's pointless now. Don't you understand that? What will he tell you—what will you learn—now that you've already given him everything he might have wanted?"

"*Might have* wanted?" she hissed.

She straightened her back and stiffened her limbs, preparing herself for the obvious rebuttal. Instead, he did something much worse: he turned and moved toward what appeared to be the cannery's only door, the heavy, steel portal opening with the push of a single outstretched finger.

7

DREAMS, VIOLENT AND VIVID ONES.

Animals fighting on top of the kitchen table, the blood flying onto the papered walls, onto the grease can and the ants. Their old home in the Channel Islands and their neighbor's greenhouse, her body bound and gagged in the corner, the plants using their strange, snakelike tongues to lick her as she struggled. The fog suffocating her, the sand eating her alive, the salt water in the bay dissolving her limbs and torso until all that was left was an otter-mauled head that bobbed on the surface and paddled around with the help of ear-shaped fins. When these dreams woke her in the middle of the night, she would sit there on the sofa and rub the scar as if trying to erase it, promising herself that when morning came, she would retrieve the sketchbook from her satchel and record whatever she remembered and then finally commit the evidence to the flames. The sketchbook, however, couldn't be found—a casualty, most likely, of their hasty departure from the hotel—so the things she might have drawn remained indefinite and free-floating, filling her with an apprehension that persisted well through breakfast, well past the moment at which her father descended the hill and left her alone on the porch yet again with nothing but the bougainvillea for company.

This time, however, she didn't find any sort of peace. What she had tried to say to her father outside his cannery had been right. By his own admittance, he had never cared about the *lesser mammal* aspect of things, or at least he had never seemed to. Her physical self and the way in which she managed it: none of it had ever attracted his concern, much less his critique. A different sort of father might have shown escalating signs of nervousness as the years passed, as the biological determinants made themselves apparent, but even on the day she first began to bleed, Anders had remained professional, expedient, her new bodily complications assessed as drily and succinctly as if he were calculating the depreciation on a piece of factory equipment. But now he was angry about it, and his anger seemed deeper than logic: a fact that, as the days passed, made their interactions twice as distant and volatile as before.

And then there was Ricketts's strange comment, the one about the Methodists and the butterflies, the hymns and the tents. It seemed to imply something impossible: that Anders had been to Monterey before and had voluntarily returned, a choice that went counter to everything he had always told her about how lives should progress.

So, restless with confusion and sour with dreams, she took the only action she could. She gathered information. She left the house and began to explore the town much as she had once explored the manor in the Philippines: mapping it out in her mind's eye, alert for patterns or aberrations. She went up and around the hill on which they lived, she saw the richest neighborhoods at its peak, the poorest neighborhoods at its base. She went over the hill and down Pacific Street, where she encountered the big, Federalist-looking anomaly that had once housed the state's constitutional convention. She dipped down into the badlands at the head of the wharf and watched the prostitutes melt away into the old adobes when they saw her approach. She paced the perimeter of the large Chinatown on Washington Street and the smaller one on McAbee Beach. She even went back to the Hotel Del Monte to see if it was still empty of guests, which it was.

The only place she didn't go was Cannery Row. As long as everything was still so flammable, such proximity seemed unwise. So she went only as close as seemed strategically advisable, to a little outcropping of land at the base of David Avenue beneath which lay a small beach and a small building with what seemed like too many windows. Here, she sat on a rock and read the local paper, absorbing whatever details seemed most relevant: about how there were battles under way between the reigning Italian fishing conglomerate and the unions; about how the Japanese and the Chinese were also in the mix, fighting for a share of what seemed to be a dwindling cache of spoils. Something was happening here. Something much like the cycle of abundance, exploitation, and famine that her father had once taken such pleasure in describing.

The next morning at breakfast, she broke several days' worth of silence to voice the obvious concerns.

"Permission to speak candidly?" she asked.

"Granted," her father replied, his eyes boring holes into his toast. They weren't cooking together anymore. Instead, they were cobbling together ad hoc, unplanned meals or, whenever that felt too intimate, not eating at all.

"The canning industry seems like an unworthy target. Too complex. Too corrupt."

"Like I said before, my interests lie elsewhere. Dramatically so."

"Reduction, then. More profit, less labor. And the laws still haven't caught up. Did you know there are floating reduction plants just offshore? Domiciled at sea to avoid municipal regulations?"

"A compelling opportunity," he hummed. "But not for me."

At this, a brief thrill. For the first time since their squid dinner, he was challenging her, goading her into playing along, and the urge to continue was almost irresistible. But she didn't want to give him what he wanted. She didn't want to surrender to his momentum, especially when she knew that by the time they finished, everything would probably remain unclear. So she put her dishes in the sink, went outside, and remained standing as she made her usual inspection of the hill, her eyes drawn inevitably to the street at its base. It was why people climbed mountains, she realized, or at least why they should: the clarifying loneliness of altitude, the resulting shift in perspective, the question of her father's work suddenly paling in comparison with the question of Ricketts's lab. As if in answer, a familiar cannery whistle: short, long, short. And the impulse that followed was one she was eager to indulge: jumping from the porch to join her neighbors on their downhill sprint, the cannery workers rushing headlong toward the sea as the sardines rushed headlong out of it.

At the Del Mar cannery, she stopped, caught her breath, and let the crowd move ahead. If Arthur had come here from the lab, which was most likely, he would already be inside, which meant she would have to wait. So she waited. She waited beneath the white sky, the air cold and foul. She counted the rats as they zipped between the buildings. She heard more whistles, she watched more cannery workers run. And what would happen, she wondered at some point when the crowds became unmanageable, if they didn't stop? What would happen if they simply ignored the canneries and just kept running down the full length of the Row, past the Coast Valleys tanks, past Lake El Estero, past the Hotel Del Monte, until they collapsed from exhaustion among the dunes, the sand reluctantly conforming there, wherever a good-sized clump of entrails had been washed onto the beach, opportunistic clouds of flies formed: mobile, black tumors that refused to disperse even when the seagulls swooped nearby. The guts and the flies were very interesting to her, as guts and flies tended to be. Even more interesting, however, were the half-dozen men combing the filthy sand with boots on their feet and buckets in their hands, just like Ricketts on the morning they first met.

When she felt Arthur's presence at her side, she made a point of not looking at him.

"You know," he said. "I sleep down there some nights. Pretty well sheltered from the wind. And when there's enough dry driftwood to make a bonfire—"

"What are they doing?" she asked, indicating the men.

"The scientists? Same thing as Doc, I guess, only they get paid a little better for it. That building over there is Stanford property: the Hopkins Marine Station." He gestured to the multiwindowed structure she had noticed on her prior visits. "Top-notch research facility, modeled after the one in Woods Hole."

"Why doesn't he work there instead of at the lab? If the pay is higher and the reputation is better . . ."

Arthur laughed. "Pay and reputation are probably the two things in this world he cares the least about. And there's no way they'd buy into his theories. Not yet."

She remembered the manuscript and its odd, energetic phrasing. Most of all, she remembered the *Styela* resting in her palm,

to their bodies? She remembered something her father had once told her about her mother's death—about how even after the fire had finally consumed her flesh, the bones remained aloft in the mud like leaves on a pond—and this, she cautioned herself, was how it would end if she didn't start being more deliberate, more clever. Mud and bones and collapse: all of it in service to ambitions that might not even be hers.

"Cigarette?"

She wheeled around. When their eyes met, she expected him to smile, but he just stared at her with a dishonestly straight face, as if he were physically suppressing something. The first few times she had seen him, she hadn't really noticed his appearance; the magnetism of Ricketts's presence had made such lesser observations impossible. Now, however, she was able to take stock. Seventeen years old, she guessed, possibly eighteen, short for his age yet solidly built, as if, had it not been for the stunting effects of poverty, he might have been taller than she and a good deal heavier. His clothes were old and colorless and almost insolently ill fitting, and his bearing was humble and nondescript. It was only his hair—wild and orange—that had any hint of extravagance to it, the curls sprouting from his skull like mutant carrots.

"I don't smoke," she replied.

"Me neither. I just tell the foreman I do so I can take a break when everyone else does."

He jerked his head toward a cluster of women standing behind him in the cannery's shadow. They were studying Arthur and her with an exhausted superiority, cigarettes pinched between thumbs and forefingers.

"Don't mind them," he whispered. "They think Sicily is the center of the universe."

"Then they probably should have stayed there."

Arthur winced, stepped forward, and drew her aside.

"Please," he said. "They've only just stopped hiding my boots in the steam cookers. I don't want to start anything."

At first, his hand on her elbow felt menacing. It reminded her of that moment in Ricketts's lab: her father holding her shoulders and shaking them. *Say it. Say it in words.* Arthur's grip, however, was neither strong nor coercive. If anything, it had a gentleness to it that almost seemed grateful, as if the threat of the steam cookers had been little more than an excuse to touch her. To confirm, she looked in his eyes and there it was. A dopey, irrepressible gladness. A crush. Unrequited, naturally, and more than a little sickening. But useful nonetheless.

"I wonder if you can help me," she said.

"I'm sure I can."

"I need my job back."

"Oh." He let go of her elbow and glanced conspiratorially in the direction of the lab. "I heard the whole thing was pretty nasty."

"What else have you heard? Has he found someone new?"

"To do the drawings, you mean?"

"Of course that's what I mean."

"Not that I know of. There's a man in Carmel who sometimes does photographs. . . ."

"But not drawings."

"Like yours?" His smile was so sweet, it made her stomach hurt. "No. There's no one around here who does anything like that."

"Then you'll ask him. As a favor to me."

"I'd be honored. But only if you're certain."

"Certain of what?"

He puffed out his cheeks and shuffled his feet. Then he dipped his head and took a step closer. She braced herself for another unwanted touch and was glad when it didn't occur.

"Don't wait here." He indicated the Sicilian women. "If they start to suspect something, I'll never hear the end of it. Go to that little outcropping above the beach where you read the paper every morning. I'll meet you as soon as I can."

By the time they reunited, it was late afternoon.

From the agreed-upon location, she watched the water. The tide was low in the yellowing light, the refuse from the canneries shining on the surface. Sardine scales glinted like flecks of tarnished silver. Sardine heads rolled in and out with the modest waves, grayish pink intestines trailing behind. Here and

there, wherever a good-sized clump of entrails had been washed onto the beach, opportunistic clouds of flies formed: mobile, black tumors that refused to disperse even when the seagulls swooped nearby. The guts and the flies were very interesting to her, as guts and flies tended to be. Even more interesting, however, were the half-dozen men combing the filthy sand with boots on their feet and buckets in their hands, just like Ricketts on the morning they first met.

When she felt Arthur's presence at her side, she made a point of not looking at him.

"You know," he said. "I sleep down there some nights. Pretty well sheltered from the wind. And when there's enough dry driftwood to make a bonfire—"

"What are they doing?" she asked, indicating the men.

"The scientists? Same thing as Doc, I guess, only they get paid a little better for it. That building over there is Stanford property: the Hopkins Marine Station." He gestured to the multiwindowed structure she had noticed on her prior visits. "Top-notch research facility, modeled after the one in Woods Hole."

"Why doesn't he work there instead of at the lab? If the pay is higher and the reputation is better . . ."

Arthur laughed. "Pay and reputation are probably the two things in this world he cares the least about. And there's no way they'd buy into his theories. Not yet."

She remembered the manuscript and its odd, energetic phrasing. Most of all, she remembered the *Styela* resting in her palm,

the beating of its primitive, unseen heart. She finally looked at Arthur. In one of his hands was yet another bucket. In the other was a mostly empty fish-meal sack.

"So. He wants me back?"

Arthur grimaced. "Yes and no. He wants you to steer clear of the lab. But he also wants you to work."

"Pictures for the specimen catalogs?"

"Yes."

He offered her the bucket. There was a damp dishrag stretched across its opening.

"Your first assignment," he explained.

"Thank you."

"Oh, don't thank me. I barely had to ask."

"And the sack?"

"Oh. That one's mine, I'm afraid. Empty coming up the hill, full coming down."

In the silence that followed, he gawked at her like a child.

"With a sack full of cats," he clarified, "it's a whole lot harder going down than coming up."

Silence.

"Going up, it's easier without the cats."

"Yes. You mentioned that."

He frowned and looked at his feet. "I suppose I did."

"Until next time." She turned away.

"Wait!"

When he reached into the fish-meal sack, she half expected

him to withdraw something furry and dead, teeth bared in protest. Instead, he produced her satchel, the heft of the sketchbook visible inside. She snatched it from him, took out the sketchbook, and ruffled the pages under her thumb. Some of them still felt wet.

"You left it at the lab after your accident. He wanted to return it to you the other day, but you and your father left before he got the chance."

She packed the sketchbook away and slung the satchel over her shoulder.

"And between you and me," he continued, "there's some funny stuff in there. Almost gave me nightmares."

"Then you shouldn't have looked."

"Oh, I'm glad I looked. It just seemed unusual, that's all. That such a lovely person could draw such ugly things."

She glared. He cringed. The scientists from Hopkins were retreating now, the gulls seeming to chuckle at them as they walked up the beach and toward the building on the point. In the distance, she could see the canopy of a dying kelp forest, its fronds transparent and sparse.

"Just this?" she asked. "Just what's in the bucket?"

"That's right. I'll come up the hill to collect it in a couple days."

"I'll be done tomorrow morning."

"That soon?"

"Yes. Best of luck with your cats."

When he was gone, she waited a bit to make sure he wouldn't return. Then she put the bucket on the ground and tore away the wet dishrag. At first, she couldn't even guess at what she was seeing. It was plantlike in shape, a thick, tapered, semi-coiled, leafless frond. In color and consistency, however, it was all animal: a disruptively fleshlike appearance to its pale skin, an asymmetry to it that implied a former attachment to something much larger.

It was only once she had taken the hill at a run, climbed the front steps, and dumped it out onto the porch that she understood. In her travels, she had heard of such things, but only from people whose penchant for superstition had made their tales fundamentally implausible: tales of a boneless beast, a creature of the darkest depths, a monster with a vulture's beak, with suction cups the size of dinner plates. She poked the tentacle with her pencil and flipped it over. Dinner plates, no, but large nonetheless, large enough to be frightening, large enough to hint at the dimensions of something as incredible as it was evil. Shivering, she retrieved the bucket and placed it upside down over the bloated squid arm, concealing it from view. Then she began to draw, filling page after page by memory until the sun had set, at which point she looked up from her drawing and out at the ocean. The sky was lit as if with a strange, gray fire. The trees were making the sound of arthritic joints, the air sharp with pine sap and salt. Her father was halfway home, halfway through his daily climb. She closed her sketchbook and began to tuck it beneath her. At the last moment, however, she re-opened it and put it back onto her lap, its pages turned to her most recent and most accurate work.

When he reached her side, he paused and looked down. "Started doodling, I see."

Something small and hard appeared in her throat: something that was difficult, but not impossible, to swallow down.

"Tasty looking, isn't it?" he said. "I should fry it up for dinner."

8

1998

HIS NEXT MESSAGE, MUCH LIKE HIS FIRST, COMES at her from beyond the aquarium's walls.

Outside on Cannery Row, the crowds gather and roll. The little squid's internal spillage is still fresh on her hands, the food room's brightness still blinds her. An unrest. An imbalance of power neither unpleasant nor new. Her first and last nights with Ricketts.

And more recently—but not too recently—the aquarium's opening day. Almost fourteen years ago now: October 20, 1984. There was a festival to commemorate the occasion, which she had specifically designed to appear homey and nonthreatening. A Dixieland jazz band made up of local musicians. Kids in hand-sewn sardine costumes, tinfoil scales falling from their arms and legs as they sang and danced in what barely resembled unison. Speeches by a handful of surviving cannery workers, all of them visibly inebriated. Balloon animals. Food trucks. Beneath it all, though, beneath the rough-hewn feel-goodery and Sicilian-style calamari, there was an unmistakable taste of something sleek and epic, audible whispers of the double-edged reward of impending world renown, of just how long it would take for the entire town to become unrecognizable as a result.

And has it come to pass? Is it unrecognizable? It's a question she asks herself often, especially now that historical preservation has come into vogue. Yes and no, she always says, like how a fingerprint does and does not resemble an actual finger. Sometimes you have to look hard—you have to look beyond the T-shirt shops and the laser tag—but the past is still there, a past even more necessary than Steinbeck's: the Costanoans and their lost, peaceful, shellfish-hungry tribes; the Spaniards who conquered and catholicized California, their fervor outwardly attributable to divine right and the glory of a distant throne, but that on closer inspection emitted the wet, fragrant heat of personal vendetta.

As for his message, it's not hard to spot. In many ways, it's as obvious as the beaching of the Humboldt squid. This time, however, it has taken human form: the two aquarium employees entertaining the visitors in line. The first is an intern in a full-body otter costume. The second is a banjo player singing well-known popular tunes rewritten in honor of the aquarium's residents: the Beatles' "Eight Days a Week" rewritten as "Eight

Arms and a Beak," referring to the eight arms of the octopus and the calciferous mandible concealed therein; the Kinks' "Lola," which is about a transvestite, rewritten as "*Mola*," which is one half of the scientific name of the *Mola mola*, the gigantic fish she still needs to figure out how to release.

Work, then, is calling: loud as it ever has, loud as it always will. But so is he. *Stay*, he says. *Watch and listen.* And she'll be damned if he isn't right. The intern is a girl of fifteen. The banjo player was once Monterey's only known homeless man. To anyone else, it would seem like an unfortunate pairing, but not to her. It reminds her of the good times—of October instead of May, of mammals instead of cephalopods—which means she's now following his instructions and then some. She hurries to the sea otter exhibit, right there among the paying public. She watches the little captives float and flip, somnolent one moment, clownish the next, fiddling with the hamster balls full of prawns and the tangled lengths of neoprene kelp: toys that are supposed to keep them from going mad in captivity.

Then, suddenly, she's on the aquarium's roof, standing in the shadow of a very different sort of tank. None of the otters up here are on display. Rather, they are on probation, undergoing a stint in rehab in the wake of maternal abandonment. The whole thing is very scientific, very sound, designed with the noble intention of eventual rerelease. The aquarist surrogate wears a welding mask, a poncho, and rubber gloves, all of it smeared with seaweed to obscure her human scent. The person, in other words, remains separate from the otter. The mother remains separate from the mothering.

There was a time, however, when it wasn't like this. Not at all. In the aquarium's early days, it happened right there in the little man-made cove below the deck. The aquarist surrogate—usually a woman, undisguised and unfragranced—would teach the poor orphan everything a mother otter would have. How to dive, how to hunt, how to get the clam and the rock, how to bang them together, how to clean up afterward. When the lessons were over and the final test was administered, the losers would be put on exhibit while the winners would be fitted with orange flipper tags and sent on their way. But then one day, disaster. A released otter returned to the cove, heartbroken and homesick and vengefully jealous, and charged the aquarist surrogate as she swam with her newest pup, biting down onto the ex-mother's face, thrusting ineffectually, and refusing to let go.

And as she stands here now—the Humboldts beginning to rot on the nearby beach, their corpses filling the air with a scent that is both inadvertent and authentic—she can turn her back on the rehab tank and look down onto Cannery Row from above. She can see the intern and the banjo player, she can imagine them failing and being placed inside a tank of their own. Tourists are everywhere, invasive and necessary, giving the street life and taking it away. There is a desperation to their desires, which she supposes would be all right except for one thing: the fact that desperation never arises out of certainty. Beneath all of this—beneath all the tributes and distractions and renovations—is a deep and fundamental doubt, and the aquarium is not immune. The real version can never peacefully coexist alongside its imagined twin, which is why the real bay and the fake one probably fight each other when the doors are closed and no one is looking, two thirsty giants battling for ownership of the night.

In her own life, it's happened before. She can trace the scar on her forehead to several verifiable sources, some obvious, some not. Some imagined, some actual. Today, however, only one seems to matter, only one seems to provide a rebuttal to his assertions. A collecting trip not in his tide pools but in the Amazon—she plus three other aquarists in search of arapaimas and *traíras* and peacock bass—during which a botfly bit her on the head. For the week following the implantation, she endured. She allowed the egg to gestate within a walnut-sized lump directly beneath the old scar tissue, the irritation growing each day, reaching heights she had never anticipated, until one night, alone in her tent with the river outside sloshing its way through the sort of mud that starts and ends civilizations, a tragedy took place, a tragedy even worse than the prodigal otter. The subcutaneous squirming and itching became too much and she was forced to expel the little embryo with a long, sad breath and a gentle application of the fingernails. Two lives at a mutually exclusive crossroads. A parasite and a host, a tourist and a local, and it's up to her to determine which is which.

9

1940

"YOU GET THEM WITH A KNIFE," ARTHUR EXPLAINED. "Slide it under the foot. I've got a Japanese friend in Chinatown who dives for them and eats them alive."

Margot continued to draw. An abalone today, a mollusk about the dimensions of a rugby ball, a scythe-shaped trail of pinholes marking the uppermost curve of its terraced shell, dark feelers emerging from the holes like tendrils of spilled ink. Yesterday, it had been an orange sea star, its plumpness veined with a net of prickly white. The day before, a turban snail, its black spiral topped with an opalescent crown. And in the days preceding it had been worms, what seemed like hundreds of them—flatworms, roundworms, polychaete worms, tube worms, fat innkeeper worms—their interminable numbers accompanied by Arthur's equally interminable monologues about the local sea life, the detail and enthusiasm of which stunned her. It was clear he was trying to imitate Ricketts: his unrushed cadence, his casual erudition. Most of the time it didn't work, but sometimes it did. Sometimes she would listen and respond, especially when the information seemed exotic or violent. Mostly, though, she kept to her sketchbook as he yammered on, his voice acquiring the same bland omnipresence as the surrounding fog.

And the fog. The fog. Always the fog. It was the most persistent phenomenon, meteorologic or otherwise, she had ever seen. Each morning as she stepped out onto the porch, there it was. Occasionally, it burned off in the afternoons to reveal a porcelain-like blue, but most of the time it stayed put, causing each passing hour, each passing day, to appear identical to the one before it. In any other instance, it would have been intolerable. Here, however, it meant something. It was a blank canvas on which she could envision a huge and glorious design, an abstract blueprint of her future inside the lab. With each new creature she was asked to draw, she could feel her desire taking shape again, her earlier doubts fading into something as useless and desiccated as the squid tentacle, which, after she had finished drawing it, had been kicked off the porch and into the dirt beneath the bougainvillea. And it was only a matter of time, she reassured herself whenever it caught her eye. Only a matter of time until she was once again in the center of things, until the right opportunity presented itself, until she could reclaim what had been promised her and unpack it with gratitude and greed.

"Once you hit bottom, you have to start running along the

ocean floor. You have to run or else they'll have time to hide in the rocks. And then there are the sea otters, which are another problem entirely."

She lifted her pencil and made a critique. Yes, success was imminent, but it wouldn't be easy, especially with work this deceptively simple. Seeing an object, isolated and context free, and then drawing it: a path that looked flat and straight on the map but that, once traveled, proved itself aggressively otherwise. The abalone, for instance. Its shell was correct—big, rough, oblong—but its foot was not, so she turned to a fresh page and began again.

"And that's why you should never trust Chileans. Because what they call an abalone is actually a rock snail, even though—"

Arthur fell abruptly silent. She continued drawing.

"Look," he resumed. "Down the hill."

Reluctantly, she lifted her eyes from the paper. Her father was making the climb to the house, which wouldn't have been remarkable except for two things. First, he was returning midday instead of in the evening: a dramatic disruption to his usual routine. Second, he was not alone. He was flanked by a woman and a boy, the sight of whom caused Arthur to fidget with nervousness. They didn't move like rich people, she noticed as the visitors continued to ascend, but they took great pains to dress like it: in clothing as well made as it was ill suited to even the mildest exertion. The woman, especially, seemed atrociously uncomfortable in her high-necked linen dress, the crisp fabric wilted with perspiration and clinging to her round limbs like butcher paper. She clutched a delicate straw boater in one substantial fist. The other fist dabbed at her forehead with a pink silk handkerchief, using the sort of care normally lavished on an open sore. She was panting from the effort of the climb but laughing, too, which produced something akin to the noise of the cannery whistles.

The boy, however, didn't make a sound. Like the woman, he was dressed in a way that indicated a specific type of masochism, but he didn't seem nearly as amused by it. His shoulders were hunched, his hands were clenched, and on his pale, sunken, strangely pious face was the pained expression of a convalescent forced from his sickbed instead of being allowed to die in peace.

"Oh no," Arthur said.

"Who are they?"

The trio came to a stop at the foot of the porch. She closed the sketchbook and wedged the pencil between its pages. Her father gave Arthur an obscure half smile and then turned to Margot.

"Allow me to introduce Mrs. Agnelli, my new business partner." He was speaking slowly and deliberately, giving his subtext ample time to sink in. "While we're inside, I trust you'll entertain her son, Tino."

Tino gave what Egon Schiele might have deemed a smile.

"I'll do my best," Margot said.

Anders escorted the woman up the porch steps and into the

house. Arthur exhaled loudly. Tino remained standing in the street, his gaze aimed sullenly at the treetops. Margot opened her sketchbook and began working again. The interruption was inconsequential, she told herself; she would return to her sketches undeterred. But the sudden urge to do something decisive and physical was too strong, so she drew back her hand and lined it up with the bucket. A slapping contest, as Ricketts would have said, that would send the abalone down into the dirt alongside the tentacle. Before she could make contact, however, a cannery whistle was sounding and Arthur was jumping to his feet.

"I'll be back," he said.

"No hurry."

"Tomorrow?"

"If we must."

He gave a manic smile and what almost looked like a curtsy, then sprinted down the hill twice as fast as the neighboring workers. When he had disappeared from view, Tino cracked his neck and unbuttoned his topcoat with a flicker of his thin-fingered hand. One eye seemed to be studying her sketchbook while the other eye scanned the perimeter of the house.

"My mother's people should stop torturing him." He sighed. "He'll end up just like my father."

She remembered the Sicilian women with their cigarettes: a school of sharks toying with their next meal.

"Your mother owns the Del Mar cannery," she guessed.

"Indeed."

"Is my father buying that one, too?"

"Likely not." He frowned. "But let's find out for sure."

Then, with an abrupt and reptilian speed, he was on the move: sprinting around the side of the house and disappearing within the rearmost branches of the bougainvillea. She stood and followed, the leaves scratching against her face. There was a window here, just above eye level.

"You're bigger," he said. "Help me up."

"No."

"Only for a moment. I need to see how they're sitting."

She squinted at him and then knelt down, hands basketed.

"Longer than a moment and I'm letting you fall," she warned.

He raised a well-polished shoe off the dirt and into her palms. When he lifted himself to the height of the window and transferred his full weight onto her, she was surprised at how light he was. He was the same age and gender as Arthur, but in terms of their individual physicalities, they couldn't have been more different: one of them sturdy and inert and almost impossible to get rid of, the other quick and insubstantial and seemingly on the perpetual verge of disappearance.

"Done." He hopped down without a sound.

"Well?"

"They're both on the sofa, which means no new business is under way. If there were a potential for that, they'd be across a table from each other. And there would be cake."

Margot nodded. She, too, could have intuited this at a glance, but she wouldn't have been able to explain it, which was an important difference.

"So," she said. "You're apprenticed."

"Apprenticed?"

"It means to—"

"I know what it *means*. I just don't know what you mean *by* it."

She gave him a look meant to convey forthrightness, not pride. "My father has been training me to take over someday."

"Preserving the legacy." He winced. "A noble path."

"And you?"

"Unlike my brothers, I'm not the sort of brute who can endure the canneries. So she totes me around with her instead."

"Then you should make yourself of use."

He eyed her disapprovingly. She looked at the dirt. The tentacle was just inches away, pill bugs nestled into its suction cups.

"Let's go back to the porch," she said.

"No. I prefer it here."

He perched himself on a branch that didn't look capable of supporting a sparrow, much less a human boy. She sat on the ground and gave the tentacle a little kick, which caused the pill bugs to wake and scatter. To an onlooker, it would have seemed like a childish thing—hiding in a bush, eavesdropping on the grown-ups—and at first, she felt that way, too. But the longer they sat there, the firmer her contact with the cold, hard earth, the more it appeared that Tino's preference had been the correct one. Their discussion was about to take a delicate turn, and she was grateful for the darkness and containment the foliage provided.

"So why is she here?" Margot asked. "If there's nothing new to talk about?"

Tino regarded her mournfully from above. "That's just the way my people do it, I'm afraid. A signed contract is only the beginning. A true alliance means socializing. Endlessly."

"Cake must be eaten." Margot nodded. "Children must meet."

"Don't forget all the trips to church."

He gave a terse, cynical smile. She offered one in return. He thought he wasn't like her, but he was wrong. They were exactly the same: offspring dragged around by powerful parents and treated as heir or prop depending on the circumstance; captives who, despite their protests, were surprisingly conversant in the language of captivity.

"Tell me about the contract," she said, rising to a crouch. They were looking directly into each other's eyes now, the bougainvillea blossoms arranged wreathlike behind Tino's head, as if by meticulous design. "What are the terms? I heard the cannery went for a very low price."

"*Outrageously* low, but only because he agreed to certain conditions."

"Such as?"

"He can buy sardines from my mother's fleet, but no one else's."

"She owns a fishing fleet, too?"

"The biggest one in town."

"So by selling the cannery to my father, she now controls both supply and demand."

"And effectively profits from each step of the production process while simultaneously avoiding the unions' antimonopoly nonsense."

"Not bad."

"I suppose. The only piece I don't understand is your father. What on earth could be in it for him?"

There was an especially large flower just above Tino's left ear. She reached up and tore it away, crushing the petals in her fist. Then she lowered herself back onto the ground. Again, Ricketts's strange words and their sticky echoes. The Methodists, the butterfly trees. Her father as a young man, asleep in a tent.

"I don't know," she answered.

Tino cracked his neck once more, the sound like corn popping.

"Well, my advice is to not care too much," he said. "There was a time when all that mattered to me was what she did and said and where I stood in relation to it. But now I realize it's a losing game. I'll succeed only if I escape."

She wiped her hand on her trousers. "Easier said than done."

"Is it, though? The way I see it, the only real problem is money. Just because our parents are rich doesn't mean we are."

She nodded and looked up. The green leaves looked perfectly

black against the white patches of sky; an occasional seagull swooped by to disrupt the pattern. A shrillness from inside the house. Mrs. Agnelli's laugh.

"That means they're done." He jumped from the branch. "Quickly, now."

They uncaged themselves from the bougainvillea, ran up the front steps, and sat side by side on the porch. Tino's clothes, she noticed, were still spotless even though hers were peppered with mulch. She tried to brush herself clean but stopped when the door opened behind them. The elders were already halfway through their formal, prim farewells.

"Speaking of money," Tino whispered, leaning closer. "You could sell those. Right here in town."

"Sell what?" she whispered in reply.

"Your drawings."

She retrieved the sketchbook and moved it onto her lap. "I've already got a buyer."

"Who?"

"Ed Ricketts."

Tino huffed in amusement. "Oh, Ricketts won't pay you. At least not in cash."

"Until Sunday," Anders announced loudly. "I look forward to Mass."

He guided Mrs. Agnelli past the children, down the steps, and onto the street. Here, there was another round of leave-taking: hands shaken, blessings offered, plans made.

"For your information, I plan on charging him," she replied, voice still low. "Three dollars apiece."

"Careful." Tino stood and rebuttoned his coat. "Don't price yourself out of the market."

She looked past their parents and down the hill.

"I'll price it however I want."

That night, Anders and Margot had steaks for dinner. Steaks so bad that even Ricketts might have thought twice before touching them.

When they were done eating, they sat on the floor across from each other in front of the sooty stone mantel and played a self-invented, two-man version of belote: an odd, complex French card game her mother was known to have favored. It was the first time since the episode at the lab that they had attempted something this companionable, and they both seemed a bit agitated by it. Anders was taking off his eyeglasses too often and buffing their lenses with too much intensity. Margot was tugging at the waistband of her trousers, as if it had become too tight.

"Now," her father said after the eighth and final trick. "Where does that leave us?"

He gathered up his cards. Margot hesitated. The game's scoring process was convoluted and specific, and she wasn't allowed to do any of the calculations on paper.

"I'm at seventy-three," she said. "And you're at eighty."

"That doesn't include my *carré* of tens."

"No. I suppose it doesn't."

"We have a winner, then. Shall we call it a night?"

For a moment, she felt like agreeing. The day had already been long and she was unusually tired. What's more, she was eager to be alone on the horsehair sofa, where she could shuffle through her thoughts and play them with far greater skill than she had just played her cards.

"One last game," she said instead.

He glanced at the clock on the mantel, waited out a few loud ticks, and then passed over his cards. She reassembled the deck, cut it, and gave it back to him.

"So," she said. "The Agnellis."

The words had come from her sharply and loudly, which she regretted but couldn't help.

"Yes," her father replied. His voice was calm and his eyes were fixed on the cards as he dealt them, flipping them onto the floor in near perfect piles, turning the proposed trump faceup. "Quite the situation. I don't think I've ever wasted so much time on snacks and pleasantries, but I suppose that's the price one pays when things are run by women."

"Pass," she said, leaving the trump untouched.

"Me too." He collected the cards and redealt them. "But I must say we were both amused when her son's face appeared in the window. It was like watching a Buster Keaton film."

She gritted her teeth. "Accept."

"*Coinchée*, then."

"And I, in turn, was amused to learn you signed a contract that, on the face of it, offers you no upside at all."

He looked up from his cards. She held her breath. His back was very straight now, the chipped, glass-shaded lamps etching black amber half circles beneath his eyes, and for some reason, she was thinking of her mother. It wasn't a thought that came to her often, that of the woman who had barely survived long enough to warrant a parental designation. Mourning, in particular—the process of purposefully summoning a memory in order to subsequently demolish it—had always struck her as far too much of a winnerless game. Tonight, though, it was as if she could finally see her mother's features clearly enough to miss them: a huge, white, disembodied head floating up to the ceiling, looking down on her with pity and affection, waiting for the signal to swell and explode and release fifteen years' worth of accumulated pressure.

"I was right the first time." He retrieved the card tin from the side table. "We're done playing."

She caught her lips between her teeth. She was ready. She was ready to know exactly what was at stake. She was ready to force the issue, to harpoon it and drag it from him, alive and growling.

"You've put me in exile," she snapped. "And the entire town knows it."

"You're out on that porch all day by your own stubborn choice."

"You told me not to go back there."

"Because you're better than that."

"I'll always have a scar." She gouged at the wound as if carving it anew. "I'll always look like this."

"You're right."

She threw down her cards and instantly regretted it. It was the most anemic-possible tantrum: eight small rectangles of paper, splayed in impotent disorder. Anders, however, seemed moved by the gesture. He scooted an inch closer to her and picked up her mess. Then he returned all the cards to their tin and tapped it with his forefinger.

"There's a reason I haven't told you yet," he said. "And it's not what you think."

"Does Mrs. Agnelli know?"

"No. I haven't told her, either. At least not the truth."

"Why not?"

He looked at the low, stained ceiling and then at his stocking feet.

"Because while I'm not planning on violating the letter of our contract, I'm certainly planning on violating its spirit." Here, a jittery pause. "And there's also some superstition involved, I'm sorry to say. I can't quite shake the feeling that, by speaking frankly about my hopes, I'm inviting the universe to ruin them."

She was gaping at him now, but couldn't help it. She had never heard him speak like this. She didn't even think he was capable of such a thing—addressing the mystical, much less using it as an excuse—and the resulting bafflement was so great that when he reached into his vest pocket, she was certain, somehow, that he would withdraw a weapon. And she was half-right. She had seen the switchbladed penknife hundreds of times before, usually when he was slashing open an envelope or severing the head from a cigar, but it had never looked as lovely or as old as it did this evening: glowing like a burnished nugget of bronze, the family name—the original, multisyllabic one—engraved on it in swirling, oversize script.

"You know what this is?" He placed it on the floor between them.

She nodded, her rage dissipating.

"It's the only gift I've ever given myself." He picked it up again and extended it in her direction. "And tonight, I'm giving it to you."

She hesitated. The reversal in his mood had been sharp and swift, which made his affection seem more perilous than his displeasure.

"You are? Why?"

In response, he took her hand, opened her palm, and placed the knife into it. It felt infinitely heavy against her skin, infinitely useful. She reached for her satchel and tucked the knife inside, right next to the sketchbook. He sighed but didn't smile.

"You want to return to his lab?"

She nodded.

"Then you should be properly armed."

"That's not—"

"It's late," he said briskly, standing. "You'll have to excuse me."

And then he was gone, the bedroom door closing noiselessly behind him.

For the next hour, she sat there, alone.

Then she returned to the horsehair sofa and unrolled herself as long as possible across it, propping up her ankles on one of the arms. Time seemed to be moving very fast now, the clock on the mantel ticking louder than ever, the seconds falling away. She imagined the world continuing to go on without her, the lights coming on inside Ricketts's lab, Ricketts behind his desk, her sketches spread out before him. She considered her desire for him and the manner in which it seemed to be growing with almost nothing in the way of fuel: just the buckets coming up the hill, the drawings going down. She thought of every decision her father had ever made, especially the ones she didn't understand. She thought of her mother's legacy, disfigured by the white-hot disturbances of death and birth; and when the last noises from the bedroom had subsided, she retrieved the satchel and withdrew the knife. She opened the knife to reveal the blade. She yanked up the cuff of her trousers and drew a line of blood across the side of her calf: the fleshy part where, no matter how deep she went, she was unlikely to hit bone. Then she wiped the blade clean and put the knife in her pocket.

And when she rose to her feet, opened the door, and began to run, there was no pain or fear. There was just excitement. The excitement of a world captured and contained and under her exclusive control, the taste and texture of it filling her mouth like food.

10

CANNERY ROW AT MIDNIGHT.

On her way down, she had avoided David Avenue, the most direct and well-lit route. Instead, she had kept to the side streets and alleyways, dropping onto the train tracks and lurking behind a steel storage cylinder until she was certain she hadn't been seen.

Now, at the outer walls of her father's cannery, she moved to the middle of the street. The air seemed green, vaguely bacterial, the fog wet and heavy and unnaturally close to the ground. She could hear the skittering sounds of pigeons and mice: those smart, dirty creatures that can both confirm debasement and foretell it. Somewhere, a machine was still in nocturnal operation, a boiler epileptic with captive heat, a processor stamping fish meal into oily cakes. The door of the lab was there in plain sight, solid and real. The building behind it, however, seemed as untrustworthy as a mirage.

Inside, she found a similar strangeness. She had been to working-class parties before, she had witnessed their pandemonium. This, however, was a new breed. Men and women assaulting each other before falling into prolonged embraces. Clothes dropping away with neither shame nor exuberance, but with the instinctual, businesslike inevitability of snake-shed skin. There was an old hobo squatting on the beer crate and pretending to read an upside-down volume by Hegel, a woman wearing a sardine net as a dress, sheaves of typewritten pages turning to a beer-soaked pulp beneath dozens of stamping feet. And then there were the people not contributing to the melee but observing it instead. They stood in the corner near the file cabinet; they were urbane, well groomed, remote. One of them in particular—a busty woman with lacquered blond hair—seemed particularly detached, looking down on the scene in sleepy amusement, cooling herself with a fan that had been folded from one of Margot's best sketches.

Enraged, Margot began to struggle through the crowd until a large form blocked her path.

"Don't worry. He's already hidden the good ones away."

She looked up. Steinbeck was heavy eyed and nearly motionless, the stiffness of his posture that of someone who was either completely sober or just moments from blacking out. The last time she had seen him he had been so vengeful, so irate. Now, under the influence of what was probably a gallon of beer, he seemed to have softened to her, or at least to the idea of her eventual reappearance.

"They're *all* good." She crossed her arms in front of her chest. "And I wasn't worried."

"Well, you have that look about you. Like you're sizing everything up and figuring out how much you can get for it."

Instead of replying, she indicated the woman, who was now using the sketch to blot her lipstick.

"Tell her to stop that."

"Oh, she won't listen. She's an actress. Here from L.A., on account of that goddamn movie." He clutched the sides of his waist. "She and her friends told me I'm getting fat, and I'm absolutely terrified they're right."

"Is Ricketts here?"

"Girls. Booze. Where else would he be?"

With that, he made his way back into the pit of the mob. She followed. It was crucial, suddenly, to feel that she wasn't succumbing to the pull of masses but fighting against it instead, and the music seemed to agree. It had been slow and rhythmic upon her entrance, but now it was emitting the high, bright squeals of an experimental style of jazz, the partygoers responding as if controlled by it. For a moment, she was afraid of being dragged underfoot and trampled. But as Steinbeck led her toward the kitchen, she remained completely untouched. Despite the density and animation of the crowd, she was able to move autonomously, securely, as if she were separated from the others by a thick yet invisible pane of something far more durable than glass.

When she and Steinbeck were a yard or two from their destination, a projectile sailed through the kitchen doorway and onto the dance floor.

"Watch out," Steinbeck groaned, continuing to push forward.

"Was that a steak?"

"There's no controlling them unless they're properly fed."

Another steak flew past her face and into the herd. She pressed herself against the wall.

"And it's nice of Ed," he admitted, "if a little lavish. Usually it's just a few cans of sardines, but I suppose he's feeling reckless tonight."

"Reckless?"

Steinbeck couldn't hear her, though. The crowd's excitement had grown too fierce, too deafening, so she just stood there and watched as half a dozen more steaks were flung through the doorway. For the next several minutes, there was audible chewing and swallowing, greasy hands wiping themselves on greasy shirts, mouths opening and closing around bottles and jugs, an endless volley of belches harmonizing to the music, which had changed yet again, this time to a wistful, foreign duet of singer and mandolin. A man in a woman's bathrobe began waltzing with a coatrack. The blond actress continued to look on, smug and immaculate.

"Beer?" Steinbeck asked.

"No."

"You'll want to reconsider that at some point."

And then he turned away, stomping heavily toward his rocking chair, the crowd trying and failing to eliminate his looming shape from view.

She looked in the direction of the kitchen. She sucked in her stomach and started walking. He would be inside, she told herself, standing in front of a fry pan, cloaked in fat and steam. But the kitchen was empty, so she spun around and scanned the front room, and that's when she saw him. He was moving quickly, past the desk and the file cabinet, past the fern in the Coast Guard buoy. She shouted his name, but he didn't seem to notice. Instead, he kept his head down, his expression both cheerful and pensive as he hurried out the rear door, an earthenware bowl in hand.

She followed, fighting what she knew was an idiot's smile. Outside, the night blinded her. On her journey down the hill, the streetlights had glowed yellow, obscuring the absence of the moon. Now the darkness seemed saturated, absolute, the densest fog she had ever seen settled over the land and water, the moisture in the air so thick she could feel it beading on her arms like sweat, clinging to the hairs and making her shine like something that had just recently been plucked from the sea. She was standing on a narrow balcony. Beneath her was a strange hybrid of a space: a back lot that merged seamlessly with the ocean and that was framed on two sides by the towering walls of adjacent canneries. The area closest to the lab was marked with a grid of concrete tanks, some of which had wooden lids, some of which did not. On top of one of the lidded tanks sat a bald man and his gaunt, homely female companion, their heads surrounded by a cloud of fragrant smoke. Wormy, the woman who had been there on Margot's first two visits to the lab, stood beside them. And Ricketts was leaning on the next tank over, the earthenware bowl perched on the tank's uncovered rim, a beer in one hand and a chunk of raw meat in the other.

Margot froze. The bald man held a pipe to his lips, inhaled deeply, and then passed it to the thin woman. Wormy coughed delicately and brushed something from the front of her dress. A spot of blood fell from the meat and onto Ricketts's boots.

"And to make matters worse," Ricketts said after pausing to take a sip of beer, "Zanuck gave him a private screening. Can you imagine it? Our John sitting there trying to be polite?"

"I've heard it's quite good, actually." The bald man shrugged. "And John gets along just fine with the L.A. types. Have you seen it in there tonight? It's like he's auditioning twenty-two-year-old blondes for the role of 'Most Likely to Make Carol Kill Him in His Sleep.'"

"Oh, let's not be too hard on him." Ricketts laughed. "He never expected this sort of thing, so he was unprepared when it happened. As far as I'm concerned, he can hide out in the lab for as long as he likes. Long enough to mend fences with his wife. Long enough for the world to forget all about *Grapes of Wrath*."

A noise from the lab—a loud, delighted shriek—and when he looked up in the noise's direction, his eyes instantly met hers, his expression so tranquil and steady that it was almost as if he had expected to find her there.

He tossed the chunk of meat into the tank, watched the resulting commotion within the water, took another drink, and then moved in the direction of the balcony.

"Mademoiselle Fiske."

His face was still impassive, unsurprised, but there was a glint in his eyes that was visible to her even in the darkness. The bald man frowned and nodded. Wormy smiled, her lips a bright and appealing red.

"Fiske?" mused the thin woman. "The family who . . ."

"That's right."

And she wasn't sure, but he seemed to be winking at her. Not in the louche, crude manner of some of her father's former colleagues, but in a way that made her feel as if she had just said or done something clever. Wormy took a long drag from the pipe, a heavy certainty clouding her eyes as if she already knew the outcome of the scene under way and was deeply, deeply pleased at the prospect of it repeating itself.

"Perhaps a beer?" Ricketts asked.

"No. Thank you."

"A puff or two?" He glanced at Wormy's pipe.

"Edward, she's a child."

"Or so they keep telling me."

Another wink, another shot of warmth running through her. Men and their compulsive need to offer things: Arthur and the cigarette, Steinbeck and the beer, Ricketts and everything else. Tonight, he bore none of the mute, inapproachable, ferocious qualities he had acquired as a result of dreams and distance. He was attentive and witty, and as the foursome resumed their conversation, she could feel her nervousness peel away. It no longer seemed dark. Instead, everything was illuminated as if by a searchlight: their shapes on the concrete tanks, the smoke swirling around the bald man's ears in direct imitation of a fleeting and translucent head of hair, all of it framed by the black skin of the bay upon which nearly a dozen sardine boats were skating with tectonic slowness. And had anyone else ever felt even half of what she was feeling now? she wondered. The dread and dizziness? The longing that waved from her chest like an extra limb? The desire to sit with someone on top of a desk and stare at him until something explosive was unearthed?

"What's in the tanks?" she asked.

Their conversation stopped midsentence. The thin woman giggled. The bald man crossed and recrossed his legs.

"Come down and see," Ricketts said.

She paused and then began to move down the stairs, her descent a marvel of luck and physics. When she reached his side, he smiled and took another swig of beer. Inside the tank, a dorsal fin periodically broke the surface, the shadow of a small, tense body beneath.

"What kind of shark?" she asked.

"Spiny dogfish. *Squalus acanthias.* Would you like to feed her?"

He offered up the earthenware bowl. She selected the largest morsel it contained and felt her skin flush when his mouth made a click of approval. When she dropped the meat in, she saw a tremor and a curl, muscles seizing up with pleasure, the underwater implications of working jaws and flexing gills.

"Edward," Wormy noted, "she's bleeding."

She looked at her fingers, at the red leavings of the shark's meal. Then she remembered the penknife. She looked down. As before, she felt no pain, but her right trousers leg was crimson from knee to ankle.

"Indeed she is." Ricketts turned to his companions. "Will you excuse us, please?"

Inside, the crowd had thinned considerably.

The tourists from L.A. were gone, as were most of the others. Only a dozen or so guests remained, most of them gathered around Steinbeck's craggy height like a family of squirrels praising a redwood, all of them singing in a language she couldn't place. The man in the bathrobe was alone, the coatrack abandoned and upended, his affections redirected toward a large glass jar with a brownish liquid inside. The desktop was bare of everything, including papers.

As they entered the bedroom, he removed his coat and tossed it on the floor.

"Take a seat on the bed, please, and roll up your trousers," he said, disappearing into the bathroom.

She sat and tried to steady herself. Her sketch of the young mother was still on his wall, its presence thrilling, auspicious. When he reappeared and sat next to her on the bed, there was the urge to push him down and stake her claim, but she clenched her fists until it subsided. From beyond the door, she could hear the final notes of Steinbeck's chorus, the melody drifting off into hums and moans.

"How did this happen? It's deep."

"I don't know."

"You don't *know*?"

He smiled, shook his head, and wiped a pair of nail scissors on his shirtsleeve.

"I can give you some ethanol if you'd like."

"No. I don't need it."

"Well, in that case, try to do better than I did at sitting still."

She nodded. As the needle entered and reentered her skin, she tried to pretend it hurt, but it still didn't, even when he tugged the sutures into a knot and pressed a strip of gauze firmly against her leg.

"You probably should have taken that ethanol. You look a little green."

"I'm fine."

"Glad to hear it. Let's hope I didn't botch this one quite as badly as the first."

She leaned toward him.

"I thought I told you to sit still," he warned.

But when she touched the back of his neck, he didn't move away. He just laughed quietly, as if remembering a particularly filthy joke, and she could feel the vibration of it as she put her mouth against his. When they moved apart, he wasn't smiling anymore.

"Fifteen," he said, shaking his head. "Fifteen years old. Am I imagining things, or aren't they making girls like they used to?"

"My mother was married at seventeen." Her fingers were still on his neck, pressing into the notch at the base of his skull, tracing the line of demarcation between his skin and hair. "I was born a year later."

"And look what happened to her."

She removed her hand.

"I'm sorry. All I'm trying to say is that these are different times," he said. "Far different. A young woman of your caliber should have more useful things on her mind."

"You sound like my father."

"Your father's right."

"Then let me work here. With you. Inside the lab."

He laughed again, but still no smile. "I trust you'll understand why that's completely out of the question."

"I won't be a bother."

"I don't believe that for a second."

They exchanged a long stare, and then she backed away just enough for him to see her fully. She had never attempted this sort of thing before—this arch and this tilt, this throwing back of the shoulders, this parting of the lips—but she knew she had done it right when his eyes briefly wandered down to her waist and then back up to her face, his breath coming through his mouth instead of his nose.

"Tomorrow morning," she said.

He squinted at her and tried to stifle something: a giggle or a whistle, or possibly a groan.

"I won't get arrested?"

"I'm sure of it."

"Fine," he said, making for the door and allowing himself one half of a grin. "Mind your manners, though. I'm not the sort of man who stands for being harassed."

11

1998

HIS THIRD MESSAGE ARRIVES AT A BAD TIME.

Everyone is here, every last aquarist, in a conference room that is slightly nicer than a nonprofit should allow. She sits at the head of the table. The aquarists sit along the sides in a hierarchical phalanx determined mostly by tenure and a bit by skill. They are all dressed exactly like her, all of them in uniform, their blue shirts extending out to a vanishing point of which de Chirico would have been proud. She's assembled them well over the years; she's kept them to a certain type. Mostly men. Odd but not ashamed, or even particularly aware, of their oddness. Unkempt, ruddy, resilient, amenable to camping, bathing in rivers, repeated exposure to ticks, ingestion of iodine-treated pond water. Dressed as if for action: bleach-stained jeans tucked into black rubber boots that stomp across the wet floors with a specific sort of casual, unwarranted bravery. Most of all, though, there's the fact of their relationship to their work. To a less enlightened soul, it could seem like drudgery: those endless loops of routine maintenance, knuckles permanently abraded by fiberglass and salt. They, however, treat it with a palpable sense of purpose, their aims so noble that they give her faith by proxy. Whenever she can, she invites herself along on their collecting trips. She's afraid of seeming useless, so mostly she just watches them in admiration disguised, for the sake of her reputation, as evaluation. She watches them blast tube anemones from their sandy burrows with a gasoline-powered pump and a hundred feet of garden hose. She watches them catch half-moons with pieces of candy-colored yarn on barbless hooks. She watches them lure garibaldis and señoritas into their nets with the luxuriant stink of fresh sea urchin roe, and by the time they return to the aquarium with their prizes in tow, she is drunk with secondhand excitement.

As for Arthur and Tino, they sit to her immediate right and left. Unmatched bookends, exceptions working overtime to prove the rule. Sometimes she wonders what her father would have done, but there's no way of telling. He could have gone either way, embracing them as comrades or vanquishing them as rivals. As it stands, she's pleased with her choice. They've each served their purpose nicely: Tino, in his long-ago willingness to turn over a crucial piece of property, to defuse the tension among the fishing contingent; Arthur in his jack-of-all-trades gregariousness, which in his old age has blossomed into something downright beatific. It seemed only fair to take them in, to give them titles, to pay them for a loyalty she appreciates but can't explain.

Which is why she bites her tongue when the two of them begin talking. As boys, they were never friends. Their personalities were too different, their communities too segregated. In their old age, though, they've grown close. They come alive in each other's company, they relish the tag-team retelling of old stories, which is what they're doing right now: relating how in August 1984, two months prior to opening day, a complication arose.

"The wharf pilings exhibit was missing its . . . ," Arthur begins, eyes big and vaudevillian.

"Wharf pilings," Tino concludes, deadpan.

But not for a lack of planning. Almost two years earlier, Arthur and Tino continue, they had begun to prepare. They had commissioned the fabrication of fake vinyl-polyester-fiberglass pilings, instructed a dive team to submerge them in the bay and secure them to actual pilings in the hope that the fakes would acquire a similar decorative cloak of invertebrate life. It was only much later, with the aquarium at the cusp of completion, that they realized their mistake. The desired populations—colonies of mussels and barnacles and anemones—had become so well established that it was impossible for even the most observant, capable aquarists to physically separate the fake pilings from the real ones, much less tell them apart.

And this is where she stops listening, because when they tell the next bit, she knows they will tell it wrong. They won't talk about how, when they broke the news to her, she didn't speak and she didn't sigh. Instead, she removed the penknife from her pocket, placed it on the blank, spotless expanse of her desktop, and spun it on its narrow end like a top, Tino and Arthur watching in horror as the knife took a handful of tight revolutions before falling with a clank.

"What should we do?" Arthur asked.

"We'll move forward precisely as intended. We'll remove the pilings and put them in the tank."

"But the whole wharf could collapse if we take the wrong ones," Tino protested.

"This entire town could collapse," she replied, aware of the ensuing hyperbole but doing nothing to stop it, "and I wouldn't care. As long as my aquarium remains standing."

At midnight, then, the team reassembled, ready to do as instructed. The divers descended and made their best guesses, their cleanest cuts. The aquarists attached floats to the severed pilings and towed each of them over to the launch ramp. Tino and Arthur backed the boat trailer into the water and helped maneuver the pilings on board. The collectors covered the pilings with seawater-damp burlap sacks. When everything was loaded, they all waited for a moment, wincing. They expected to hear the creaks and snaps of breaking wood, the jarring, sonic-boom splashes of big things falling into an even bigger body of water. But they heard nothing, so they began the slow, careful journey back to Cannery Row, Tino and Arthur in the tow truck, the others in a motley fleet of vehicles following close behind, Margot sitting protectively astride one of the shrouded pilings on the trailer, her jeans cold and wet, the night wind weaving through her hair as she guided the secret, merciless parade away from the shore and into town.

The conference room is silent now. They are all looking at her: Arthur and Tino and the aquarists, looking at her and grinning in a way that reminds her of Ricketts. And she wants to say something that will express her gratitude, maybe even her love, but the moment has already passed. The meeting is under way again, the staff's attention precisely where it should be: on more urgent, more *Mola*-related matters.

And it's a shame, because the story of the wharf pilings has been left unfinished. Not in a strictly narrative sense—beginning, middle, end—but in terms of its lesson. For a while there, in the years immediately following the incident, she could barely contain herself. She was so pleased by the grand gesture, so proud of it. She honestly believed the retrieval of the pilings was the sort of anecdotal monument outlandish enough to send a ripple through space and time, theatrical enough to change things, powerful enough to reach him in that place beyond life. In the years since, however, she's recognized an upsetting pattern, a certain scorched-earth mentality. The self-inflicted leg wound comes to mind, as does the time she traveled to Key

West to hunt down and seduce the reclusive designer of a revolutionary new jellyfish tank. There was also the time she insisted on using her own two hands, instead of a trained professional's, to weld the surge machine for the kelp forest exhibit. So loud, these actions. So dramatic and unsubtle. And she regrets them not because she's embarrassed, but because Ricketts's latest message is now so clearly in opposition, so clearly laid out on the surface of this big, expensive table.

"You'll have to excuse me," she says, standing.

"But we were just about to—"

"Not now."

"But we need you to decide about the—"

"It doesn't matter. Surprise me."

And within the aquarium proper, within the spaces meant for tourists—tourists who observe and mock and praise and sometimes imitate, tourists who think it's all for them, all for show—she feels, for the first time in years, like a failure. The darkness she sensed on the rooftop, the darkness at the perimeter of the otter rehab tank, is now falling in earnest. She's seeing shapes in the periphery, the shadows of doomed company, eerie black profiles against the vivid, backlit blue, the ghosts of people who once felt this same thing and couldn't crawl out from under it. Outside, the banjo player offers up an acoustic homage to Duran Duran entitled "Hungry Like the Wolf Eel." Inside, the white sturgeons trawl the tank bottom with their Confucian whiskers, giant sea bass loom midwater like obese, blue black sentries, white-plumed anemones sprout in furry, albino gardens. She doesn't hate it. Of course she doesn't. But she can imagine being someone who does. Not just the fish and the anemones and the repurposed pop songs, but the aquarium itself. She can imagine hating how its perfection and cleanliness approach the realm of parody. She can imagine hating how whenever the fish speak their own dual names—*Mola mola*, ocean sunfish—she's never quite sure which one is the alibi: the one used by the scientist or the one used by the layman.

"Oh, just put it out of its misery," she said upon first learning that the *Mola* had outgrown its tank.

"You'd honestly rather murder it than just let it go?" Arthur gasped.

"I don't see the difference."

"You're kidding, right?"

And she's frantic now and sweating, the aquarium's crowds suddenly indistinguishable from the ones that used to attend Ricketts's parties. Why, she asks herself, do both courtrooms and aquariums have the same word for the thing that contains the evidence: exhibit? Why do the visitors always—*always*—tap on the exhibit windows, even though they are expressly requested to refrain from doing so? Is it because they want the fish to acknowledge them in the same way they are acknowledging the fish? And why do they take so many photographs? Hundreds and hundreds of snapshots without a single human face in them: a thought that freezes her in place right beneath the gray whale skeleton suspended from the ceiling of the atrium, her sweat starting to cool, her muscles beginning to shake. A family photo album, she imagines, horrified, in which both people and fish are given equal precedence. Fish pouting and mugging alongside the newly born and newly betrothed. Fish exhausted by their singular, immersive knowledge, suspending mankind's breakable prism in a way that both devours light and excretes it.

12

1940

"YOU'RE DOING IT WRONG."

She lifted her pencil to shoulder height and let it fall onto the desk.

"Come," Ricketts said. "I'll show you. Again."

She gave him a narrow look. Then she rose to her feet and followed him through the lab, down the rear stairs, and into the back lot. Outside, she squinted into the fog as he retrieved a bucket from beneath the balcony's overhang. It was the most unsubtle hour of the morning, sharp and white with noise and light, the canneries running at full throttle. The sharks were restless in their tanks today, their bodies stirring the water into a chop. Her father's place of business was not far from here, the possibility of his appearance both immediate and real, but she didn't care. All that seemed to matter was the fact that for the past two weeks of coming to the lab, the only thing she had succeeded at was failing. Failing to maintain even the faintest shred of aloofness and disinterest, her excitement at his closeness still obvious and hateful. Failing to entice him in any manner, his treatment of her still formal and unwilling.

He handed her the bucket without comment. She carried it to the water's edge. The tide was well on its way to lowness, their feet surrounded by piles of cannery refuse and lawns of algae. A trio of plovers side-eyed them as they used their tweezer-shaped bills to mine the sand for bugs.

"Look down," he said. "Tell me what you see."

Her chin dropped to her chest. It was the fourth time in as many days that he had brought her here and attempted an explanation that didn't quite take, and this was perhaps the biggest failure of them all: the fact that, despite urgently wanting to, she was unable to fathom how he worked or what he was hoping to achieve by it. It was enough to make her want to crack her head open again or reempty the jug of formaldehyde: whatever would return her brain to the looseness it had possessed on her first night in the lab, to the semi-stupor required to understand him and his methods.

"The ocean." She sighed.

"What else?"

"A tide pool."

"And what's inside of it?"

She studied his face for traces of familiarity or suggestiveness, for any indication that he felt as unsteady as she did. But he was responding to her exactly how he responded to everyone else, with a happy crispness that seemed to shut the door to any possibilities except the honorable ones. And that, she told herself, was the cruelty of charisma: how it's never satisfied with the capture of an individual. How it requires the ensnarement of the masses to thrive.

"Sardine heads."

"What else?"

"A crab. A snail. A little fish."

"You haven't learned the Latin nomenclature yet?"

"You hired me to draw them. Not memorize their names."

Then an unexpected yet deeply satisfying response: a whistle and a shake of the head, an exasperation that seemed more like the product of amusement than annoyance.

"Fair enough. Just put them in the right piles and that will suffice."

"But your piles make no sense."

"Of course they do." He gestured at the three creatures, each one different in every respect save its general placement in relation to the waterline. "Things that live together should go together. And things that live elsewhere should go elsewhere."

"I don't understand."

"You don't? I feel like I've made it perfectly clear. And on several occasions."

"You find them in a certain spot today—"

"The *high intertidal*."

"You find them in the high intertidal today. But by tomorrow, they could be anywhere. All the way out. At the bottom of the ocean. Any of them could go anywhere they like."

"That's precisely it, though! They *could* go anywhere. But they never actually *do*."

She dipped a toe into the pool in question and stirred it around. She watched the fish panic, the crab scurry, the snail remain blindly in place.

"But a crab looks nothing like a fish," she muttered. "And a fish looks nothing like a snail. Or haven't you noticed?"

"You sound like the boys over at Hopkins."

"You mean the real scientists? The ones who know what they're doing?"

"For your information," Ricketts replied, his tone still alarmingly good-natured, "they keep my specimen catalogs on their shelves. They use them for their graduate course work."

He blinked and grinned. She didn't desire her father's intrusion, not in the least. She did, however, desire his clarity, his confidence, his brutal adherence to a system that had long since been praised and proven.

"I'm going back inside," she said.

"Absolutely not. You'll do it right today. Even if it kills me."

She set her jaw and met his gaze, trying to hold it for several seconds longer than usual, to finally extract something from it. He was already on the move, though, approaching the shark tanks and beginning to inspect each one in turn, seemingly oblivious to her company. For the next few minutes, she just stood there, watching. Once or twice, she tried to stop herself. She tried to do something that would convey the presence of her free will and the absence of an infatuation so deep, it had begun to border on servitude. But it was hopeless. All she could do was marvel at him: the air gathering around him as he studied his captives, the world shimmering beneath his single-mindedness, eliminating everything in its periphery.

The saddest part was that on the first morning of her apprenticeship here, she had assumed it would be easy. Bolstered by her triumph on the night of the party, she had entered the lab without knocking, eager to see the look of surprise on his face, the surprise morphing into delight. Instead, she was met with an empty room, the whole place completely abandoned save for a selection of preserved tide pool creatures already lined up on the desk, inert and perfect in their jars of yellow fluid. On the seat of the desk chair was a note written in a somewhat feminine hand, detailing both the manner in which the specimens should be portrayed and the full contents of the kitchen in case she got hungry. She sat down and tried to work but found herself unable. Her eyes wandered away from her papers at every opportunity, divining the clues that, if assembled in the right order, would help to shrink the distance between her body and his. She wanted to stand up, jump around, knock things from the shelves. She had, however, made herself certain promises: detachment, maturity, indifference, restraint. So she forced herself to remain behind the desk, her only concession to her weaker impulses the occasional visit to his bathroom, where she would stare at herself in the mirror and perform the sorts of actions that, until now, she had always considered wasteful and sad: the fluffing of hair, the pinching of cheeks, the releasing of the top two buttons of her shirt, anything to ensure her attractiveness when he eventually found her sitting there with his jars, one living body among the dead.

The morning came and went and still he failed to appear. At around noon, she put her sketches into an immaculate pile and rose from the desk. She went into the kitchen and cut a chunk of salami from the links that hung above the stove top like stalactites. She opened a can of the same sort of sardines her father either was or was not in the process of canning. She washed one of the dirty glasses in the sink and filled it from a pitcher of milk in the icebox. Then she took her meal out to the balcony that overlooked the shark tanks and the shoreline, and that's when she finally saw them: Steinbeck and Ricketts and Wormy, all of them out as far as the tide allowed, all of them bent over the same patch of water as if whatever was inside of it required three grown humans to successfully subdue.

Her lunch forgotten, she descended the stairs to the back lot and positioned herself in the most obvious spot: sitting on one of the lidded concrete tanks, faced in their direction. She could hear Ricketts guiding the others as they rummaged through the water and filled their buckets. Occasionally, there was a small spark of excitement or humor: a rogue wave dousing them with spray, a slapstick stumble on the rocks, a sea cucumber eviscerating itself onto Wormy's hands, Steinbeck insisting he had been bitten by a periwinkle until Ricketts reminded him that on a purely technical level, periwinkles didn't have teeth but, rather, a rasplike tongue called a radula that was used to scrape algae from the rocks. Otherwise, it was meditative in the extreme, the spell unbroken until, about an hour into Margot's observations, Wormy suddenly looked up from the water and into her eyes. It wasn't a long glance and it wasn't a combative one. But it was enough to make her retrieve her lunch and return to the lab, mortified.

"Don't mind me."

Arthur was rocking in Steinbeck's chair, one of Ricketts's essays sitting on his lap.

"I won't," she replied.

She put her dishes in the kitchen sink and reclaimed her place behind the desk. Before stopping for lunch, she had been sketching a clownish, misshapen little gastropod called a sea hare, and now, as she resumed the task, she could feel the cold, unwelcome spark of Arthur's surveillance.

"They mate in orgies, if you can believe it. Hundreds of them sometimes. Right there on the seafloor. They're hermaphrodites, so it doesn't really matter if—"

She looked at him sternly. When he scratched his scalp, she could hear sand falling from his hair and onto the manuscript.

"Have you read that before?"

"What?" He swept the sand from the papers. "This?"

She nodded.

"Sure. Plenty of times, but not this particular draft. Every time he rewrites it, I learn something new."

The wisest course of action, she knew, would be to leave it at that, to express no further interest. But she couldn't help herself.

"Like what?"

"Well, like this." He cleared his throat and took on a deeper, more authoritative tone. "'Not dirt for dirt's sake, or grief merely for the sake of grief, but dirt and grief wholly accepted if necessary as struggle vehicles of an emergent joy—achieving things which are not transient by means of things which are.'"

She frowned. He beamed.

"Almost makes you want to cry," he said. "Doesn't it?"

And when she returned to her sketches, she expected to feel just as scattered and uninspired as before. It was, however, the opposite. The images were flowing from her with such frantic accuracy that she almost thought herself possessed, and this, she realized, was how she would eventually win him. Long hours, half-empty rooms, dirty hands, wet feet, watching and being watched until she appeared, especially to herself, to be the sort of person he might want.

So it was for the next thirteen days: sketching in the morning, lunching alone from her spot on the shark tank while the others searched and collected. She tolerated Arthur's presence in the afternoon. She listened to the sound of Wormy typing on the typewriter in the bedroom. Most of all, she waited for Ricketts to acknowledge her in even the most cursory way, and in this regard, she sometimes got her wish. He would nod at her from the tide pools or offer a polite, dimensionless hello as he wandered into the kitchen for a bottle of beer, and the thrill of the encounter would be just enough to sustain her until that evening, when she and her father would both make their separate returns to the house on the hill. At dinner, which was still being prepared without conversation or camaraderie, they would stand at the kitchen counter and Anders would look at her in a way that seemed heavy, that sought to convey something; but he never asked any questions or voiced any suspicions, and she was never forced to lie or brag or defend herself. For some reason, she was no longer expected to play the spy, which meant her days in Ricketts's lab remained unnoticed, unquestioned, and began to acquire a dreamlike quality as a result.

Today, though, she knew it was real. As she stood there tracking his progress through the grid of shark tanks, she knew the universe was solid and verifiable, and she wanted to do something to prove it. So she reached down and grabbed the nearest object she could find: a small, sharp-edged rock that landed in the bucket with a clang.

He whipped around, hurried to her side, and held out his hand.

"Let's see."

She passed the bucket to him. As he peered inside, she watched his face closely, desperate to see something—anything—that would replace that look of epic, imperturbable calm. So when he smiled broadly, it was contagious, the last remnants of her reserve mutating into relief.

"I've been trying so hard to—"

"Come here," he said. "Slowly."

She bent down next to him, as near as she could come without touching. His face was just inches from hers, so close that she could practically feel his beard against her cheek. When he extended his hand to retrieve the rock, she saw the source of his sudden happiness: two worms, flat and pale and oblong, their bodies covered in blue, branchlike markings that reminded her of trees in winter.

"Large flatworms," he said.

She nodded. *"Alloioplana californica."*

"I thought you hadn't bothered yourself with the names."

"I lied."

Another smile, another seizure in her heart.

"Well, everyone has a different idea of the truth, I suppose." He shrugged. "As for these two little miracles, there's no doubt. They're excellent finds but delicate ones. So much as brush them with a fingertip, and they'll split in two."

He reached into his pocket and extracted a glass microscope slide. Then, with what seemed like an excess of caution, he maneuvered the slide directly beneath the bigger worm's head and remained motionless, wordless, as it recoiled slightly before oozing its full length onto the glass. He secured the rock between his knees, careful to leave the second worm untouched. Then he removed a glass vial from his other pocket, filled it with seawater, and eased both the slide and the worm into it.

"God, I love these," he said quietly. He plugged the vial with a rubber stopper and then tilted it up toward the sky. "Most people think they're appalling, but I just love them, I really do."

In the high, bright glare of the shore, she could see, more clearly than ever before, the evidence of his age. There were wrinkles—deep ones—across his brow, a stubborn quality to the way he held his mouth. In his eyes, though, was that flintlike spark, the glow of the fog internalized.

"You try the next one," he said, resting the vial beside the bucket and producing another microscope slide from his pocket.

"I don't think—"

"Just do it. Nice and slow."

He passed her the slide, retrieved the rock from between his legs. She did her best to mimic him: holding the slide with a light grip, approaching the worm with a reverence that seemed wholly disproportional to the task at hand. For a moment, the worm seemed unwilling, its body contracting, its branches rippling, but she didn't flinch. Instead, she remained perfectly still as the worm began to pour itself incrementally forward, making its deliberate transition off the rock and onto the slide.

"Oh," he said. "Very nice."

He held out his hand. She passed the slide to him. He slipped the second worm into the vial alongside the first.

"I'll draw them," she said.

He looked away from the worms and into her face. And there it was: the expression she had been trying all this time to cultivate, waiting all this time to see, a new sort of wickedness framing his grin, a glad darkness born from the type of pain that, if you endure it long enough, eventually turns to pleasure.

"Yes," he replied. "But first, we need to kill them."

They were in a room she had never seen before.

"Sit over there, on the Buick," he instructed. "I'll let you know when it's time."

"Can I—?"

"A moment, please. Only a moment."

His voice was brisk and methodical, as unfamiliar as her surroundings. She took a seat on the hood of the car. They were in a garage: a ground-level chamber flush with the back lot and one level below the main building. There were two metal sinks against the far wall, dozens of bottles on a series of warped, poorly hung shelves, all of them labeled in a chemist's obscure script, an icebox just as dilapidated as the one in the kitchen, lidded trash barrels filled with what she could safely assume was not the usual sort of trash. On the raw-wood countertops was a variety of scientific equipment: microscopes, flasks, burners, tongs, an abundance of glass slides like the one she had used to capture the worm, all of them stored upright in a box marked PROPERTY OF HOPKINS MARINE STATION. What really drew her eye, however, was the old china hutch at the base of the staircase. It was filled with what looked like hundreds of bottled specimens, many of which she had seen in isolation before, but never all together.

"Come here."

She looked away from the hutch. He was standing in front of the sinks. She slid down from the hood of the car, and went to his side. Most of the morning's collections had already been sorted and categorized into metal bins: hermit crabs cowering in their pilfered shells, snails stretching their gooey feet up the sides of their enclosures, small sea stars curling and uncurling their slender, spiky legs as if desperate to signal something. The worms, however, were still alone in their vial, untouched and alive, resting quietly on their microscope slides.

"Well then," he announced, his voice perfectly amiable now, but also too jaunty, too official. "We'll start with one part menthol to nine parts seawater, which should get them nice and relaxed. And because we're feeling fancy, we'll add a dash of magnesium sulfate, but not too much because we're running low and my current supplier is one of those shortsighted types who insists on being paid."

He let out a snort, but she remained straight-faced, intent.

"Awfully serious today, aren't you?" he said.

"I thought this was serious business."

"It is."

"So what happens next?"

"Like I said, a nice splash of menthol."

He selected a bottle and held it directly beneath her nose. When she inhaled, there was a brain-flushing odor halfway between pine and mint, the strength of it almost enough to push her over the edge.

"Into the bin?" she rasped, eyes watering.

"That's right."

She took the bottle from him and let a glug or two escape. Then she watched him uncork the vial that held the worms, and as the worms slid from the vial and into the liquid, she expected something intense and purifying, something like the burning sketchbooks. But the worms barely moved, their edges making a slight upward curl before falling from the slides and stiffening into gradual paralysis.

"Are they dead?" she asked.

"No."

He uncapped another bottle and poured its contents into the bin.

"Now they are."

They both coughed, the smell in the garage unthinkably foul. Eyes watering, she searched his face, but he just smiled with the same vacant brightness as before and turned toward the icebox.

"And now we'll just give them another minute." The ease in his voice was an insult now. When he opened the icebox door, she could see a stack of dead cats, a tapestry of bared teeth and stiff tails. "And then we'll rinse them down and get them into the formalin: a five percent mixture, just to be safe. As for the rest of our little friends, I suspect we'll use some Bouin's fixative on the mollusks, or maybe some Zenker's. And the brittle stars should be easy enough. Seventy percent alcohol and just a splash of glycerin. It's important to remember the glycerin. Keeps the articular membranes nice and flexible so there's no risk of—"

She backed away from the sink and reclaimed her seat on the car.

"You disagree?" he asked, shutting the icebox. "About the glycerin?"

"No."

"Then what's wrong?"

She looked at the hutch again. She wasn't sure if it was the euphoria of working alongside him or the lingering effect of the menthol. Either way, the sea creatures in their jars seemed to be moving slightly. She blurred her eyes, hoping to erase what she was seeing, but they came even more alive as a result. And she wanted to say something about it, but how to phrase it? How to put it in a way he couldn't possibly discard or misinterpret?

"I've been having dreams," she said.

At that, his face finally darkened. He wiped his hands again, removed his apron, and joined her on the Buick's hood. Their legs were almost touching, both of their feet propped up on the front fender, and it reminded her of sitting on the bed with him, both of them admiring her sketch, both of them fully aware of what would happen next.

"'The dream is the aquarium of the night,'" he said.

"From the new draft of your essay?"

"No. From Victor Hugo."

"I don't like it when people quote things. It's better when they just say it for themselves."

"I disagree. I feel like I always sound better when I sound like Jung."

"Jung is even worse than Hugo."

"Have you read either of them? No lying this time."

"I haven't. And I don't intend to."

"Really? I think you'd benefit highly from a little dip into the collective unconscious."

She put a hand on his knee. He gently removed it.

"Margot Fiske," he said. "You promised."

There was a fast, sharp pain in her lungs, her eyes once again glued to the specimens in the hutch. They weren't moving anymore. In fact, it was as if they had never been alive at all.

"It never should have happened," he said softly. "I'll never forgive myself."

"Forgive yourself for what?"

"For disrespecting . . . for dishonoring . . ."

"You don't actually believe that, do you?"

"I don't know. I might."

"You weren't my first," she lied.

"I wasn't?"

"In Manila, I drank a flask of *lambanog* one night and ended up passing out in the pickers' shed. With one of the pickers."

He looked at her closely but not admiringly.

"Not that it's any of my business," he said. "But there are some women you can talk to, aren't there? Friends? Neighbors?"

She shook her head.

He nodded. "As long as we're in the process of confiding, I must admit that I still don't know what to do with you. You seem to enjoy drawing these creatures, but you don't seem especially fond of the creatures themselves."

"I do," she replied. "And I'm not."

She looked down at her balled-up fingers. To have once touched him, she realized, felt strangely like handling the microscope slide, and now she was sorry she had followed his guidance so carefully, that she hadn't just slid the worm directly off the rock and onto her palm.

"I want to be the one who kills them," she said at last. "I'll still draw them. But I want the other part, too."

He swallowed loudly.

"Is that wrong?" she asked. "Does it make me bad?"

"I hope not. Because it would make me bad, too."

And when the noises started from upstairs, she thought it was her father again, here to drag her out of the lab and back up the hill. But then she heard Steinbeck's voice echoing down the stairwell.

"Oh no." Ricketts jumped off the hood of the car and rolled down his sleeves. "I thought he was still up in Los Gatos."

"Ed!" came the voice from above. "Ed!"

"Down here, John."

Seconds later, Steinbeck burst through the doorway, a pink invoice clutched in his hand. Ricketts fiddled with his cuffs and studied the ground as Steinbeck approached.

"I should have known as much. First chance he gets, he's bending you over the front of his Buick."

"John!" Ricketts sputtered. "Enough."

"Oh, I'll tell you what's *enough*." Steinbeck waved the invoice above his head. "Fifty dollars! On syringes! How much, exactly, do you think I'm worth?"

"The book did so well. And now there's the movie . . ."

"That's not the point!"

"I'm good for it. You know that, John."

"You haven't had an order in months!"

"We needed them, John."

"Fifty dollars!"

"We needed them for the octopuses. Immersion won't work on cephalopods. We have to inject. You know that."

Steinbeck lowered his hands to his sides, let out a moaning exhale, and then squinted at Ricketts. Margot watched them both very closely. She had never witnessed the full arc of a domestic dispute before—from the initial explosion to the eventual rapprochement—but this was precisely how she imagined one taking shape.

"Can't argue with science, I suppose," Steinbeck said at length.

"No." Ricketts smiled persuasively. "You cannot."

"Christ, my head aches. I think I'm coming down with the flu."

"You always think that."

"Doesn't mean I'm wrong."

"Well, in that case, I know just the cure!"

Ricketts reached for a crate labeled SHARK LIVER OIL.

Steinbeck took a large step backward. "Unless that's where you've started to hide the tequila, I want no part of it."

Laughing, Ricketts turned away from the crate and grabbed the bin that contained the worms. He held them out for Steinbeck's inspection.

"Look! Aren't they delicious? Margot found them. Turns out she has something of a knack."

"Of course she does."

A noise escaped from her: something that sounded like a giggle but wasn't.

"Ed, please tell her I'm in no mood for levity. Or an audience."

She looked at Ricketts. He jerked his head firmly in the direction of the stairway, and she didn't protest. She did, however, envision something seditious as she began to climb: that she was bottled up alongside the largest and rarest of his specimens. That she was still in the garage, watching and hearing their private conversation from the strange comfort of the china hutch.

Upstairs, she could, in fact, still hear their voices: loud yet entirely indecipherable, like a radio tuned just a few notches in the wrong direction. Arthur wasn't there, and she was unspeakably thankful for it. The canneries next door were an earthquake that never stopped. From the bedroom behind her, there was the sound of typing. On the desk, an unfamiliar tube of lipstick was serving as a paperweight, its cap missing and the red paste inside crushed down to a sore-looking nub. She could feel the wounds on both her forehead and shin as intensely as if they had somehow been reopened.

She sat down, moved the lipstick to where she couldn't see it, turned to a clean sheet of paper, and began to sketch. And just as she had expected, the worms appeared there with twice the accuracy and intention of anything she had ever drawn. When a wide-angled shadow fell across the floor, she was certain Ricketts was in the doorway, ready to claim her. But Steinbeck was there instead.

She leapt from her chair and stood beside it.

"I'm not that monstrous, am I?" he asked, shaking his head. "Sit down. Just sit down."

Watching him carefully, she reclaimed her seat. His face was red and shiny, a veil of moisture across his mustache.

"It's hot down there," he moaned. "Why are we out of beer?"

"I don't know."

"Run and get some, will you?"

She shook her head. He frowned at her and then looked blankly around the room as if trying to remember where he was. Then he walked over to the desk and began to study her sketch of the worm. He stood there for several seconds in silence, his face and neck gradually regaining their normal hue, leaving only his large, jutting ears a vengeful shade of red.

"He told me to tell you to go home."

She nodded in understanding but didn't move.

"You're working for him now?" he asked. "In the tide pools?"

"No. I'm doing the sketches. And the embalming."

"But you're hoping for something more, is that it?"

She held his gaze for a second. When she was afraid her face had turned the same color as his ears, she returned her attention to the sketch and made a few swipes of her pencil, unsure as to whether she was making things better or worse.

"Well, keep at it." Steinbeck sighed. "From what I can tell, you've already done an admirable job, and not just with the drawings. He likes to make things complicated, to put up a little fight, but at the end of the day, it's always the same. Like a goddamn goldfish, round and round the bowl, thinking he's found the ocean when he's really just mucking around in the same old puddle as always. And the worst part is that I believe him. I believe him every damn time. I believe him because I've never met anyone as smart or as good as him, and besides, I'm far too busy to be doubting things all the time. Do you have any idea how terrible it is? To have created something people care about? To get rich on account of it? We used to make fun of people like me but, my God, how times have changed. These days, I'm little more than a bank account. Without my money, I'd be even less useful to him than Arthur."

He fell into another extended bout of silence. She stopped drawing and, in lieu of considering his words, reappraised her sketch, hoping for the same feelings of pride. Something about it had changed, though. Something had been vanquished as a result of Steinbeck's grim company.

"And I tell him," he resumed suddenly, the sharpness of his voice making her jump. "When you've collected every little creature from the Sea of Cortez to Alaska, when you've fucked everything in lipstick and a Catholic school uniform, when all your jars are finally categorized and cross-referenced and organized to some lunatic's version of order, when that damn essay has been revised and rewritten for the one-millionth time, do you honestly think you'll be any better off? Any wiser? Sure, you'll know the ocean inside and out, but people will still be a mystery, and there's nothing in this world more tragic than that."

That night, she didn't return home right away.

Instead, she went to the place where Arthur had once given her the sketchbook and the bucket: the small promontory just south of her father's cannery, just east of the train tracks, the spot from which she could see not only the terminus of the Row, but the marine station on its outskirts. There were no scientists on the beach this evening, but there were lights on in the station building, and the lights were something she envied.

And this was the real crux of the matter. Envy. Earlier that afternoon, when Steinbeck had finally left her alone, she had succumbed to it. She had shuffled through Ricketts's desk drawers, looking for a draft of something she hadn't read yet, something Wormy had typed. Another essay or perhaps a poem: anything strange and dense enough to bang her head against. But the only thing she found was the carbon copy of a letter that had been penned years before her arrival and that seemed like a remnant from a different lifetime. *All quiet,* he had written, *until the glass case gets broken either from the outside or inside. And then maybe it's sleeping or comatose instead of just an exhibit. I mean the dream.*

And, God, how she hated her tallness. Sometimes, it was a longing even more painful than her longing for Ricketts: the wish for a complete bodily distillation, a retraction into a more adorably compact form. Her father had always told her to take pride in her vertical inheritance. He had taught her to let it speak for her, to give her authority by proxy. But lately she had become convinced of a more evolved way of being. She imagined Ricketts and Wormy in bed together, their small bodies a perfect match, their union muscular and efficient and happily confined to a cell of its own devising, a cell in which she couldn't possibly fit. If anything, she was more like Steinbeck than Wormy. She was big and sour and needy, and what if Steinbeck's fears were true? If he were no longer the lab's sole patron, would he be cast aside and forgotten? Would someone else come in to take his place? Could that someone else be her? And that's when the realization dawned: an answer that caused her to turn away from the ocean and sprint up the hill.

Back at the house, she paused briefly in the sitting room. With the exception of the sofa and the good china and their personal belongings, most of which were still in trunks, there was nothing material that spoke to their presence here, nothing that could have told a curious observer who they were or what they prized. Similarly, there could have been nothing extrapolated by examining their neighbors, all of whom differed from Anders and Margot in every possible way. And perhaps this was why she had been so resistant thus far to Ricketts's categorization of the world. She didn't glorify the distinction between those who lived here and those who lived elsewhere—the distinction between the locals and the tourists, the distinction between those who watched the party and those who joined it—because to do so would be tantamount to denying the boundaries of her own existence.

"Margot?"

When she entered the kitchen, she was alarmed at how bright it was.

"Did you get a new lamp?" she asked.

"No. I brought in the one from the bedroom."

The can of grease was still on the windowsill, as it had been for more than a month now. Normally, she wouldn't have even noticed it. Tonight, however, it had company: first, a vial of shark liver oil similar to those Ricketts was always trying to convince people to drink; second, a Chinese joss stick jammed into the flesh of an unripe peach, the burned end releasing an irregular curl of musky smoke, its presence somehow both placating and aggressive, like the warning shot that comes before deadly fire, like the line in the proverbial sand.

"I heard you lurking," he resumed. "I don't like it when people lurk. It means they want something but are too cowardly to ask for it."

Heroes advance when it makes sense to retreat, she quoted to herself. *And cowards retreat regardless of what makes sense.*

"I'd like to ask your permission to visit the Agnellis."

He put down his pencil and arranged his documents into a pile, the resulting déjà vu making her head swim. A newspaper sat on the far edge of the table. A headline read, FISKE CANNERY TO CEASE OPERATIONS: UNIONS TO SUPPORT.

"You didn't seem particularly fond the other day," he replied. "I'm surprised you're so keen to socialize."

"Oh, my interests aren't social."

"You've a new plan in place. Good girl."

She adjusted the strap of the satchel.

"Would you care to discuss it?" he asked.

"No. I think I've become a little superstitious, too."

He smiled, but not gladly.

"I'm joining them for Mass again on Sunday," he said. "You can accompany me."

She nodded at the newspaper. "Soon we'll both have reason to celebrate."

"Yes." He leaned back in his chair. "I think you're right."

13

1998

NO MATTER WHERE SHE GOES, THOUGH—NO MATter which part of the aquarium's public spaces occur to her as a refuge—there's music. Music designed at her own behest. Music meant, if she's honest with herself, to replicate and revise how it once felt to be inside his lab.

She remembers sitting down with the composer, showing him the blueprints, describing the main exhibits, playing him a few examples of what she had in mind. Bach, of course. A well-known *kirtan*: "Hay Hari Sundara," the 1926 Carnegie Hall version. Some Debussy, embarrassingly enough. That part in "Take It on the Run" where the guitar does a high altitude burn. To all of these, he nodded in time to the beat, scribbled down notes. When she reached the last song, however, he stopped writing. It was "Get Ready," perhaps the Temptations' strangest offering. To be fair, she knew it was weird. For one thing, it was about a stalker. For another, it didn't start out like all the other Motown relics, with a jolting, percussive call to arms. Instead, it began with a dirge of horns, persistent and menacing, followed by some violins gasping for breath. Then there was the part with the saxophone, notes stabbing the air in what should have been a solo but instead seemed like the disembowelment of one. On top of it all, the singer: a voice that sounded neither male nor female, neither completely sane nor completely unhinged, neither dangerous nor safe. *I don't want this kind of trouble*, the composer's face seemed to say. *Who would?* She, however, was sitting there with her eyes half-closed, certain that, had he lived long enough, this song would have either pleased Ricketts greatly or upset him to near madness.

So in addition to her infantile excitement about his messages, there's also a reaction far worse: the need to prove she's received them. In a sense, this was why the aquarium was created in the first place, to make his most famous, most accessible theory flesh. Instead of arranging things the traditional way—by species or taxonomic relativity—she's arranged things by habitat, by place of residence. *Things that live together should go together,* he once said. *And things that live elsewhere should go elsewhere.* She's even taken it one step further. She's demanded that, with the exception of special temporary exhibits—the one about the Amazon basin, for instance—everything in the aquarium must be indigenous to Monterey Bay. Every animal, every plant, every alga, every fungus. No cheating, except when she permits it.

And it's not something she will ever question. It's not a position from which she will ever back down. The problem, however, is that the bay is getting warmer and the skies are getting bluer, and not in a cyclical, El Niño–type way. No, this is something permanent, which means that species from the south—species that would have previously found Monterey unlivably cold—are moving in. The Humboldt squid and the *Mola mola*: two animals that were once seasonal visitors but now take up year-round aquatic real estate. *Accept it*, she tells herself. *Accept it and move on.* But her artist's eye won't quite allow it. If everything is embraced, nothing is said. A crowded canvas is proof of an empty mind. There's a moment at which even the most purehearted tribute becomes an ode not to the person being honored, but to the person doing the honoring. *And I'd be honored in return*, she tells him, the aquarium's ambient sound track egging her on, *if you'd quote me on that.*

14

1940

"AN ANGEL. SHE LOOKS LIKE AN ANGEL IN THAT dress."

Mrs. Agnelli's voice was gentle, off-puttingly so. The laugh, however—the one Margot had heard that day at the house—seemed ready to surface at any moment and break the veneer of her goodwill, like the air-raid sirens that had punctuated their last days in Manila.

"Thank you," Margot muttered. "It's new."

She yanked at the skirt. Yesterday afternoon, in anticipation of churchgoing company, her father had taken her to Holman's, the local department store. She had expected to be able to find something sturdy and anonymous and reasonable, like what the First Lady wore when she was photographed making speeches or visiting disaster sites. The store, however, offered women's apparel of only one style: lightweight, lace-trimmed frocks so spectacularly ill suited to both Margot's tastes and the local climate that even Anders had been amused on account of it.

"Now I know why you always wear that sport coat," he had said, chuckling.

Margot, however, hadn't laughed. She had suspected it would happen in time—her chest and hips and stomach resigning themselves to a puffier inevitability—but she hadn't expected it to happen so fast, and now, looking at Mrs. Agnelli, she could imagine the horrors with which it all might progress.

"Speaking of angelic," her father redirected, "the Mass was sublime. So many kind tributes to your husband."

"He is ailing, yes," Mrs. Agnelli admitted, eyes downcast. "But the prayers of our community will lift him up."

Anders nodded and appeared to contemplate this in silence. Margot, too, considered the service. In the Philippines, the natives had also practiced Catholicism, but a very specific version of it: riotous and colorful and brutally hierarchical, its practices closer to voodoo sometimes than Christianity. On some of the smaller islands, men fought each other for the honor of being nailed to a cross and paraded through the village streets on Good Friday. Here, however, there was none of that. The bread was not quite flesh, the wine was not quite blood. The same was true of the church's immediate surroundings. The homes of the boat and cannery owners could have been large and showy, but they weren't. Instead, they were modest and well maintained: stucco beachheads with red-tiled roofs that looked sturdy and immortal against the white sky. Children played calmly on the porches. Street vendors made their rounds. Big, iron cauldrons bubbled in the backyards atop flaming beds of pine, the intestinal lengths of sardine nets tanning within.

"We had hoped to offer up a blessing for your imminent venture," Mrs. Agnelli continued. "But I'm afraid it slipped Father Paraino's mind."

"No matter," Anders replied. "I'm not superstitious in the least."

Mrs. Agnelli's face flickered with distaste before returning to its previous serenity. She was in her prime today: surrounded by her own kind, proud and at ease, her face absent of perspiration, her breathing unlabored. As for Tino, he looked exactly as sharp and fragile as before, especially in comparison to his brothers. All five were just as burly and bulletproof as he had implied, standing open-mouthed behind their mother in order of descending height like an unpacked set of giant Russian nesting dolls.

"Shall we, then? Our girl has cooked a wonderful roast."

The brothers turned and began to clomp uphill.

"I'll be glad to accept your hospitality. Margot, however, will be staying behind. She has business with your son. The small one."

And there it was again: a shadow of distaste. "In that case, I'd like to speak with her first."

The brothers froze in place and closed ranks around Tino.

"By all means," Anders replied.

Mrs. Agnelli reentered the church. With a glance in Anders's direction, Margot followed. Inside, it was quiet and cool, the walls white and bare. Father Paraino was fiddling with something on the lectern. The candles on the altar had just recently been extinguished, wicks still smoking. She remembered the séance in the lab. The broken circle.

Mrs. Agnelli sat heavily on the nearest edge of the rearmost pew. At the noise, Father Paraino looked up, bowed to her, and scuttled out of sight.

"There's been some trouble," Mrs. Agnelli began, her voice even kinder than before, even softer.

"I'm sorry about that."

"Oh, I don't want you to be sorry. I just want you to help."

Margot shifted her weight to one foot and then the other, noticing how the dress swished timidly across her knees in response. In a situation like this, it was important to equalize the balance of power. She should be sitting next to the older woman, side by side as equals. But, on account of the space Mrs. Agnelli had chosen to occupy, this was nearly impossible. To join her on the pew, Margot would have to climb right over her or walk all the way around to the other side of the nave and slide down to meet her, both of which were too awkward to even contemplate. So she remained standing and took a small step forward, which ensured that, when Mrs. Agnelli began to speak again, it would be to Margot's back and not her face.

Mrs. Agnelli giggled as if in understanding, and then continued.

"At first, you see, I thought your father was to blame, but then I realized it was most likely a shortcoming of my own. The truth is, I'm unaccustomed to the company of men. They're always out on the boats, often for weeks on end, which means they have a different way of seeing the world than we do. A different way of finding satisfaction."

A rogue sunbeam shot through the stained glass window above the altar, the effect identical to what it looked like when light shone among the leaves and blossoms of the bougainvillea.

"You have six sons," Margot countered. "All of whom work with you."

"Yes, but working with someone and feeling bettered by their company are two different things entirely. I'm sure you understand."

Margot resisted the impulse to look behind her. Mrs. Agnelli produced a short, crackling cough and then resumed.

"And I might be flattering myself, but I like to think that, when I put my full trust in my real allies—my fellow mothers and daughters, the ones who understand life's bloodiest battles and how to win them—I can see it all much more clearly. Both the big picture and the small one. Or, as your friend Ed Ricketts might say, both the ocean and the tide pools on its border."

From where she was standing, she couldn't see the sacristy, but she could hear a subdued commotion occurring inside of it: chalices clinking, robes shifting on their hangers, uneaten communion wafers being returned to their tins. There was a strange, unpleasant sort of pressure in the air, as if she were about to enter a tunnel. She turned around.

"What's your question?"

Mrs. Agnelli broadened her smile, her nose crinkling.

"Oh, I have several. The workers he's hired, for one thing. Not a single Sicilian—or even a Genoan—on his payroll. He's taken in all the mongrels instead: the Japanese, the Chinese, the Portuguese, the Filipinos, the Okies, all the people that live even lower on the hill than you do. He's even allowing them to fully unionize, which is something I've been fighting against for years."

"None of that was in the contract. So it's fully within his rights."

"Oh goodness! You *are* clever! No, the real problem isn't the people he's hiring or the bureaucratic mess he's allowing them to make. It's what he's *not* having them can."

She looked beyond Mrs. Agnelli at the iron-studded front door, biting the insides of her cheeks to keep from smiling.

"You see, my most valuable property sold at a pittance. There's an absurd surplus of product on my hands, and the biggest buyer in town refuses to buy." She rose from the pew, the wood creaking. "And unlike you, I don't find it particularly funny."

"He isn't buying from anyone else. He hasn't done anything wrong."

"That depends on who you ask."

"I'm unclear on what you want me to do."

The sound of a car sputtering down the street outside, the jovial hollers of someone selling ice cream or peanuts. For a moment, Mrs. Agnelli seemed pinned to the floor. Then, without warning, she was smiling and laughing, pitching forward and pulling Margot into a hug.

"I'd like you to think carefully about your own interests. And then tell me what you decide."

Margot couldn't see. She was in the tunnel now, and Mrs. Agnelli's voice was bouncing against the walls and her smell was, too: warm and thick and lovely. Margot held her breath. She tried to move her body but it wouldn't listen, so she called on her mind. *Run,* she told it, *before it's too late.* But it was just like that first morning in the tide pools: her limbs dead with panic, the unwanted memories rapidly surfacing. The discovery of the fake paintings in the root cellar. The bestowal of the penknife. The ghost-balloon of her mother's floating, omniscient head. But also something from much further back, from before she was of use to her father, from before she was of use to anyone. A toy made of tin and held aloft on little wheels, its mouth clattering behind her as she pulled it across terrain that was far too rough for either of them to safely navigate.

When the embrace ended, she took a step back and stared at the floor.

"My interests are the same as my father's."

Mrs. Agnelli waited for a second or two, lungs rattling. Then she brushed past her, footsteps weirdly silent. "Let me know when you change your mind."

When she was gone, Margot sat down on a pew across the aisle from where Mrs. Agnelli had sat. She waited for a new noise, a new smell. She waited for the bare walls to suggest a color or a pattern. When she finally went back outside, everyone was gone except Tino, who was still standing on the church steps, just as she had left him.

"I'll do more sketches," she said. "But only if you're still certain we can sell them."

He considered this and then nodded. "You're financing an escape, too."

"No. The opposite."

He frowned in confusion.

"I'm pursuing some new business," she explained. "With Ricketts."

His eyes brightened. "Well, then you were right before. We should start at three dollars apiece. The Woolworth's on Alvarado will give you a discount on supplies if you purchase in bulk. I get fifteen percent of net."

"Three seventy-five apiece. You buy supplies. Your percentage is ten."

"Fine. But no sea creatures. Just people. Portraits on commission."

"Come on." She hurried down the steps. "Let's get started."

"Right now?" he replied.

"Yes. Unless you can give me a reason to wait."

15

"YOUR FATHER HAS STRANGE FRIENDS."

She decapitated Arthur with her eyes and then turned her attention to the real work in progress. *Styela*: their bodies like little lumps of alien excrement. Since her first encounter with them, they had grown no more appealing to her aesthetically. In a practical sense, however, they had become indispensable. At first, she had considered other, more expensive species: the dog-fish, or the red octopus, or Ricketts's beloved flatworms. But all these creatures had seemed too rare in a relative sense, too labor- and time-intensive, too vulnerable to unwanted scrutiny. The *Styela*, by contrast, were plentiful and unremarkable and something the lab was extremely eager to divest: so much so that it was only now, as the tenth order had been placed, that someone was thinking to question it. And that someone was Arthur.

"Not his *friends*," she snapped. "His associates."

"Either way, I don't understand why they need so many of these things."

"No one expects you to understand anything."

"Settle down, children," Steinbeck drawled in a broad Great Plains accent. "Else you'll get the whip."

Ricketts laughed and then leaned close to her.

"It's wonderful, you know," he confided. "I never could have flushed out so many buyers on my own."

She fought back a smile and grabbed a bottle of fixative from the shelf above the sinks. Ever since the orders had started rolling in—orders she had placed in another name using the proceeds from her portraiture—it had been like this: his affection more brilliant than usual and aimed more often than not in her direction. Today it was especially obvious. In a subversion of the lab's usual hierarchy, she—not Steinbeck—had been chosen to stand next to him at the countertop while Steinbeck and Wormy packed and labeled the boxes that Arthur lugged broodingly from the garage to the curb. The message, therefore, was clear. Money wasn't everything, but it was something. And now, just as Steinbeck had predicted, allegiances were shifting on account of it.

So there was satisfaction: a surplus of it that rivaled the *Styela* themselves. But there was another feeling, too—a less jubilant one—that resided several layers lower. As she measured out the chemicals and slew each little tunicate in turn, she probed this feeling and stirred it up a bit so that its contents could swirl and separate and make themselves known. She had struggled and she had prevailed. She had proceeded exactly as Anders would have. Why, then, did it feel less than perfectly earned? Why did she suspect there was a better and more admirable way: one that her intellect was too dull or her character too weak to fully discern?

"Well," Ricketts announced, "that appears to be the last of them. Arthur, you wait for the shippers. Wormy, you update the accounts. John, you tidy up."

Steinbeck huffed through his nose and slapped a paste-damp shipping label onto a box. At some point, they would figure out the truth. They would realize that her father's *Styela*-hungry colleagues were nonexistent and that the money was actually hers. By that point, however, it would all be settled, she reassured herself as she buried the bad feelings even deeper. She would be a fixture inside the lab. She would be essential to Ricketts's ambitions, a prize within his heart, and the elaborateness of her ruse would be fodder for the best sorts of stories, the best sorts of songs.

"And Margot. Please come with me."

In the passenger seat of the Buick, she continued to congratulate herself.

From the very first portrait, she knew Tino had been right. There was a gold mine here, and she was just the one to mine it, which is not to say she had proceeded without caution or forethought. Her drawings, in their unaltered state, would not have appealed; they were too ragged, too raw. So she had blurred the rough edges on purpose, she had improved on nature's design instead of representing it faithfully: a compromise she expected to sicken her. But it didn't. It was an opportunity, she reasoned, not a surrender. She was giving something to the masses, and they were giving it back. Her inaugural client, for instance—a new mother with a baby less than two weeks old—was so overcome by the exceptional portrait of her subexceptional child that she wept with pleasure and offered Margot three times the agreed-upon fee. An old, mute crone, thrilled with a depiction of her face that made her appear several decades younger, gave Margot a gilt pocket watch that, according to a flurry of unofficial sign language, had been in her family for over a century. Margot thanked her in a Sicilian subdialect, just as Tino had taught her, and then placed the watch into her satchel alongside the penknife. Later that afternoon, she had Tino take both items to the pawnshop on Munras.

"You're sure about the knife?" he asked, noting the inscription.

"Yes. I'm sure."

The next Sunday was the same: up and down the hilltop streets, in and out of small, dark, overdecorated parlors, curtains drawn to conceal the net-tanning cauldrons out back, garages open to reveal the chrome-limned shadows of new cars. One of her clients—all of whom were women, most of whom bore a passing resemblance to Mrs. Agnelli—offered her a sip of anise liqueur, which she smelled but didn't drink. Another client was so satisfied with Margot's rendering of the suggestive look on her face that she took off her blouse and asked Margot to continue farther south, to which Margot agreed until she reached the breast region and found her pencil frozen in unexpected horror. On the third Sunday, when she ran out of good paper and her last pencil had worn itself to a nub, Tino was dispatched to the store on Alvarado for supplies, and so it went until the sky dimmed and the families gathered for dinner. Alone on the street now, the two of them returned to the steps of the church and stood there for a moment in silence. It was the time of day Margot had always liked least: dusk, everything too sharp, everything too orange, the day's accomplishments, no matter how grand, withering under the aspersions cast by the sun's dying light. Nevertheless, the sense of achievement was electric. All these homes. Not only had she been inside them, she had left something of herself within. She had shaped these dwellings in a way that was more than just transactional, in a way that was apparent only to her. Power and possibility and beauty, and this time it wouldn't be taken from her.

"Can you get the penknife back?" she asked Tino as the sun set into the bay, its vermilion snuffed like a candle.

"Consider it done."

Now, as the Buick began to sputter, she traced the outline of the penknife through the leather of the satchel and watched Ricketts guide the car onto the road's dusty shoulder.

"Goddamn it." He gave the dashboard a little slap. "Arthur told me it was fixed."

He leapt from the car and peered under the hood. From the other side of the windshield, she couldn't see the whole of him, just a collection of representative parts: his shoulders in his cotton shirt, the back of his sunburned neck. The bay wasn't visible from this stretch of highway. Rather, it was artichoke and lettuce fields as far as the eye could see: hypnotic, gray-green striations of them. The sky seemed to be fighting for its blueness, the sun for its warmth. She crossed her ankles and buttoned up her vest, watching the two flaps meet and merge with a mental click. If there was any downside to the past several days of near-constant sketching, it was this: the clicks, the machine-symphony of verification when two shapes joined correctly. Usually, it was something she could turn on and off at will, but it no longer seemed voluntary. The shape-clicks now sounded whether she summoned them or not. Even worse, the colors were mixing themselves without her instruction or permission: a phenomenon that seemed to intensify in Ricketts's presence. The car was repaired now and they were back on the road, but it didn't feel like they were moving. Rather, it felt like the world beyond the windshield was outlining itself, smudging itself, and filling itself in with browns and greens and blues while she remained perfectly separate from the process, perfectly still.

When the scenery finally became inert, she looked over at Ricketts. He had brought the Buick to another stop: intentional this time.

"Where are we?" she asked

"Elkhorn Slough. About twenty miles up the coast." He exited the car and she followed. "There are some canneries over there on the island, just like on the Row. And rumor has it they're going to build an honest-to-goodness harbor here. A wharf even bigger than the one in Monterey."

As he opened the trunk and began to unload it, she tried and failed to appraise the property without imagining how she'd draw it. A pocket of brackish marshland, an estuary snaking through the low, dry hills before slipping into the mouth of an industrial marina. A series of conjoined mud flats, clusters of yelping gulls, a dense patch of pickleweed separating the land from the water.

Then she considered Ricketts's face. He was still happy, but not as happy as he had been inside the lab.

"If the harbor was a good idea," she said, "it would have happened already."

"Excellent point." He gave her a bucket of bait. "The same can probably be said for their plans for a power plant and a yacht club."

"Maybe the power plant. But not the yacht club."

"I'm glad you think so, because I don't have a yacht. Just a canoe."

"You don't even have that."

"Guess again."

He pointed to the pickleweed, in which she now perceived the shadow of an elongated wooden watercraft.

"Technically, you're right. It's not mine." He went over to the vessel and began extracting it from its hiding place. "But Manuel's more than happy to let me borrow it, provided we bring him back a bat ray."

"He's a collector, too?"

"No. He uses a cookie cutter to punch little circles from their wings. Then he fries them up and sells them to tourists who think they're eating scallops."

She wasn't sure if she was supposed to laugh, so she didn't.

"Bow or stern?" he asked, when the canoe had been packed with gear and carried to the waterline.

"Bow."

"Naturally."

She boarded. He handed her a paddle and hopped in behind her. When they pushed off and began drifting through the marina, it was with the practiced ease of people who had known each other for years. The clicks in her head were silent now and the colors were respecting their own boundaries, and it felt like a reprieve. But it also felt like an emptiness that needed filling.

"What's the marina called?" she asked.

"Moss Landing. Which I'm sure you'll find hopelessly obvious."

Instead of replying, she dipped her paddle and watched it work. For a while, the water justified its name: soft, green, inert. Then, as he steered them away from the marina and into a channel, everything changed. A fast, clear current was pushing against them now, the canoe slipping into reverse, the landscape wheeling by in the wrong direction. She began to paddle faster, spurred on by the sound of him doing the same. Soon, she could feel blisters stinging on her palms like cigarette burns, her arms threatening to give out, until, all at once, the current vanished as quickly as it had appeared. The canoe moved effortlessly into the gray brown funnel of the slough's midsection, into the black green of the eelgrass that reached out from the banks like fingers. She lifted her paddle as the canoe slid ashore. The water here was still and murky again, the dunes wet and fat. The shore curved around them in a lazy crescent, the half-submerged remains of an oyster farm dangling from its southern tip.

As they disembarked and unloaded the gear, she tried to keep her arms from shaking.

"Didn't think we'd make it, did you?" he asked.

"Seems like a great deal of trouble for a handful of worms." Her voice was overloud, but she couldn't help it. She was far more fatigued than she should have been, and there were two strange, symmetrical pains throbbing between her hips.

"Oh, we're not looking for worms today." He unrolled a gill

net and began to bait it with squid. He, too, seemed spent, but not physically. His earlier brightness was now almost totally extinguished, an odd flatness moving in to take its place. "In fact, I'm not sure what we're looking for. I just needed to escape for a bit, I suppose."

"From what?"

"From the lab."

He handed her one end of the net, which she held in place as he got back into the canoe and rowed across the cove. He jumped out, secured his end to a section of the old oyster farm, and then returned to where she was standing. He tied her end to the beached canoe and then sat down on the slough's wet banks, the mud receiving him with an audible squish. She raised an eyebrow.

"Ah, yes. I'm in the presence of a lady. I keep forgetting."

He stood and retrieved a tarp, which he unfurled with a snap. Sitting next to him now, the tarp beneath them, she watched him watch the net. As always, the prospect of a capture had him completely focused, and she, too, felt certain something extraordinary was within seconds of happening. This time, however, his attention proved a poor predictor of action. For a long stretch, there was nothing: just the minutes ticking slowly by, the morning starting to deepen and shift into noon, the only sound that of the occasional car rattling up or down the distant road, that of the seals flopping their beefy shapes into the mounds of shattered clamshells that lined the lower edges of the slope.

"What did you bring for lunch?" she asked.

"Hungry?"

"No. Just curious."

"Fried chicken and hard-boiled eggs."

"And which shall we eat first?"

His eyes were widening now, his mouth curling, a portion of his good humor starting to resurface.

"Can it be true? Has Margot Fiske attempted a joke?"

"No good? You should have invited someone funnier."

He wrenched his gaze from the net and let it fall on her face. "Funny or not, you're the only person on earth I would've wanted to come along."

She looked down and pretended to examine the blisters on her palms, which had begun to surround themselves with little hoods of clear fluid. He was a charming man, and he likely would have said the same thing no matter who was sitting there beside him. To Steinbeck, to Wormy, maybe even to Arthur. She didn't care, though. She had goals in mind, and none of them would be achieved by convincing herself she wasn't special.

"What did you mean about the lab?" she asked. "About wanting to escape it?"

He tucked both legs beneath him and then reconsidered, stretching them out to their full length, the heels of his boots digging into the mud.

"I don't know," he replied. "It just feels different in there all of a sudden. I wish I could explain it better."

"Money's no longer a problem. That's probably a relief."

"Oh, money's never really a problem." His focus was on the net again, but a shred of it had been left behind with her. "Yet it's always a problem. I'm sure you understand."

She nodded vigorously to conceal her confusion.

"And with the trip coming up, I suppose we can use every penny we can get our hands on, even though I can't shake the feeling we're doomed no matter what."

"What trip? And why is it doomed?"

He gave her a perplexed glance. "I could have sworn we already discussed this at length. Just yesterday, in fact."

"No. I would have remembered."

"Hmmm." He frowned. "Must be mistaking you for one of the girls at the Lone Star. Anyhow, we're leaving for Mexico in March. A couple of months in the Sea of Cortez, gathering material for the new book. John's lawyer is finalizing the lease for the boat as we speak and Wormy is preparing the cargo manifest, which is mostly beer, which I'm sure comes as less than a shock."

She prodded at a blister to make it burn. "Sounds like a productive journey."

"That's the idea, but things have gotten so complicated. John is worse than I've ever seen him, the poor fellow. He just can't seem to concentrate and I don't blame him. The Hollywood contingent is driving him mad. Carol is up north, screaming divorce every time he blinks. As for Wormy, well, she has obligations of her own, which never comes as a surprise to anyone but me. To be honest, it makes me wonder what we're trying to prove, taking off to sea when everything on land is falling to pieces."

When he stopped talking, she paused to weigh his words. With only a few luminous exceptions, he had never unburdened himself like this before; he had never dropped the scrim of his friendly optimism. For several seconds, she had no idea what to say. Then, as she looked in the direction of the bay, a useful memory surfaced: the departure from the Philippines, the decisive enormity of the cargo ship, the sea putting a measurable distance between her and happiness, but also between her and defeat.

"Some people think the ocean means freedom. A new start."

"I'll bet fish think the same thing about land. And oh, how wrong they are!"

"I'm not sure fish care one way or another."

"And that, I'm afraid, is where we part ways."

At this, he shimmied his rear end deeply into the tarp, as if trying to reestablish contact with the mud beneath.

"Should I tell another joke?" she asked.

Still brooding, he looked up at her. "You know why I'm out there every day, don't you? On the very borderline of the metaphysical?"

"Breaking through with the limpets? Staring the life out of hermit crabs?"

"I had a dream about you last night," he continued, ignoring her incitement. "Or, more accurately, about your father. He was a Nazi. And you were a Jew."

"How silly."

"Is it? I feel like Anders has more than a bit of latent sadism trying to push its way through."

"I would assume most fathers do."

"Not mine. Most of his people were ministers."

"God brings no guarantees."

"You're quite right. But in this instance, the book matched its cover." His smile was sad but thankful. "His mind wasn't especially keen, I'll grant you that, but his soul was good. He encouraged me to read and exercise. To sleep out in the snow, to harden myself a little. When I dropped out of school with the intention of walking through the southern states by day and sleeping in graveyards by night, he didn't question it. He saw me off with encouragement and pocket change, and then, in the lab's early days, he even worked alongside me for a spell. It was wonderful."

Another flurry of confessions. How to best receive them? she wondered frantically. How to keep them coming?

"And where is he now?" she asked.

"Dead."

"Oh."

She expected him to sneer at the grief and shove it aside, as she usually did. Instead, he put a hand over his heart, as if palpating the ache.

"Almost four years now, but it's still pretty fresh. Same year as the fire in the lab—the one that destroyed practically everything I owned—and, even now, it's like two halves of the same terrible thing. It's like the two events are related. Not in terms of one causing the other, but in terms of being linked in some primal, *toto* manner. I'm sure you know what I mean."

Fire and the death of a parent. Yes. She knew.

"But there are plenty of good people left," he continued. "That's what I try to remind myself every day, especially when things seem dark. John, Wormy, Joe, Ritchie, Tal, George, Xenia: they understand and that's what matters. Even if the boat sinks, I'm still out there doing good work, and that's something even a failure can be proud of."

She watched him shut his eyes and then reopen them.

"I'll come with you," she said.

"Where?"

"On the trip to Mexico."

"What?" He laughed. "No!"

"Why not?"

"Oh Christ." He leaned across her and peered mournfully inside the picnic basket. "And to think I forgot to pack the beer."

"I'm serious."

"So am I."

"Tell me what I'm up against."

At this, the net gave a twitch, but not one big enough to warrant attention.

"You're not up against anything, that's the point." If he was annoyed with her now, he was doing a decent job hiding it, his eyes fixed on the net's false alarms. "You've made yourself completely essential and I'm not sure if I like it or not."

"Of course you like it."

He looked insulted. But then his mouth broke open, the day's first genuine smile lighting up his face.

"I need to pee."

"You're in the presence of a lady. You said so yourself."

"I know. I always use the word *pee* around ladies because it's so much more elegant than *piss*. Everyone knows that only horses piss."

"I'll wait here and pretend I'm not listening."

He groaned and scratched his beard. "If John doesn't write a book about you, he's a goddamned idiot."

He stood, climbed the slick dunes, and half disappeared behind them. She heard the intimate, expected sounds—the unzipping of a fly, the splashdown of an elevated stream—and then there was a tremor of the net that made her jump. She sprinted to the water's edge. In the net, only a few steps from shore, was a bat ray nearly four feet long and equally as wide, thrashing and brown and cat-eyed.

"Ed!"

For the first time ever, she had called him by his given name, and the sound of it was like a gunshot. The commotion in the net mirrored the commotion at her back—the tucking, the zipping, the scrambling—and before she knew it, he was at her side, lunging for the captive, bringing it out of the water and into his arms, not in the competent way he handled most things, but with an almost vengeful, disorganized force. He looked desperately around him at the mud and the weeds, and then at her.

"The knife in the picnic basket," he grunted. "Get it."

She bent down and snatched up the implement. In her hand, it felt insubstantial and weightless, unlikely to survive a passage through a stick of butter, much less through living flesh. So she tossed it into the mud and withdrew her father's penknife from the satchel. She flicked it open.

"From gills to gills, right below the jaw," Ricketts said, unaware of the blade's substitution. "And then stand back."

"I'll ruin it."

"No, you won't. Manuel just needs the wings."

As if in response, the animal sucked Ricketts's hand into its throat, its tooth plates grinding down, its mouth curled permanently upward as if smiling. Ricketts yelped and tore his fingers free. She stepped forward and paused for a second, waiting for the right opportunity, and when it arrived, there was no hesitation. It was just like the flatworms and the microscope slide: total precision, total inevitability. The flapping of the wings made it more difficult than expected, as did the puppylike softness of the ray's skin, as did the puppylike roundness of its skull. She proceeded, however, cutting right where he had instructed, right below the jaw as if she were making a second mouth. There was a gush from the arteries, her fingers suddenly hot and wet and red. Stunned, she stepped away and let him manage the death throes on his own, the ray flapping against his chest like a big, featherless bird.

When it was all over, she wiped the blade against the eelgrass and washed her hands in the water. He lowered the ray into a patch of mud that had turned mauve with blood.

"When I die," he said quietly, watching the animal make its final twitch, "I'm nearly certain they'll all be waiting for me. Everything I've ever killed, waiting for me in one big room."

That's crazy, she wanted to say.

"That's beautiful," she said.

He picked up the dead ray as if it were a sleeping child, wrapped it in the tarp, and then placed it inside the canoe.

"Normally I use a rock," he said, still looking at the animal. "Just a quick smack to the head. But I couldn't find one."

She retrieved her paddle and the picnic basket. His eyes shot over in her direction.

"What are you doing?" he asked.

"Packing up and going home."

"No, you're not."

He caught her by the wrist, shook the paddle from her grip, and dragged her down.

And this time, it wasn't slow and it wasn't careful. Also, there was the mud: a surface far less reliable than his rope mattress and far more eager to involve itself in the intricacies of the movements under way. She could feel it on every inch of her skin, even the parts that were still covered with clothing: how the mud's temporary wetness both facilitated and impeded the force with which they slammed into each other, and she knew he wasn't claiming her, not for good. But the land was. For a moment, there was fear and trepidation, but then an opening unlike anything she had ever experienced. He could talk all he wanted about where things lived and why, but the fact of the matter was that wanting something meant nothing unless you actually took it. People, places, things: all of it so fragile, so easy, so obtainable. So infinitely up for grabs.

Later that evening, she took a bath fully clothed.

Her father was a room away, sitting at the kitchen table, as usual. He had seen her come home. He had seen how she was a chalky gray from head to toe, the mud dried into a flaking shroud. He didn't mention it, though, nor did he disturb her.

Hours passed, maybe even days. He remained in his part of the house and she in hers, and by the time she drained the tub, undressed, and toweled off, the kitchen was empty and his bedroom door was closed.

She sat at the kitchen table and pretended it was Ricketts's desk. On the canoe trip back to the Buick, they had spoken only once.

"Latin name?" she had asked, referring to the dead body at their feet.

"*Myliobatis californica.* As if it could ever exist anywhere else."

And how perfect, she realized now, to have two names for the same thing, each of them nonsensical based on your perspective. The streets in Manila had been like this. They had had an official name that appeared on the maps, but also a colloquial name to which the locals obstinately clung. In Monterey it was like this, too: Ocean View Avenue, Cannery Row. And then there was the woman who had wanted a nude portrait of herself, her impulses so desperate and broad, Margot had almost pitied her. Now, as she opened her satchel with loose, prune-y hands, the pity was gone. She sharpened her pencil with the penknife, which was still flecked with dried blood. And the sketches that ensued were things that could have been hung in museums, but never in family homes: exotic, acrobatic pairings that showed not only lust and its aftermath, but also the void in which lust occurred. This time, there were no corners cut, no edges blurred. This was the harsh, contained, ancient survivalism of the tide pools, but magnified into human dimensions, its beauty that of the huge, disembodied tentacle: invisible to everyone except those who felt compelled to seek it.

The following Sunday, four weeks to the day after first acceding to Tino's offer, she stood with him on the church steps again, just as before.

"You'll be able to find some buyers for these, I assume." She handed him her most recent portfolio, her confidence half-feigned. It was ugly and sad, she feared suddenly, to put one's private thoughts so clearly on display. As he skimmed through the images and recognized their pornographies, however, her uncertainty faded. A redness was rising into his neck and across his face, his expression soft and awed.

"These are all men with women. Can you do men with men? And the other way, too?"

She nodded.

"We'll sell out within a day," he replied.

And he was right.

16

1998

IT'S NOT NECESSARY ANYMORE, AND SHE WANTS him to know it.

There was a time when it was fuel. There was a time when she was certain that, in its absence, she might stall out midjourney, just like his old Buick. Now, however, the machine is one that feeds itself, that offers pleasures other than the punitive. If anything, the love she once felt for him is like one of those chronic diseases that starts with the letter L: lupus or Lyme. She can go weeks, months, years, without an outbreak, but then something weakens her defenses—usually a dream—and suddenly he's with her again, offering old flatteries, opening old wounds.

Which is precisely why she's come to the cephalopod gallery, the room behind the octopus tank. Darkness and silence. Raised, plastic-grated flooring. A ceiling so low that her head almost touches the water pipes above. If Anders ever taught her anything of value, which she doubts, it's this: the price of hesitation. So she wastes no time. She submerges herself from fingertip to shoulder. She scratches the fiberglass rockwork that lines the back of the tank. At first, nothing. But then an almost imperceptible shift from somewhere within the rockwork, a series of telltale flashes from the cameras on the other side of the glass. She leans forward as far as she can, her back and hips beginning to protest, her blue aquarium-issue shirt soaked now from neck to navel. When the tentacles appear, it's with a drama that seems to demand a sound track: the suction cups expanding and contracting with audible pinches and pops, sliding along the window with a sureness no terrestrial appendage could ever possess. When she first came to Monterey, she despised it. She found it cold and sad, especially compared with Southeast Asia. But first impressions are rarely final ones, and now this town is, without rival, the most beautiful place she's ever seen. And so it is with the octopus. At first, Margot's existence is repellent, the tips of the octopus's tentacles curling backward in dismay. But then love strikes like lightning: the octopus rising from the tank using Margot's body as leverage, its skin blossoming from orange to red, an orange-black quality to the way it inhales and exhales through its flapping siphon. A ballet of braided limbs, swirling together and apart and together again as if choreographed. She begins to laugh—not in the manner of an old woman, but in the manner of a child who has just seen something intended for adults—and by the time it's all over, she's happy and sure. Not everything about it was bad, she tells him, despite how badly it ended, and here's the proof: this map of the octopus's progress, this Morse code of angered capillaries, these small red kisses on her skin.

suits you far better than that Agnelli boy. I should have seen that from the outset."

She scowled and shrank down into her collar. His mood was worse than usual tonight, callous and sarcastic and fierce, and there was a part of her that longed to fire back with a barb of her own. But she remained silent as they moved away from the house and in the direction of the wharf, the night sky reminiscent of an El Greco.

She, too, felt on edge. She had acquired so many of Ricketts's specimens that she didn't know what to do with them. Before, when her income had been modest and her orders small, she had had the boxes shipped to a nonexistent address in Chicago. But then, as her portraiture took its darker turn and her profits spiked, she was forced to deal with the shipments at their source. She instructed Tino to bribe one of his mother's men on the railway, who destroyed the boxes instead of loading them: a solution she knew to be temporary. Any day now, the volume would become too great, the specimens too interesting, the curiosity of their hired conspirator too intense, and she would be required to handle things another way. She began to covet spaces for their existing size and quality. Her father's cannery, for instance. It was a building so vast, it could have easily concealed every specimen she could ever hope to buy, every specimen Ricketts could ever hope to kill, its functionality as a hiding place so theoretically perfect, it almost hurt her to look at it.

There was also the matter of Arthur, just as her father had

17

1940

"IT SEEMS TO ME," ANDERS SAID, PULLING HIS TOP-coat tight against the fog, "that love is in the air."

"Pardon?"

"And I'm sure he's a fine young man. Smart, loyal, hardworking. Although he could certainly stand to do something about that hair. Remind me of his name."

She looked down at her shoes, at their sea-hardened leather. They had just crossed Lighthouse Avenue and were walking alongside the train tracks now, passing over a smelly bit of earth where, on her way to Ricketts's lab that morning, she had seen the hobo from the party pleasuring himself in the weeds.

"Arthur."

"That's right," her father scoffed. "Well, I caution him to remain gentlemanly, but otherwise, I give him my blessing. He implied. Lately, his company had become incessant, his affection full of strident concern. He appeared at the house each morning in order to escort her to the Row; he appeared at the lab each afternoon in order to escort her back home. During the day, whenever she thought she was alone behind Ricketts's desk, he would materialize at odd and inconvenient times, his smiles too quick, his frowns too broad, the mere fact of his presence annihilating whatever concentration she was able to summon.

Then there was the lab's other male hanger-on: Steinbeck. Before, the writer's attentions had been sporadic and mildly resentful, as if Margot were a small pile of dog shit he couldn't quite keep himself from stepping in. Recently, however, he had become as vicious as on the morning they'd first met. He would groan at the mere sight of her. He would sit in the rocking chair and scrutinize her as she worked, his gaze hateful and unsparing. Arthur would sometimes make excuses for him, but Margot knew the truth. Steinbeck's anger was real and his envy was justified and she felt sorry for him, but not nearly enough to follow a different course of action.

Ricketts was the real problem, though: the one that made her stomach buckle, her chest hurt. Two days after their trip to the slough, Wormy disappeared from the lab. No excuses were made for this, no explanations offered. She was simply there one day and gone the next, which pleased Margot immensely until she realized the consequences. Wormy's absence weakened Ricketts like an illness. He began to drink more than usual and wander the coastline in his Buick. Sometimes he invited Margot on his sojourns: poorly planned excursions hunting for specimens they didn't quite need, carrying picnic lunches that would go uneaten, finding a mostly level, mostly concealed patch of ground on which to up the ante of their pseudoromance. She learned about nuance. She learned that not everything in life could be self-taught. She learned that there was a place several miles down the coast, on the tip of Big Sur's Hurricane Point, where the southern sea otter, once thought to be hunted to extinction, had made a small yet triumphant comeback.

"I'd like to build something here," she said, standing alongside him on a ledge above the water. The wind was almost strong enough to rip out the manzanita bushes by their roots. A mother otter and her pup were trussed up in the kelp beneath the cliff, enduring the swells with tucked chins and closed eyes. It smelled like sage and wet stone, and there were cattle in the distance, diligently picking their way down the uneven hillside. Behind them, hidden in the land's damp folds, were redwood groves, dense and soundproof.

"If I didn't know better"—he slurred—"I'd say you enjoy being uncomfortable."

In reply, she pulled him down into the dirt and tasted the alcohol on his tongue.

And it was on that afternoon that a difficult notion occurred to her. It was entirely possible that, all this time, she had been aiming for the wrong thing. She had assumed that having him was a goal in and of itself, that the fact of the capture would provide her with all the satisfaction she would ever need. But now she was wondering if what really mattered was what occurred after. Their bodies were joined now, several times a week. His mind, however, still resided in a place she would never be able to visit, except as a tourist.

Her only clarity, therefore, was in her work, and in this sense she had never been more successful. With the exception of her and Ricketts's field trips, her days were split precisely down the middle, anesthetizing and preserving his collections in the morning, drawing them in the afternoon, a schedule as predictable as the tides. In the garage, the air was rough with menthol and brine, her blood warming with each little death; behind the desk, she would perform her artistic resurrections. During these times, she could almost forget how awful it was to be in love. It was only at night on the horsehair sofa that the truth came to her: the day's disappointments lurking, her adoration of him and her abhorrence of herself so suffocating, so monotonous, that it felt like a measurable physical weight. It made her want to give up entirely, to never go down the hill again, to remain in the house until her father's work was done and it was time to leave Monterey for good. But then she would remember the mud, the otters, the smells of sage and stone. She would remember how much money could be made and how much power forged in the gratification of primitive desires. She would remember her father's teachings about persistence and worth, cowardice and heroism, and she would find herself descending the hill yet again, wondering if today was the day when she would kill the animal or draw the corpse that would finally tip the scales, that would bear a fruit that wasn't so outrageously small and bitter.

Her father's work had also taken a turn, although in what way she still didn't know. His vexation was sharper and louder than ever before, and his schedule had become irregular. Instead of departing for the Row in the morning and returning in the evening, he was now coming and going at unpredictable times—the middle of the night, the middle of the day—which made her uneasy because it deepened the mystery of his ambitions. There was a small, unhappy part of her that rejoiced in his aggravation, that extracted a modicum of pleasure from what seemed to be his long-awaited comeuppance, but his despair was much like Wormy's disappearance: there was something about it that prohibited real schadenfreude. The covert inspection of his papers soon became a habit, no longer in an attempt to undermine, but in an attempt to assist, which was how, on a night he failed to return home, she found something she hadn't consciously been looking for but that seemed inevitable the moment it caught her eye. Wedged within a roll of blueprints were three of her rawest, most troubling sketches. It gave her plenty to think about, certainly, but among the first considerations was this: that somehow, in the multiple transactions that had allowed them to pass from her hands to his, the message of the drawings had changed entirely. Of course there was disgust and suspicion and fear. But mostly, there was disappointment of a very specific sort: that of the angler hooking a fish long considered too elusive and intelligent to catch.

So when he had invited her to join him on this evening's visit to the Agnelli warehouse, she had accepted despite deep misgivings. Now, as they proceeded to the wharf, deep into Sicilian territory, she knew her misgivings had been warranted. The boats lurched in their slips. The night crews went about their labors in ghostly silence, condensing and scattering around the perimeter. When they stopped in front of a large, corrugated metal structure marked with the Agnellis' blunt-lettered logo, she shivered. Her father, too, seemed to feel a chill, rubbing his hands together as he peered through the single salt-pocked window. He began to knock at the door but then thought better of it and entered unannounced.

"My God," he whispered. "I haven't seen a place like this since I demolished those olive oil presses in Puglia."

Inside the warehouse, it was dark, but not too dark to see. A pale light was trickling in from an indeterminate source, painting the walls and floor a sepulchral gray, and it was against this backdrop that she gradually became aware of the room's contents: hundreds of crates filled to overflowing with oval-shaped sardine tins, and a ten-foot-tall plaster saint standing on an ornately decorated platform, several gardens' worth of paper flowers wilting at her feet.

Her father rapped on the wall: a cold, tympanic sound.

"Anders Fiske," he announced. "For Giana Agnelli."

When there was no reply, her father began eyeing the sardine tins as if counting them. Then there was a noise from the far end of the warehouse—a clearing of the throat, a launching forth of the resulting by-product—which caused Anders to move a step or two closer to the building's innards. Seconds later, Mrs. Agnelli and Tino appeared from the shadows, both of them attired more expensively than ever.

"There's a reason they call it an *embarrassment* of riches," her father whispered.

If Mrs. Agnelli heard the comment, she gave no sign. She continued to move in their direction, her speed leisurely and unaltered, her head tilted toward the saint as she coughed and spit again. It was only Tino who seemed to acknowledge them, assessing both father and daughter with a gaze that seemed to imply his great regret not only at the fact of their presence here, but in the entirety of the cosmic plan that had given birth to it.

"She looks fatter," Mrs. Agnelli said. This was not her cajoling, reverent, hilltop voice. This was a voice from somewhere far beneath. A voice that matched the laugh. "Which begs the question of what, exactly, you've been stuffing into her."

A gossipy murmur from the bowels of the building. Margot moved closer to her father. On account of the echoes, it was difficult to estimate the size of the audience, but she could imagine the brothers lurking nearby, fully concealed from view behind the towers of crates. She glanced fearfully at Tino. Tino blinked and crossed his arms around his waist.

"My daughter's dietary habits," Anders replied, "are her business entirely."

"I was just trying to lighten the mood. But I forgot that your people aren't known for their sense of humor."

"And your people aren't known for their ethics. So many lies, so many distractions. Wouldn't it be easier to just rob your countrymen in the night?"

A new tightness passed across Mrs. Agnelli's face, an expression that made Margot certain someone or something was within seconds of being hit; but then the tightness collapsed into a frown, and for the first time, Margot could see the resemblance to the son, who was now standing behind his mother and slightly to one side.

"So you're done being polite," Mrs. Agnelli said. "What a shame."

"The permits. Where are they?"

Her frown deepened. "What makes you think I know? I'm a fisherman. Not a bureaucrat."

Anders lifted his chin and clasped his hands in front of him. "The workers, then. Why haven't they shown up? Have they been threatened?"

The sorrow on Mrs. Agnelli's face looked irreproachable.

"My influence reaches only half as far as most people think. There's no mafia here. Unless you count the Chinese."

Margot took a deep breath and then released it without a sound. She looked over at the saint. Her arms were outstretched in a gesture of simultaneous menace and supplication, a glint in her glass eyes that Margot recognized. The workmanship here was crude but passionate, and there was something about it that reminded her of taxidermy. But she didn't want to think about that right now.

"You know her, my dear?" Mrs. Agnelli was using the other voice now, the sweet one. Margot remembered the hug, then shook her head to clear the memory.

"Santa Rosalia," Mrs. Agnelli continued. "The patron saint of the sardine fleets. Last year her blessings were unprecedented. And this year is certain to bring more of the same."

"Not according to Ricketts's estimates," her father interjected. "Which I'm assuming you haven't read."

The name made Margot twitch.

"Oh, I read them," Mrs. Agnelli replied, the sweetness gone. "But I found them less than sane."

"His methods are unorthodox, yes. But I'm certain he's right."

"And I'm certain he's out of his mind. Him and his writer friend, that bloated communist. Stomping around in those tide pools, slobbering over each other and bickering like a married couple. Your daughter knows what I mean."

Her father looked at her. Her heart almost stopped.

"He's the only good biologist in town," Anders replied. "Miles ahead of everyone at Hopkins."

"He has no degree. Biologists have degrees."

"He runs a legitimate business."

"Oh, Anders, that business hasn't been legitimate in years. The only reason it's still afloat is because Steinbeck supplies all the funds that Ricketts and his army of sluts and vagrants sees fit to drink away."

"He's done the research. He's got the numbers. He knows things are changing and you're a fool if you think you can—"

"A fool?" Mrs. Agnelli shrieked, the last traces of her earlier gentleness falling away.

Then, a commotion from the rear of building, an assembling of bodies. It was not the brothers, Margot realized, who had been hiding in the darkness. It was a squadron of women—many of whose portraits Margot could clearly remember sketching—emerging now from the blockade of crates and cans, arranging themselves in a line behind mother and son. She looked at her father's face, expecting to see the blank, emotionless scrim it usually acquired during moments of challenge or confrontation. Instead, she saw his cheeks turn bright red, his eyes sparking with anger and uncertainty.

"If anyone's a fool," Mrs. Agnelli continued, "it's you. And your kind."

"My *kind*?"

"Blustering and preening like you've made the world and

everything in it. Never even the barest understanding that there was something here before your arrival, and that there will be something here long after you depart."

"Come, Margot. We're done."

"No, no! She should stay. She should know the truth." She turned to Margot. "He had been here before, you know, when he was just about your age. Made an absolute mess of himself."

She couldn't look at her father anymore. All she could do was guess at his response: the color in his face fading away, his eyes going dark.

"And I'll be happy to paint the picture for you, even though that's usually your job."

"One more word to her, and I'll—"

The women made a collective step forward. Anders fell silent.

"It was squid back then, wasn't it?" Mrs. Agnelli began again. "And it was Chinamen who fished for them. They would usually start up around midnight. A lighted pine-pitch torch on the bow to draw the shoal of spawning squid to the surface, two skiffs following behind the boat, towing the purse seine. The skiffs would circle the shoal and then pull the line to close the purse. Then they would drag the net to the shore by hand, if you can believe it, down there in the water with all those little copulating monsters."

When Mrs. Agnelli coughed again, Margot could feel the sensation in her own lungs, her own throat.

"And there were women working alongside the men, running

into the water to help the men bring in the net, all of them tanned and half-undressed and bareheaded. If you think it smells bad now, you don't know the half of it. When they would split the squid and dry them on the rocks outside their village, it smelled like the world was coming to an end."

Mrs. Agnelli paused for a moment and inhaled deeply, as if the smell were still present somewhere, still captured inside the warehouse walls.

"And your father—our dear, young Anders—would sit on China Point and watch them fish. When he wasn't doing that, he would hang around the Hotel Del Monte. He couldn't afford a room there, of course, but he would slip onto the grounds whenever he had a chance, pacing the gardens, pretending he belonged. One night, he even crept into the ballroom. Everyone was so happy and drunk they didn't even notice the poor boy in their midst. He could have done anything he wanted. He could have eaten their food, sipped their wine, but all he wanted to do was confess himself. All he wanted to do was unburden his poor Methodist soul to the Chinese girl who, when she wasn't busy gutting squid, was busy breaking his heart."

"I was young," her father insisted. "And very confused."

"As was I, once upon a time. But now my name is on the biggest boats in the bay. I own a house ten times as large as the one I was raised in. So tell me: what could you possibly know of this place that I do not? What scheme of yours could prove half as successful as what I've already been able to accomplish? What

sort of salvation do you plan to grant those of us who have already been saved?"

"I'm doing something I should have done far sooner."

"What the hell does that mean?"

Anders removed his eyeglasses. The air inside the warehouse seemed to spasm. The women shifted, the saint stared. Outside, a sea lion began to howl. When he started speaking again, his words were careful and slow and almost modest.

"It means I'm building an aquarium."

The walk home was quiet and strained.

She stayed a few steps behind, allowing her father to seethe in peace. Every once in a while, a car would rattle past, headlights flickering as the wheels crunched across a patch of gravel. Otherwise, the only sound was of the ocean, the hiss of its tides growing fainter as they climbed, the sky a rolling swath of green and black. At certain points, it felt as though they were being followed, but she couldn't tell for sure.

When they returned to the house, Anders retreated to the kitchen and Margot followed. She watched him from the doorway, hoping the additional confessions would pour forth of their own accord. He was already thumbing through his files, though, already consumed by his work.

"Why are you—"

"Where's my pencil?"

She removed her own pencil from her satchel and handed it to him. He instantly began to scribble something on the nearest sheet of paper, his handwriting illegible.

"I didn't realize—"

"Please, Margot. Not now."

Heart racing, she went to the cabinet, withdrew a frying pan, and set it on the stove. Then she opened the icebox and desperately scanned it for something to cook, but it was empty.

"Not now!"

She turned to look at him. His eyes were small and red.

"What can I do?" she asked.

"Leave. And don't come back until I'm asleep."

Outside, Tino was sitting on the porch, chin cupped in his hands.

"Were you following us?" she asked.

"An aquarium," he mused. "That's wonderful."

And how could she possibly respond without sounding foolish? How could she possibly tell him there was a part of her that had known it since the beginning? Not the conscious, striving part, but the part that refused to be taught. The part of her that, upon entering Ricketts's lab for the very first time, honestly believed it had already occurred and that she had been taken captive alongside the fish.

"The new drawings," she replied instead. "The dirty ones. Who bought them?"

"The brothel."

"The one on the Row?"

"No. The one on Washington Street."

"In Chinatown?"

"That's right. They give them to the customers on their way out. Like souvenirs."

"I can't work with you anymore."

When he winced and rubbed his neck, she was glad of it. Someone else was in pain now, not just her.

"But it's so much money."

"I can't."

"You'll proceed on your own, then?"

"I don't know."

"Can I make a suggestion?"

She shrugged.

"Get a camera," he said. "Sell the real thing."

This time, the party in Ricketts's lab could be heard from halfway down the hill.

As before, she stopped in the middle of the Row before entering. The curtains were fully parted in every room except the bedroom, so she could see what was happening inside, all of it misty with booze and lamplight. Once again, it was a segregated mix: the locals carrying on with an almost pitiful lack of self-

awareness, the tourists behaving with the expectation of being recognized and celebrated from the shadows. Steinbeck was happy for once, radiantly so, his arm around the same blond actress who had once used Margot's sketch as a fan. Arthur was sitting in Steinbeck's chair, staring at the empty space behind the desk, the drink in his hand making him look just a tragedy or two shy of a grown man. Ricketts, yet again, was nowhere to be seen.

She went around the building and into the back lot, but he wasn't there either. So she picked her way down to the waterline and found a rock that was mostly dry and adequately flat. Someone would come to her. She knew it. Ever since her arrival here, it had been like this: someone on the hill, someone on the porch, someone in the garage, someone behind the wheel of the Buick. At times, it felt like she barely needed to move. It felt like, if she waited long enough, the tides would bring everything she wanted and everything she didn't, and the world would wait patiently for her to figure out the difference.

A minute later, Steinbeck appeared. He was holding two beer bottles, one of which he extended in her direction.

"Please don't say no this time. It'll make me feel bad about myself."

She held up a hand and let him deposit a bottle into it. When she drank, the taste was bitter and weak, almost like nothing.

"We don't do our best collecting out here, to tell you the truth," he continued. "He prefers a spot in Pacific Grove, tech-

nically beyond the boundary of Monterey Bay. I'm sure he's shown you by now."

"No. He hasn't."

He nodded, as if noting something and filing it away for future use.

"Why are you being nice to me?" she asked.

"Wormy's back. I thought you should know. She's in the bedroom."

"With Ricketts."

"That's right."

She took another sip. It still tasted bitter, but this time in a way that seemed to suggest something. "She knows what she's doing."

"She sure does," he replied.

"You sound angry."

"No, I don't," he grumbled. "I'm in favor of sex. I like it. It's just that I expected a bit more from Ed. I thought he was too smart for small distractions. I thought he enjoyed our little conspiracy against Venus. But I suppose the good days never last, which is precisely why they're good."

And where, exactly, did these strange urges come from? she wondered. Why did she want to run into the lab, not in search of Ricketts this time, but in search of Arthur and his stricken reliability? Such an unfair, unwanted ache, as if her body were now host to needs and unions she had never considered before, that had always been rejected purely on account of their unfa-

miliar color and volume. Steinbeck, she knew, felt it, too, but in a different way. There was the young woman inside with her big, stupid smile, but there was also Ricketts, the potential of love incompatible with love's actual existence.

"You'll write about him?" she asked.

He looked at her with heavy eyes. "How can I not?"

"Are those essays any good?"

"Yes. But they'll never get published."

"Have you told him that?"

"No. It would crush him."

"He seems pretty resilient to me."

"Well, then you don't know him at all. I shouldn't be telling you this, especially since I've been against your little dalliance from the beginning. But for a while there, when Wormy was missing, he wanted another loan from me. He said that for a few extra thousand, in addition to all the money he's been making on your mysterious dogfish orders, he could purchase a little parcel of land in Big Sur. A place right off of Hurricane Point. He said he could imagine building a house there. And living in it with you."

He gave a long, baritone sigh and then chucked his beer bottle into the sea.

"What do I do now?" she asked, brain on fire.

"Well, I don't tend to give advice, especially to people I don't particularly like, but try not to take it too hard. You're different and maybe even a little bit evil, and talent like yours is a lonely,

sickening thing. Someday, though, you'll find your own spot, a place where you can burrow in with a handful of souls who don't make you feel like the world's ending. And suddenly there you'll be. Home."

She watched the beer bottle come back in on a wave and rebound hollowly against a rock.

"Do you know where I can find a camera?" she asked.

"There's one in the garage. Right next to all those goddamn vials of shark liver oil."

And then she started laughing. She knew it was a bad sound—unnatural and spooky, just like Mrs. Agnelli's—but she couldn't stop, even when Steinbeck recoiled in confusion. She couldn't stop when he left her alone at the water's edge, or when she slunk into the garage like a chastened animal and found it there, just as he had promised: a Kodak 35 Rangefinder, still in its box, a canister of film accompanying it. Laughing, she loaded the film. Laughing, she left the lab and sprinted in the direction of downtown.

She fell silent, however, when she stepped onto Alvarado Street. She remembered it from her earlier explorations: how the streetlights dropped off into an incense-tinged darkness once a certain corner was turned. At the intersection of Tyler and East Franklin, she slowed down. Then, as she proceeded onto Washington Street, it revealed itself: a purple-curtained, two-story building with an anachronistic gas lamp out front. There was a window in the alleyway that would have been inaccessible to

most voyeurs but that, on account of her height, gave her a direct view of the brothel's most well-trafficked chamber. And although she had to endure the proclivities of seven other clients before finding the client she sought, she didn't lose courage or stamina, she didn't start to laugh again. Instead, she worked with the calmness of a professional, making sure her father's face was in the frame whenever possible, the woman beneath him little more than a compositional afterthought: beautiful and foreign, thin with work and want.

18

1998

THROW THE FISH, THROW 'EM GOOD. FISH FOR THE fish. Eat or be eaten. Sardines in the bay? Not anymore, but they're sure as hell inside the aquarium. She stands above their tank on a catwalk. She throws them their food the way Ricketts used to throw his steaks. "Broadcast feeding," one of the aquarists named it, as if there's a message being transmitted and received, and she can't see the delight of the crowd on the other side of the glass, but she can feel it. She can feel the vacuum of drawn breaths as the sardines tighten their school, as they begin to move as a single undulating tongue, curling around the meal and flashing with satisfaction, a mass of pure instinct shattered and rejoined. The urge to start yelling is nearly uncontrollable. Of course she once saw the horses fight! she wants to yell at him. Of course she did! A clearing in the orchard, a makeshift fence, the snap of torchlight, the waxy leaves of the mango trees

catching the breeze like tiny, black sails. A bad, sweet smell in the air, like a pie being baked from rotten fruit. A crowd of men, her father's long, pale form a crude oddity among the darker, smaller ones. Then the horses, three of them. One: a skinny, nervous mare tied to a stake in the middle of the clearing. Two and three: a pair of stallions, circling the ring, sizing each other up. An involuntary flick of the mare's tail. A hoof to the chest, a gargle of anguish. Teeth sinking into a throat and pulling away a sheet of bloodied hide. The loser falling to his knees, the winner limping forward to claim his trapped prize. After that, she couldn't watch anymore, but she could listen and she could smell. And that, of course, was more than enough.

19

1940

FOR THE NEXT TWO WEEKS, WAR.

It started out slowly, somewhat prosaically: the defacing of the exterior walls of Anders's cannery, the breaking of windows.

Then there was a brief truce, just long enough for Margot's father to relax, followed by a barrage of vandalism as inventive as it was disturbing. Live squirrels were put inside the pump house, clogging the mechanism with bones and fur. Human excrement—what seemed like tons of it—was piled up in front of the cannery's main door. She expected him to retaliate, to do whatever he could to inflict an equal degree of suffering upon his rival, but he continued on just as before, utterly immersed in his work, eerily unmoved, the ill will aimed in his direction little more than a distraction that, with the right combination of denial and willpower, he could endure unscathed.

Then one night she awoke to a strangely familiar smell, and

when she rose from the horsehair sofa and opened the front door in search of the smell's source, she was hit with a blast of angry, orange heat. The statue from the Agnellis' warehouse was on the porch, the saint's body bright with flame, the bougainvillea bush similarly alight. She ran inside and roused her father, who sprinted to the porch in nothing but his undershorts, and for the next hour they fought the blaze with bedsheets and bowls of water, slapping the plaster woman and leaving the bougainvillea to its own pyrotechnic devices, conscious that their neighbors had also been awakened by the fire but had not found it prudent to help.

In the lab, too, her hope was being incinerated. Until the night of the second party, the night of Wormy's return, the lab had been quiet and sparsely populated during the day. Now, however, the activity was unceasing. Wormy herself spent hours at a time drifting in and out of Margot's field of vision: shuttling from the kitchen to the Chinese grocery and back again, stocking the icebox with crate after crate of unlabeled beer. Fleets of neighborhood boys entered with twitching, snarling sacks and exited with pockets full of nickels. Steinbeck loitered in the front room, choosing a book and then changing his mind and choosing another. Prostitutes from the Lone Star arrived on the doorstep with vague yet urgent medical complaints to which Ricketts gladly tended, his dry, upbeat professionalism belying his continued lack of traditional expertise, before disappearing on collecting trips on which she was no longer invited: expedi-

tions that kept him away from the lab all day and well into the evening.

And Margot stayed behind the desk. She had stopped drawing humans, so now it was only sea life. For a while, she tried to take an obliterative comfort in it, her stack of sketches ballooning to dimensions that in any other instance would have made her proud, but her sense of dread was so all encompassing that nothing seemed able to puncture it. The entire town seemed to understand it just as well as she did. The cannery workers eyed her with an odd combination of regret and triumph. Arthur moped around the lab as if it were his life, not hers, speeding toward some nameless yet certain upheaval. Even Steinbeck offered what he could in the way of condolences, nodding at her whenever he passed by the desk. It was only Ricketts who remained seemingly unaware of anything ominous, his behavior detached and jovial, his treatment of her totally uninflected with even the barest hint of desire or melancholy. There were times when she considered saying something, pressing forth. For the first time in her life, though, she didn't have the heart for it. She had become weary and full of self-doubt, even the smallest challenges suddenly insurmountable.

Which was why she couldn't even think about her father. She couldn't even think about the film canister in her satchel. She couldn't even think about his aquarium and the extent to which Ricketts might have assisted in the idea's creation. It was gro-

tesque and, like most grotesqueries, she wanted to both wallow in it and run from it. As she continued to kill and draw the little tide pool beasts, the lab's mayhem roaring around her, she imagined the same animals entering her father's cannery and staying there, the bodies rotting, Ricketts and her father congratulating each other on the resulting stench, the resulting violation, a crowd cheering them on by torchlight, their allegiance reopening a wound that had been inflicted long before her birth, that long since should have healed.

It was with little in the way of optimism, therefore, that she arrived at the lab one morning to find it vacant once again. The tide pools were devoid of interlopers, the front room was free of cat hunters. Wormy wasn't in the kitchen and Ricketts wasn't down in the garage, so she ventured to the tide pools alone and selected something that seemed worthwhile: a sculpin that almost immediately allowed itself to be pinned against the rocks and scooped up with a net. In the garage, she tended to its demise with a heavy, distracted mind and then took it up to the desk to draw it, its furry head still cocked in what seemed like amusement at its own ruin. Then she added it to the pile Ricketts had reserved for what he called the *tourists*, the animals that didn't quite belong in the tide pools but often claimed territory there nonetheless. Then she stood to retrieve her things.

"You're learning."

The voice seemed to come from nowhere, and when she

turned around, she half expected to see nothing. But there he was: smiling at her from the bedroom doorway, the undershirt beneath his suspenders threadbare and yellowed with old sweat.

"I thought I was alone," she said.

"I've been trying to rest up. It's bound to be a long night in the tide pools. The first proxigean spring tide in more than a decade."

When he approached the desk, she wanted her feelings of apathy to remain. His nearness, however, was still as potent as the chemicals in which his specimens met their end.

"I feel as if I've barely seen you lately." He picked up one of the piles and began to shuffle through it. "You work so hard, you practically disappear."

"Things have taken a turn. With my father's project."

"I know. And just when everything was going so well!"

There was the urge to contradict him, to speak of Anders's predestined failure, to speak of her own. But he was sitting on the edge of the desk now, his body closer to hers than it had been in days.

"Yes," she said.

"Stay for a drink. Drown your sorrows."

She looked out the window.

"I should go."

"Tonight, then. At eleven. Come back and help me collect."

For a moment, everything was finally clear, finally predictable: the efficacy of restraint, the value of dignity.

"No," she replied calmly.

"There must be a way to convince you."

"There's not much—"

And then he was touching her scar, running the tip of his index finger along its numb length and then down her nose until it came to rest between her lips.

"Eleven," she said.

"That's right." He nodded, removing his finger. "Wear your boots."

That night, she watched the clock with an executioner's eye. With the proper focus, she told herself, time itself could be bullied. It could be bullied into moving faster, so fast that by the time the agreed-upon hour arrived, she would be a grown woman capable of everything and answerable to no one.

When she poured her fourth cup of coffee, Anders put down his cards and glared at her.

"You keep drinking that," he said, "and you'll be up until dawn."

She took another sip and stared even harder at the clock's pendulum. Its swinging looked especially rhythmic tonight, in a way that spoke not of mortality but of mortality's opposite: the universe winding itself up with such intense tightness that it might never be able to wind itself down.

"It's your move," he said.

"I think I'm done."

She placed her cards on the floor and stood.

"Giana Agnelli was right."

She sat back down. She looked at the ceiling. Her mother's head was there again, and it was looking at Anders, but it didn't seem particularly concerned with what he was about to say.

"What was she right about?" Margot asked.

"About me," he replied after a long moment. "But she was also wrong. For one thing, I wasn't a Methodist. I just lived with them because the tents were cheap. For another thing, the girl didn't fish for squid or clean them. Quite the opposite, in fact. Her family owned one of the little carts that used to park at the entrance to the Seventeen-Mile Drive and sell things to the tourists. Junk, mostly. Painted abalone shells. Driftwood whittled into dollhouse figurines. Sometimes a whale vertebra or a shark's jaw. But for the customers who were willing to pay, there were other things, too."

She held her breath.

"Sea creatures," he clarified. She exhaled. "Live ones. The girl would put them in jelly jars that you could take home with you. I bought them because I loved her. I followed her around like a dog, to be honest, and she trained me like one, too. She trained me in how the cart made and reinvested its money. She trained me in the concepts of scarcity and abundance, or at least the appearance of them. Before coming to California, I thought

I knew. I thought New York had taught me everything I'd ever need to know. But this was business on a completely different level: shrewd, elegant, discreet. When she was confident I was ready, we opened our own little sideshow just outside the hotel grounds. All of our fish and crabs and snails arranged together in one big display. The children could look for free, but the adults had to pay."

When he paused, she looked away. *So I wasn't the first,* she told herself. *And neither was he.*

"And when the girl ended up preferring one of her own kind—a man who lived in the same fishing village—I didn't know what to do. I got so jealous I poisoned the water in the jars. I busted the spokes of the wheels on her family's cart. I wasn't sure what point I was trying to prove."

He shut his mouth abruptly, an awful bewilderment in his eyes. His hair was falling down around his face and he made no attempt to slick it back.

"What happened to her?" she asked.

"Her village burned to the ground."

Her blood went cold.

"Don't worry." He sighed. "By that point, I had already been gone for years."

She nodded. He stared at the empty fireplace. Fifteen minutes passed, then thirty. At half past ten, he finally rose and went to the bedroom. She went outside without trying to camouflage the sound of her footsteps. The stars were shifting and she didn't need to look at the clock to know it was time, but she lingered for a bit longer, staring out at the bay. Her clothing—a pair of trousers in a lumpy brown tweed, a sweater with a rough cable knit the approximate width of a human forearm—suddenly felt unbearably tight, ill suited for the rounder, more specific body she had acquired since their arrival in town. So she went back inside and rummaged through her trunk in search of the dress she had worn to the Agnellis' church. She put it on and left the house. On the Row, it was silent. His front door was unlocked. The lab was empty. She went down to the garage, selected a bucket, a flashlight, and a net, and went out to the tide pools by herself, confident that when he arrived at the appointed time, he would see her standing there in the water, a beloved ghost among the sand and rocks.

And even though she was alone, she could feel the presence of others. Crawling things, shrinking things, things shutting and sealing themselves against an exposure that, to their tiny minds and bodies, must have seemed apocalyptic. The waterline, owing to a rare lunar aberration, had plunged dozens of feet beyond any low-tide mark she had ever seen, and the entire universe seemed stunned by the novelty of it. The gulls and sea lions were quiet, the moonlight wavered. She could hear noises in the lab's garage now, sounds that carried easily across the calm water. *I'm ready*, she told herself. So she put a final creature in her bucket, took a final look at the bay, its depths entirely

knowable, entirely hers, and then made her way through the grid of shark tanks and into the garage.

He was standing at the sink. She placed her bucket on the floor. At the sound, he turned to look at her. And that's when she saw Arthur's face.

"He's already gone," the boy explained.

She couldn't speak.

"To Mexico," he continued. "The Sea of Cortez, to be precise. The boat was ready a few days early, so they decided to take advantage of it. Him and Steinbeck and Steinbeck's wife and a few hired hands for good measure. Won't be back for a month or two, so he put me in charge."

Even though her eyes were burning, she could see everything clearly. In a manner too precise to be unintentional, he had garbed himself exactly like his employer: apron, visor, black rubber boots, a woolen cap obscuring his hair. His movements, too, aped the older man's gestures as he picked up her bucket and held it to his chest.

"It's strange out there, isn't it?" He grinned. "Feels like a dream."

She looked at the chemicals in their bottles, the specimens in their jars. *So much glass*, she thought. *So many things to break.* And with the shards, she knew exactly what she'd do. She'd find the sharpest edges and wield them like scissors, cutting the clothes from Arthur's body, cutting his skin and hair.

"Show me how to do it," he said.

"All right," she whispered.

But she didn't join him at the sink. Instead, she turned for the door and ran outside. The tide was coming back in now, the sea reclaiming the shore with an audible speed, the sand hissing beneath the water's sudden weight. Over the past several weeks, all the sharks had been euthanized and preserved and sold in fulfillment of her fake orders, except for one: his largest, his favorite, his pet, the animal to which she had once fed the bloody morsel of meat. She hurried to the edge of its tank, and when she plunged her arms into the water, she expected to have to fight for it, just as she had fought for everything else. But the shark's body was already perfectly aligned, its rough skin raking against hers. A moment later, its gills were fluttering across her fingers like the pages of a book, so she made her fingers into hooks and cried out with the effort as she lifted the animal into the air.

"Margot, don't—"

"Empty the trash barrel," she growled. "And fill it with as much benzocaine as you can find."

He stared at her, terrified, and then rushed back to the garage. She carried the shark inside, its body like a single, rough tendon, its jaws snapping in fear and futility. When she got there, everything was ready. Her arms shook as she dropped it into the barrel. First, the fury of recognition, mouth wide in what might have been a scream. Then the paralysis and col-

lapse, a stiffness to its shape as it sank to the bottom of the barrel like a stone. Then the relaxation that in any other instance might have felt sweet: the shark loosening and bending and returning, in its death, to the posture of its birth, curled head to tail like an elongated fetus.

"We don't have a display jar big enough," he said.

For a moment, she envied Arthur's innocence. But then she loathed it, her hands moving of their own accord now, unbuttoning the front of her dress, slipping it from her shoulders.

"What was wrong with me?" She was screeching like a harpy, her voice hateful and shrill.

"Margot . . ."

"What did I do?"

"Margot, he has a wife. She lives a few miles down the coast, up in the Carmel Highlands with their daughters. The oldest is just about your age."

"I don't care."

"And then there's Wormy, who has a husband of her own. And the dozens of women before that. . . ."

The bodice of the dress was crumpled around her hips now, her breasts bare. She looked at Arthur, expecting to see shock or desire in his eyes. Instead, she saw the same seriousness that had been on his face that very first day inside the lab.

"I'm a good person, Margot. Everyone knows that. And I've been watching successful men, men like your father. I'm figuring things out, doing what I can to make life good. I'll buy a house on the hill, get a better job in the canneries: one that will support a family. Doc says we're a perfect match, and if you'll have me . . ."

"I don't need you."

At this, he finally looked at her breasts. She looked at them, too. They were swollen, sickeningly opaque, marbled with blue veins. Her stomach protruded.

"You'll need someone."

Instead of responding, she stepped out of the dress.

Then she sat on the Buick and slowly spread her legs until the appropriate expression was on his face: gratitude, disbelief, delight. He started to remove his hat, but she shook her head.

"Leave it."

"All right."

And she could hear the shark, even though she knew it was dead. She could hear its ghost fins slapping and rubbing, applauding her as she leaned back and let him in.

20

THE NEXT MORNING, THE SMELL FROM THE CANneries reached its apex.

Just as Giana Agnelli had predicted, the winter had been one of record-breaking sardine hauls, and now, as spring creaked in, the town found itself awash on a quickly souring tide, the supply vastly outpacing the demand. The municipal authorities, recognizing that a good portion of the populace had already gone half-mad from the stench, dusted off Ordinance 106: a dictate that all canneries and reduction plants install the proper deodorizing equipment, a violation of which was punishable by ninety days in jail. When the threat of the ordinance failed to enact the sort of change the townspeople had been promised, they took matters into their own hands and formed five-man "smelling committees" that roamed the Row at peak canning hours, enforcing a haphazard type of vigilante justice that climaxed in the citizen's arrest of the seventy-five-year-old superintendent of the Carmel Canning Company.

And as the smell blossomed and bred, compelling everyone in Monterey County to consider the downside of taking from the sea exactly what they thought it had offered, Margot became a corpse. A corpse lying on the horsehair sofa, the hours inching by. Everything was merciless, aggressively lit, and all those details she had taken such great care not to notice—her earlier sickness, her recent fatness, the absence of her monthly bleeding—were insisting upon themselves, repeating themselves in the opposite of prayer.

A resurrection, in other words, didn't seem likely, but it occurred nonetheless. She wasn't sure where to go. She no longer had a mutiny in mind or a riddle to solve, so she just proceeded aimlessly, visiting all the places she knew would disturb her with their aftertaste. She returned to the Hotel Del Monte. She sat beneath the sickly palms and watched a skeleton crew of Japanese botanists dance through the pest-eaten topiaries in their small black shoes.

When she had grown tired of the hotel, she climbed the hill to the Presidio, sneaked through the gates, and gazed blankly out at the vista that, more than three centuries earlier, had been claimed under the authority of a careless empire. She loitered around the outskirts of her father's cannery and listened for the noises she feared. She went to the Agnelli warehouse on the wharf and found Tino standing outside, a bag of saltwater taffy in hand.

"Would you like some?" he asked.

"No."

He tossed the bag over the railing and into a waiting cluster of sea lions, who ripped the bag to shreds and swallowed the candies whole.

She looked at the sky. Somehow, it had become dusk.

"Are you expected at home?"

"No," she replied.

"Me neither."

So they continued the pilgrimage together, following the railroad tracks until, at the shared border of Monterey and Pacific Grove, they came to a stop.

"What's going on here?" she asked.

There were lanterns everywhere: lanterns in every window of every big, cakelike Victorian home, lanterns casting an eerie orange flicker onto the black streets.

"Let's go," he pleaded.

"Not yet."

And when the parade started, she wanted an explanation, but Tino refused, so she asked a fellow onlooker. The celebration, the onlooker said, was a local tradition that had been popular at the turn of the century but that for the past few decades had fallen a bit out of favor. He wasn't sure of the exact details, but it didn't really matter because the whole thing had been made up anyway: the story of the ancient Chinese queen who tried to drown herself rather than submit to her father's desire for a tidy, profitable marriage of convenience. There was a brass band playing what sounded like a funeral dirge. There was a bejeweled bunch of white girls dressed as the queen and her royal court, waving at the crowd from a passing float. As for the actual Chinese, there was no trace of their presence. It was just the lanterns in the windows and the sardine boats in the bay, the land and sea white with fire, the earth's skin a platinum cloak of heat and error.

"You're in trouble, aren't you?" Tino asked when the parade had ended, when most of the lanterns had been snuffed.

"I think so."

"I'll talk to my mother. She knows the right people."

She hesitated and tried to think clearly. But she no longer knew how. She no longer knew the difference between a promise and a coercion.

"Please do."

"She'll need payment, though."

She reached into her satchel and withdrew the canister of film. "She'll find this interesting."

He took the canister and gave it a little shake.

"And for you?" she asked.

"I don't need anything."

"I insist."

He thought for a moment and then glanced in the direction of the hill.

"One last portrait," he said.

And it *was* the last one, she told herself as they entered his father's sickroom, as Tino climbed into bed alongside him. After this, she would never put pencil to paper ever again. She would never create a single thing. Because what was the point? What was the point in the face of such sadness: Tino curled up against the one man who might have shown him a different way to be, his father so drunk on pain and the medication that was supposed to relieve it that, despite the presence of an audience, he was visibly terrified at having been left to die alone.

An hour later, she found herself standing outside the lab.

The door was locked for once, so she let herself in through the bedroom window. Inside, she listened for a while to make sure no one else was there, and then she sat on the bed. Then she wandered into the front room and lowered herself into the chair behind the desk. She pushed her hands against her ears, but the voices were too loud to silence, too big to suppress, so she went back to the bedroom. She lay flat on the bed and watched as night achieved its full expression, as the day's mute circus packed up and set off for parts darker and unknown. She watched the shadows on the street stamp a changing, conjoined pattern against the green curtains, the shapes heavy and absolute. There was an unfamiliar feeling between her legs that reminded her of the blank, breathtaking millisecond that occurs between pain's infliction on the body and pain's registration by the brain, and she tried to rub the feeling away, but to no avail. At dusk, she heard the sound of an automobile engine and went to the window to see if it was the Buick, but it was not. And although the prominent feeling was one of queasiness—that of having accidentally bathed in something other than water—there was also a sense of weird expansiveness. It was almost as if she could see everything from above, the entire town laid bare in all its segments, everyone confined to borders that had more to do with the quality of the light and air than the presence of any real boundaries, everyone holding down their territories as if armies would rise from the water and rob them of everything save the dense comfort of their own kind.

At around midnight, she heard the front door crash open. She set her jaw and didn't move, even when her father appeared in the bedroom doorway, his suit rumpled, his face bent with rage.

"Get up," he said.

"No."

He approached the bed. He grabbed her by the wrist.

"Where did you get those photographs? Why did you give them to her?"

He yanked her to her feet. She fought, gripping the mattress and pulling herself back down.

"I don't want to hurt you," he pleaded.

She spit at him. His palm collided with one side of her face and then the other. When her nose began to bleed, he stepped away from the bed, his face frozen in fear and amazement.

"How could you?" he said, quietly this time, almost gently. "You were my life's work."

"No, I wasn't," she replied. "I was the thing that happened in spite of it."

21

1998

THE OCTOPUS'S SUCCOR IS FLEETING.

This doesn't surprise her, though. Relief is not dry land, but a moment on the tide charts, an interlude between drownings. There was a time when she didn't know how to save herself, didn't know how to swim back to shore. A long stretch of time—the 1950s through the 1970s—when, in the wake of the inevitable sardine decline, she would pace the remnants of Cannery Row and find herself at fault. Exhibits A through Z: the warehouse fires springing up twice a year as if on schedule, milk-eyed windows, graffiti-veined walls, weeds and pigeons, the abandonment made infinitely more unsettling by the small businesses that attempted to capitalize on the few visitors the Row continued to receive. A History of Monterey wax museum in which the models "breathed" via pneumatic lungs, an antique shop with nearly two hundred doll heads in the window, an art gallery selling coarsely executed oil paintings of naked people riding dolphins, a restaurant that consisted solely of a dented Weber and a trio of lawn chairs.

Worst of all was her father's old cannery. It had come back into her possession, but she wasn't sure what to do with it. The time wasn't right. The world was far too satisfied in its conventionality and then far too satisfied in its iconoclasm, neither of which was ideal for what she had in mind. She found ways to pass the years: a marriage and a divorce, and then another round of both. She invested her father's fortune and watched the original sum acquire a tail of self-replicating zeroes, the money sprouting like polyps. She made strategic donations to local causes, kissed the occasional rear end. She made the mistake of taking a course in business ethics at the local community college. She was elected and reelected to the city council. She invited Arthur and Tino to her house every so often and pretended to listen to them talk. For a while, she even thought about leaving town again, about finding somewhere entirely new: a language she didn't know, a quality of light that confused her. But then—it was 1977; she recalls this distinctly because an aquarium called Ocean Park opened that year in Hong Kong—the tides began to change. Monterey began to lose its mind. It didn't surprise her; she had always suspected that too many years beneath the region's trademark variant of fog bore the potential not just of physical discomfort but of psychological damage, and now there were stories in the paper along these lines. The death of an otherwise unthreatening preteen, an empty swimming pool and a peaked roof and the great distance between the two, the body of a young boy found in a house in Carmel Valley high up in the rattlesnake-infested hills, the Pebble Beach woman who, bruised and cut from nightly beatings, shot her husband in the cheek and then turned the gun on herself. Stories of a failed local restaurateur attempting to stave off financial ruin by hiring an Israeli contract killer to murder his wealthy parents in their sleep. Stories of a veterinarian in Seaside slaying two waitresses and having them secretly cremated alongside a Doberman named Fancy.

The entire peninsula, in other words, was breaking apart. And she was just the one to fix it.

So she finally began to set things in motion. Arthur and Tino were on board, as were the scientists at Hopkins, many of whom were persuaded to leave the institute to work alongside her. There was some generalized resistance at first, just as there had been in her father's day. The fishing fleets feared the fickle interference of tourism; the historical preservationists wanted everything to stay the way they presumed Steinbeck would have wanted it; the residents of Monterey and Pacific Grove moaned about traffic and parking. Permits were another issue. The old cannery from which the aquarium was to be fashioned straddled the border of the two towns in question, which meant that permission had to be granted from each municipality, a bureaucratic quagmire that nearly derailed the project before it even began.

Work, then. Work unlike any that had come before, that made her apprenticeships to Anders and Ricketts seem frivolous in comparison. Dark mornings, sweaty afternoons, weepy nights. A cast of humans to manage, but also a cast of fish and plants, none of them quite as amenable as one would like. Lingcods devouring the black-eyed gobies, sea otters using any object within reach to make deep, irreparable gouges in the three-story acrylic windows, seven gill sharks bashing their snouts against the tank walls and refusing to eat unless a sushi-grade salmon steak was clipped to a pole, dangled directly beneath their mouths, and made to thrash around in imitation of a live fish. A sea turtle was acquired from an aquarium in Japan, its suspiciously low price explained when, after its painstaking installation into a million-gallon exhibit, it attempted to mate with one of the volunteer divers. And the turtle wasn't the only one. The aquarists, too, couldn't keep their hands off each other. Almost every time she went into the service corridors behind the tanks, she would find a new couple going at it in the darkness: up against the filters and fiberglass, shirts off, pants down, the fish bearing witness.

"It's not an amusement park," she told the offending aquarists as they stood before her, their hair mussed and their eyes lowered. "And I'm not amused."

When it came to matters of aesthetics, however, no one needed much convincing. The architects understood perfectly, as did the exhibit designers. The old did not bow to the new, nor did the beautiful cave to the efficient, nor did money prove an object. The original system of overhead piping was preserved despite outrageous inconvenience and expense, as was the gigantic boiler, which was made an exhibit in its own right. When it was discovered that the whistle towers—the ones that had once summoned the cannery workers to the lines—would not survive the rigors of large-scale renovation, the originals were quietly demolished and precise fiberglass replicas were assembled and installed over the course of a single weekend. Floor tiles of sparkling gray quartzite were specially ordered from Mozambique. The font on the informational placards was designed on commission and then trademarked. *Indulgences*, she sometimes answered whenever the *Herald* came asking. Secretly, though, she knew it was something else entirely. A vision both enamored of and at odds with itself, a private need made public, a dream that had both everything and nothing to do with the waking life that had inspired it.

And then there was the matter of the ocean itself. It wouldn't look good, she knew, for an immaculate aquarium to preside over the shores of a spoiled bay. So she began the long-overdue task of repairing the damage the canneries had once wrought. Anders's schooling was key. *Know a politician's needs*, he had advised her, *and you'll be more powerful than the politician.* So she pulled her strings and called in her favors and it wasn't long before environmental safeguards were recommended, legislation was written, and a sanctuary was established, the fishermen's livelihoods now secondary—and rightfully so—to those of the fish.

Then, without warning, it was almost time. They were in the final phase of construction now, the crews laying the foundation for the sprawling outdoor deck and amphitheater. Because of the tides, this work couldn't be done during the day, so she hired night laborers at an expense that seemed to necessitate supervision. Hidden in the darkness, she would stand there on concrete that was still semi-wet underfoot, her body held precariously aloft on ad hoc plywood "snowshoes," and she would imagine the bay's prehistory. She would watch the blowtorches spray and hiss, she would hear the pneumatic fire of the nail guns, and she would summon the gods, Greek in girth and temperament. How to make that first, submarine slice? A trident dragging across the earth's skin and splitting it open. Out of wounds, something must flow or else it's not really a wound. So, sulfur: sulfur spewing from huge, hollow columns, sulfur on which blind things began to feed. A richness to these depths, pea-soupy and sinister. A shift in temperature, a lightning strike of radical warmth, the gods of earth and sky finally taking an interest. The land carving Santa Cruz to the north, Pacific Grove to the south. The first inhalation of fog, the rich deepness rising. And then the feast. The filter feeders siphoned in whatever they could from their anchorages on the rocks. Fish, big and small, gorged themselves silly. Whales, too, blues and grays and humpbacks, suckling calves in tow. The blood shadows of sharks and sea lions, teeth snapping at the periphery. Then, the people. Only a few of them at first: a calm, resourceful tribe who ate the sea urchins straight from the tide pools and used their spiny tests as currency. Then, visitors from elsewhere, harbingers of thievery and sickness and faith. Gold, otters, squid, sardines, oil: bait for a new worship. And standing there on the deck, on the black edge of her own creation, she knew. She knew she was not one of the people summoned by the gods. She was a god herself. Angry, jealous, impulsive, cruel, but also possessed of more than a little magic, more than a little immortality. If she waved a hand across the water, actual waves would rise up in response. If she bled into the bay, it would start to boil. If she gave enough of herself, this town would love her even more than it loved its own children.

But then it was opening day and she wasn't a god anymore. She wasn't untouchable or vengeful or brave. In fact, she could barely approach the aquarium without panicking, much less go inside of it. So for the first few weeks, she did everything remotely. She attended meetings by phone. She wore out her fax machine. She had someone bring her the daily security tapes so she could watch them at home. She watched the fish and waited for them to give her courage. But, in the end, it was the people who convinced her. The looks on their faces. The fire in their eyes. They all understood exactly what she meant. They had all broken through.

So now what more is there to do? In the years since his death, she hasn't been shattered, she hasn't been chaste. He always hated old women, their bad smells and their thin lips, and she does, too. Tonight, however, she will share a bed with someone far better looking than she, far younger, and it's not on account of her beauty, which existed for only five months: from November 1939 through March 1940. What matters are her accomplishments and the strength of character that enabled them, although sometimes she wonders. She wonders about the women, both old and young. She wonders what her mother would have said. She wonders about Wormy. She imagines the face of her father's first love. She considers the acts of Giana Agnelli and aches with understanding. She never wanted to join their ranks and still doesn't. But that doesn't mean she would object to them joining hers. *Follow me down the stairs*, she would say. *Watch your step.* And then they would work side by side to empty the china hutch, place the jars on the garage's dirt floor, and arrange the specimens however they damn well pleased.

22

1948

A LEAP YEAR THAT SEEMED, FOR ONCE, TO DESERVE the extra day. An entire nation gripped by a sizzling postwar enthusiasm, endless cocktails and endless car rides, huge vehicles grinding through countrysides that were just now being chopped up into the staging grounds of modern suburbia.

The death of Anders Fiske, therefore, felt poorly timed on many levels. He would have been able, Margot reasoned, to harness this new dynamism in surprising and productive and potentially revolutionary ways. But his life was cut short in Colorado Springs when he choked to death on a bison steak that had been raised on a plot of grassland he had purchased in prescient anticipation of both a booming alternative-meat market and his impending retirement in the mountains; and this was how she found herself at his grave site with only his recently hired secretary for company, the Rockies looming at their backs like guests that had been invited to the funeral but hadn't particularly wanted to come.

Later that night, the secretary joined her in the mountain cabin in which her father had met his end.

"You're the boss now," he said. "If you want to be."

"I don't," she replied.

"So we'll sell it off?"

"Yes, I think that's best."

She let the secretary finish his brandy, then showed him out. She watched the road until he disappeared from it, the door open to the darkness and cold, the landscape's jagged miraculousness even more jagged and even more miraculous on account of the Milky Way's prophetic presence overhead. She shivered. For a moment, she wished for her old clothes: the ones she had worn as a child, the sturdy trousers and stiff collars and woolen sweaters that had done such an exemplary job keeping out the elements, or at least camouflaging her physical response to them. But she hadn't had the luxury of such things for quite some time. As counterintuitive as it seemed, living apart from her father's supervision had required her to become more fragile—more feminine—not less, as if calling attention to her weaknesses made them harder for strangers to exploit. There was also the fact, jarringly realized, that the imitation of power is not the same as its acquisition. So it had been skirts and blouses for nearly eight years now, even the occasional dress. Clumsily, at first—sleeves too short, waistlines too loose, proportions all askew—but then her freshman-year roommate at Wellesley had doled out a morsel of sartorial charity, and soon she was passing for normal and then some. The way she looked was not only important; it was malleable. It could be as carefully planned and executed as the pictures she had once drawn, and she began to see herself in precisely this context: as a project not unlike the ones her father pursued.

Now he was dead, though, and her perspective was collapsing. She wanted to call out into the night, to summon the secretary back to the house, to ask him to stay awake in the kitchen, shooing away ghosts while she slept. She knew, however, that her shouts would produce only echoes, and the last thing she wanted was to hear her own voice, especially when she knew it would be tinged with the most useless kind of panic. So she closed the door and reentered the cabin. Evolution despised emotion, which explained so much about life and those who lived it successfully. Now, though, it was as if the film were being shown backward, legs devolving into fins, lungs into gills. It wasn't pain and it wasn't fresh, but it was as unpleasant as anything she could ever remember feeling, which was why she allowed herself the queasy liberty of finding her father's tiny, pine-paneled bedroom, of lying down on his bed, of taking a sip from the bottle of brandy the secretary had left unfinished. The view from his coffin, she realized, must look similar to what she was seeing now: wood on the ceiling, wood on the walls, wood all around.

She spent the next day wandering the landscape, acclimating herself to the thin air and the way the tree line seemed hand stitched on the mountainsides. Then she began to work alongside the secretary to liquidate his estate. There was the subdivision and auction of the hemp fields just outside of Steele, North Dakota; the disbandment of WXRP, a radio station that broadcast one-man comedy hours from a lighthouse on the coast of York, Maine; the emancipation of nearly three hundred sled dogs in Cripple, Alaska. When the transactions were complete and the funds had been transferred, she read the telegrams with a cold eye before crumpling them in her fist and tossing them into the pines, wishing the news they contained were meant for someone else.

Soon there was only one remaining task: the resolution of a trademark dispute concerning the aborted cigar company in the Philippines.

"I'd be happy to press forth," the secretary said, "and notify you when everything has been resolved."

"No," she replied after a moment of deliberation. "I'll manage this one myself."

She gave the secretary his last paycheck. Then, for the sum of fourteen hundred dollars, she booked a seat on a DC-4 from San Francisco to Manila.

On the plane, which was different in every way from the cargo ship that had once taken her and Anders in the reverse direction, she tried to prepare herself. It would be upsetting, most likely, to see Manila again after eight long years, to witness the near total destruction she had read about in the papers. But the shock of actually arriving there, of seeing animals in the rubble fight for what she hoped was not a human bone, was terrorizing and instructive in a way she never could have foreseen. She learned the manner in which her own tragedies compared or did not. She learned the completeness with which landscapes could dematerialize and reconfigure. She learned how to take reliable refuge in smoke and drink, lighting cigar after cigar, pouring glass after glass of *lambanog*, the local coconut wine, as she wrote and received her telegrams from the lobby of the Manila Hotel, which, although it had been torched by the Japanese upon their retreat, remained partially open for business. When her correspondence had been read and attended to, she would roam the broken city and see something that, for the first time in nearly a decade, she could imagine wanting to understand.

So she did her homework. First, she returned to the manor and the mango orchards or, rather, to what was left of them. The manor was now a pile of bombed-out masonry. The fountain in the courtyard was dry and filled with soldierly remnants: condoms, cigarettes, machine-gun cartridges. The orchards were cratered and patchy, the surviving trees visibly disappointed by the burden of continuing to fruit.

"Where," she asked one of the locals in an ugly mixture of

English and what little Tagalog she remembered, "is your most beautiful bay?"

The journey from Manila to Donsol took two days by bus. In Donsol, the beach was littered with what looked like fishing shacks but that on closer inspection turned out to be ticket kiosks for sightseeing trips into the outer bay.

"*Butanding*," one of the tour guides explained.

She didn't understand but bought a ticket anyway. Minutes later, they were afloat, just her and the guide. Their brightly painted pontoon boat was little more than a canoe with wings. It was late afternoon. Her legs and back still ached from the bus's hard, tiny seats; her stomach still wobbled from the twisting country roads. The light was slanted, tropical, the beach fluttering like a white ribbon in the distance. When she saw the huge shape in the water below the boat, she thought she was hallucinating until the guide began to yell and smile.

"Pagsisid!"

She looked down at the water again. The shape was coming closer now, its size four times that of the boat, its darkness punctuated with thousands of white dots, its rearmost section tipped with what looked like a gigantic scythe. The guide shoved two objects in her direction: a pair of goggles and a curved length of bamboo with a rubber mouthpiece on one end.

"Pagsisid!"

This time, there was an accompanying pantomime. He

donned the goggles and snorkel. He steepled his hands and thrust them forward. *Dive.* Nodding, she rose to her feet, the boat rocking beneath her. She stripped down to her underclothes and took the gear from him. Without thinking twice, she jumped.

And later, she would learn the names: whale shark, *Rhincodon typus.* She would acquire an exhaustive knowledge of its habitat, diet, and life cycle. Despite the promise she had made to herself after drawing the portrait of Tino's father, she would begin to sketch again: the whale shark rendered over and over in pencil and pen and charcoal and crayon, whatever seemed to best memorialize its massive, philanthropic shape. On that first day in Donsol, however, she did none of this. She drew nothing and she learned even less. Instead, she simply hovered above the whale shark and allowed its current to pull her, its toothless mouth funneling untold trillions of plankton, its company so quiet and natural that when darkness fell and her time was up, the guide had to catch her by her bra strap and physically drag her back on board.

That night, in a borrowed hammock beneath a balete tree, she remembered Monterey.

To do so was a delayed act, foreign and fragmented, so she approached it carefully and with the buzzing of the insects as a buffer. Her father, during his remaining years, had never alluded to those last days, so she had been forced to piece it together on her own, which had left her with the following conclusions. Tino, first of all, had been good on his word. After learning of her pregnancy, he had gone to his mother armed with Margot's offering: the photographs of Anders and the whore. But instead of taking the payment in good faith, instead of offering her assistance and discretion, Mrs. Agnelli used the information to her advantage. While Margot had sat in the lab waiting for Ricketts to return, Tino's mother had gone up the hill and blackmailed Anders, who, fearing for his reputation and, to a lesser extent, that of his daughter, saw no choice but to finally admit defeat and return the cannery in exchange for his rival's silence. After this, they'd stayed in Monterey for only one more day: long enough to finalize the transaction and to prepare for a hasty departure. On the train out of town, there were no words of either accusation or apology. It was only when they arrived in San Francisco that her father managed a sour smile and an assurance that things would rectify themselves in due course.

"But I want to end it now," she told him. "It needs to be over."

"You're too far along for that, I'm afraid."

For the duration of her pregnancy, she was confined to a room at the Sir Francis Drake: a hotel that, although only a dozen years old, already seemed haunted by the same ghosts as the Del Monte. When she began to fight, to endanger herself, there were sedatives and threats and then a span of gray stillness as she watched with hatred and disbelief as her belly grew. She counted the days until the mercy of the expulsion, until the rest of her life could rise up in the spirit of a new hollowness. The birth was a question of bright lights, the tang of an unknown narcotic, forceps, and darkness. If Ricketts was partially responsible for this, she told herself, it was only in the way that God is partially responsible for hell.

As for the child, it was stillborn, which came to her as a relief and to Anders as an inevitability. No one told her what was done with the body, but she had her suspicions: a fire as wet and prolonged as the one that had consumed her mother, a notion that, for the next near decade, dragged her down like leaden weights, her depression unshakable and misunderstood.

She never worked alongside her father again. In fact, she rarely saw him. As soon as she was physically able, she was packed off to a Catholic boarding school in Marin that was as pointless as it was well landscaped. The same was true of Wellesley, to which she was admitted two years later. For the most part, the college's academic instruction was a sideshow to the core curriculum in the domestic and social arts. When the monotony became too much, she got permission to enroll in art history courses at a nearby men's college. There, she gravitated immediately to the study of the Precisionist school: an obscure sect of Western industrialism whose strict lines and robust coloring made her feel as though there were still things in this world to both fear and accomplish.

And then there was the publication of Steinbeck's book, the one about Cannery Row. She read it in her dorm room one night the way one might watch a bloody roadside scene: fleetingly and through the psychic equivalent of half-closed fingers. Did she recognize Ricketts and his predilections? His musings? His triumphs? His failures? Of course. But in erecting this monument to his friend, Steinbeck had done something unintended. Instead of creating a facsimile, he had created a hybrid. *Half Christ and half satyr*, in Steinbeck's own words. To Margot, however, it wasn't quite so mythic. She saw Ricketts's head with Steinbeck's ears attached to it; Ricketts's shortness transformed into Steinbeck's height; Ricketts's vitality reduced to stasis, to an invisible cage that allowed Steinbeck to own him and watch him forever. She wanted to tell someone about it, to announce her discoveries to a like-minded contemporary, but she had no intimates. The girls at school thought she was morbid and odd. And she knew they were right.

Then, mercifully, her formal education was at an end. Upon graduation, she secured an unpaid apprenticeship in document restoration at the Fogg Museum in Cambridge and a room in a boardinghouse on Kirkland Street. The loneliness was so instant and intense that she began roaming the museum after closing time in search of imaginary company, which she eventually found in the form of a chalk drawing by Georges Seurat. It portrayed a nameless, faceless woman hunched over a blank-paged book, an easel in the background like a hangman's scaffold. Some nights, she would pretend to be this woman. Some nights, she would pretend it was her mother and distribute blame accordingly. Either way, she was always careful to leave the museum in time to make the boardinghouse's curfew, and when she slept it was without dreams or the half-waking visions that often preceded them, her life as blank and cold on the outside as it was within. Her father, she knew, was still living out west—in Nevada, the territory being claimed by gamblers and showmen—and there were times when the notions of geographic distance and inherited pain seemed to roll themselves up like two sides of the same map. More than once, she considered writing a letter to him that sought to confess the true scope of her childhood agony and the formative fallout of it, to solicit a reply that would acknowledge his own parallel experience. But months and years passed and no such letters were received or sent, and she came to the conclusion that heartbreak, instead of drawing people together as most shared experiences did, forced them even further apart, everyone confined to his or her own private cell of untranslatable despair.

On the evening of March 20, 1948, the night of Toscanini's all-Wagner television debut, she was informed of her father's passing. She had gone down to the boardinghouse's common room to see the concert on-screen. The seventy-year-old landlady clanked in on her crutches at the precise moment in act 3 of *Die Walküre* in which, had they been watching the actual opera and not a televised special, the curtain would have risen to reveal the mountain peak and Brünnhilde's sisters, gathered in preparation for the funerary jaunt to Valhalla. And the landlady's whisper in Margot's ear sounded like something Wagner himself had scripted: the death of a god, the world rent asunder, a robed chorus howling at the justice of it.

Now, in the hammock beneath the balete tree, she breathed in the wet air and blew at the stars as if they were candles. She had known the memories would be painful, and they were, but not nearly as much as she had expected. If anything, they seemed like remnants of a very bad dream: disconnected, surreal pieces of a larger, subconscious whole. It was illogical, furthermore, to believe in payback, but here it was: the glow of what a spiritual person might have deemed a blessing. So she stayed in Donsol. She visited the whale sharks every afternoon. She learned to adjust her buoyancy so that her belly grazed their rough, speckled backs. The hammock gave way to a thatched hut on risers beneath which lived a rooster who woke her at exactly four A.M. each morning, which she didn't mind one bit.

On her tenth and final morning in Donsol, she rose at the first squawk and went outside to find a telegram nailed to her front door. The telegram was from her father's secretary and typed out on Manila Hotel stationery. Pursuant to Anders's death, it read, a probate court in Monterey had recently unearthed the deeds to two properties within the city limits: the house on the hill and a reduction plant on Cannery Row, both of which would remain in jurisdictional limbo until someone came to town to settle matters in person.

She folded the telegram and reimpaled it on the nail. Then she went down to the beach and sat on the sand. It was still mostly dark, the sun not yet risen. The ticket kiosks were still shuttered for the night, unmanned. She went into the water up to her knees and then returned to the hut, lit a cigar, took a puff from it, and stubbed it out on the boards beneath her feet. She poured a cup of *lambanog* and nursed it as the shoreline began to come to life, and by the time the chatter of the tour guides began, her decision had been made. She packed her things. She wrote a letter to Tino Agnelli. And, after running five miles to the nearest telephone, she reserved a seat on the next DC-4 out of Manila.

23

SHE ARRIVED IN SAN FRANCISCO ON A DAMP, WHITE afternoon, a flask of *lambanog* tucked into the waistband of her new skirt.

She spent one sleepless night at the hotel across the street from the Sir Francis Drake and then boarded the four o'clock southbound *Del Monte Express*, the same train that had once taken her and Anders down the coast and back up it again. The parlor car was empty save for herself and the waiter, who kept mostly to himself as the train rattled through the artichoke and lettuce fields. The banquette on which she sat had peeling leather and loose bolts. The velvet draperies across the cloudy windows looked as though they had been both shelter and sustenance to several generations of moths.

"I think you'll barely recognize it," the waiter speculated at one point. "Everything's so different down there since the war."

She smiled at him but said nothing. She had drained the flask hours ago and had since consumed several beers, not because she wanted to blunt her mind, but because she wanted it loose enough to consider things objectively. She had left the Philippines full of conviction, certain the telegram had provided as close to marching orders as she was likely to get. But now that they were creaking across the Monterey County line, the grayness of Elkhorn Slough and Moss Landing appearing through the windows like something that had been breathed onto the glass, she was met with the delayed realization that she didn't really know why she had come. The transaction, certainly—a meeting with the Agnelli scion, a signing of papers—but it would be more than that. It had to be. And so the beers kept coming, and by the time they reached Monterey, she was drunk enough to expect to find her father waiting for her on the station platform, ready with words of caution and regret. Instead, she was greeted by a teenage porter who helped her into a hired car before handing her a small, stiff note card with the Agnelli name on the letterhead.

She read the note and put it in her pocket.

"The Hotel Del Monte, please," she told the driver.

"The what?"

"The big one near the—"

"Oh, that place hasn't been a hotel in years. It's a postgraduate school now. For the navy."

She looked out the window, at the black tumor of the resting train, its doors still open.

"To the neighborhood on the hill, then," she replied. "The one where the cannery workers used to live."

At the small white house, she paid the driver twice the customary fare and allowed him to unload her bag.

Then she stood outside for a while before entering, looking at the bougainvillea. The last time she had seen it, the plant had been little more than a skeleton of ash, the victim of a rich woman's myopic wrath. In the past eight years, however, it had regenerated itself into something twice as lush and expansive as before, and at the sight of its pink flowers, she became wary of something she couldn't name.

Inside, she found everything much as they had left it. Many of the other houses on the block had been abandoned and looted and given over to nature, but theirs hadn't. The horsehair sofa was still inappropriate and cumbersome, the dust in its crevices as thick and white as frosting. A sheaf of her father's papers was still in the wastebin beneath the kitchen table, a sherry bottle was still hidden in the cabinet above the sink. She drank what little was left and then spent the next hour finding things to clean. She tied a handkerchief around her mouth and beat the sofa with a broom. She scrubbed the grout between the bathroom tiles. She polished the door handles. She mopped the linoleum until she could see her own warped reflection in its surface. When the entire house was tidied to her satisfaction, she collapsed onto the sofa, too tired to sleep. But she slept anyway and, for the first time in years, dreamed. She dreamed she was exploring her father's cannery by flashlight, its beam slipping across the barren walls like a yellow snake. There were no conveyor belts, packing lines, retort baskets, or boilers. No blood or oil or water underfoot, nothing that evoked the bio-efficient, almost intestinal quality of a fish cannery at work. Instead, there was a building as empty as it was cavernous, the floors swept clean.

When she was done looking at the cannery from the inside, she looked at it from the outside. She walked out a door and onto a narrow catwalk above the water that led from the main body of the cannery to the pump house. The ocean was angry, spitting and thrashing, punishing the shore with sets of closely spaced waves. The crescent moon was orange and blurry behind the fog. In its light, she could see Ricketts sitting on the edge of the catwalk, his feet dangling toward the water. She switched off the flashlight and sat down next to him, their legs swinging back and forth in near synchronicity. It felt good at first, but then it didn't. She considered withdrawing her sketchbook. Her satchel, however, was empty except for her father's penknife, and she could hear noises behind them, a crowd gathering on the street outside.

"Quick," he said. "The knife."

But the parade was already upon them, the hill ablaze with lanterns, the saint's waxen face glowing within the confines of her bower, a book in one hand, a human skull in the other. Tino Agnelli was at the head of the procession. Arthur was behind him, his head shaved bare. Her father was last in line, walking slightly apart from the crowd, coatless despite the gathering cold. The air was full of smoke.

"Inside," Ricketts said, taking her arm. "Before it's too late."

They ran back into the cannery. She leaned against him. For the first time, she noticed the vast difference in their heights. He was so short, he could fit his head snugly beneath her chin without bending or crouching.

"I did a bad job, Wormy," he said, reaching for her forehead.

And when he reopened the scar with the knife, the cut wasn't made on her skin. It was made on the seafloor beneath her, the earth splitting itself along a famous fault line: the one that, according to centuries of seismological fantasy, would break California free from the rest of the jealous landmass and send it floating off into the night.

The next morning, she walked to the wharf.

The waiter in the parlor car had been wrong. The town was still recognizable, but disappointingly so, like a beautiful woman without her makeup. It was only when she reached the doorway of the old Agnelli warehouse that things took a more hopeful turn. Unlike the rest of Monterey, this building had thrived since her departure. The single window had been scrubbed clean, the corrugated metal walls painted white, a crimson awning stretched over the entrance. Inside, there was no darkness, no statue, no sardine cans, no henchwomen. Instead, it was bright and tidy and outfitted in a way that was clearly meant to evoke the Agnellis' homeland but looked like a caricature of it instead: ropes of garlic sagging from the rafters, a gaudy mid-Crucifixion portrait of Jesus and the Virgin Mary staring down at her in gory benediction, tables covered in red-and-white-checked tablecloths, candles weeping streams of wax onto basket-bottomed Chianti bottles. The barman awoke with a jolt when he heard her enter. As for Tino, he was there just as he had promised in his note: sitting at a large table near the kitchen, flanked by his brothers, his chin in his hands as if presiding over the world's most anticlimactic Last Supper.

She studied him before approaching. Like the town itself, he had been eroded by the intervening years, but not necessarily disfigured by them. The primary difference was his nose, which was a good deal longer and narrower than she remembered and more emphatically wide nostriled. He had taken to wearing his dark hair slicked back from his forehead, which, in addition to highlighting the sharpness of his features, made the prematurely thin patches around his temples look as if they had been spray-painted there. He was still impossibly slim and spotlessly dressed. Even in this moment of what she assumed to be repose, he looked coiled and skeptical, thrumming with the exact same quiet, dissatisfied energy he had possessed as a boy.

When he saw her, he raised his small, bony hand in the resigned manner of a forcibly dethroned potentate. She waved back.

"You received my correspondence," he said as she reached the table, the brothers tracking every inch of her approach.

"It's a restaurant now," she replied.

"To feed all the tourists."

A lone cannery whistle blasted in the distance, its sound fuzzy and dilute, as if it had traveled across the distance of years instead of the distance of physical space. In her memory, Tino had been someone she had once known well, but now that she was actually in his presence again, she realized her mistake. She had never really known him at all. She had once put her future, and her father's, in the hands of a stranger.

"Tourists?" she asked. "But the town's a disaster."

"Interestingly enough, they seem to like it that way."

One of the brothers said something in Italian. Tino glared at him and stood.

"Come," he said to Margot, gesturing at an empty table in the restaurant's farthest corner. "So we won't be interrupted."

"Thank you. I'm fine right here."

Tino shrugged and reclaimed his seat. Margot sat across from him and removed a box of cigars from her handbag and offered one to each of the brothers in turn. When all of them declined, she selected one for herself and lit it.

"Thank you for agreeing to this," she said, taking a puff and trying to summon an unburdened smile. "The location you suggested is certainly appropriate, even if the hour is unusual."

"Habit, I guess." His eyes traced the smoke as she exhaled it. "It was my mother's custom to eat with the crew after the night's haul. I continue to honor the tradition, even though there's nothing much left to can."

"Where is she?"

"She passed away. Shortly after your father."

"I'm sorry to hear that."

"You are?"

"I don't suppose I could get a beer."

"Of course."

He nodded at the barman and made a series of quick gestures. The barman filled a glass, and when he brought it to her, she took the longest sip she could manage without gulping or coughing.

"You've changed," Tino said. "Rumor had it you were the only one who ever went to Ricketts's lab and didn't emerge blind drunk."

"I emerged pregnant. Which was probably worse."

Tino swallowed. The brothers traded glances.

"You've changed, too," she continued. "I wouldn't have expected you to want to take the helm."

"Oh, life is less about what one wants, I suppose, and more about what one is willing to accept."

"It was your mother's plan all along," she guessed.

"I suppose it was."

"And you're still willing to buy?"

"My family owes you at least that much, even though the reduction plant is barely worth the land it stands on anymore."

"It's gotten that bad?"

"It has. During the war, the government took over and then bled us dry. Requisitioned our boats for shore patrol while simultaneously forcing us to meet impossible quotas. Evacuated some of the poorer Italians and all the Japanese. When the sardines disappeared, most of the canneries went under, but we were able to stay open because we switched over to squid."

She looked down at the table. The squid boats from Anders's childhood. Orange sails. Women in the night water wrestling the heaving nets to shore.

"Are you all right?" he asked. "You look ill. Let me walk you home."

"I'll be fine." When she drained her glass, another one arrived as if by magic, full to the brim. "Let's discuss our terms."

"Whatever you think is fair."

"Market price. Minus expenses."

"For both the house and the reduction plant?"

"That's right."

"I'll have my lawyer draft something. You'll have it by this evening. I'm sure you're eager to move on."

"I am."

"Then why, if you don't mind my asking, did you come at all?"

She nudged her drink, watched the bubbles rise and gather.

"Call it nostalgia," she said, half choking on the lie.

"That's never a good reason."

"I know. Thank you for indulging me."

On the way back to the house, she chose the path closest to the beach.

At one point, when the beers began to take their toll, she found a dune and took a seat and watched how her nylon stockings—a postwar luxury that was just now becoming morally permissible—were acting like little sieves, letting the smaller grains of sand in and keeping the larger ones out. The sky was an intense, bright gray: a color that, in all her travels, had never materialized anywhere else in the world but here. After a long while, she stood from the dune and returned to the street. She was thirsty, but her flask was dry. So she went to the new liquor store on Lighthouse and bought their smallest, most expensive bottle of gin. At the house, she drew the curtains against the afternoon, sat down at the kitchen table, and drank as much as she wanted. Then she searched the rooms, looking into closets and cabinets for anything that would disprove her father's death. She found an undergarment that was still stiff with starch, the pulverized nub of a pencil. She returned to the kitchen and rooted through the wastebin, hoping to find a fugitive drop at the gin bottle's bottom, but there was nothing left. So she opened the door and went outside to her old spot on the porch, the air tightening behind her in a silent peristalsis, an expulsion of the living from the dead.

She sat there for several minutes, not thinking, not moving. When she saw a shape at the base of the hill, she rose to greet it. *Tino's lawyer*, she thought, knees buckling on account of the booze. *Right on schedule.* But as the person continued his climb, she realized her mistake. This was not a lawyer, but a boy: a young man of the same age Arthur had been, but larger and coarser and somehow unknowable looking, as if the very nature of children had changed since she was last able to count herself among their ranks.

"Miss Fiske," he said, his voice respectful and disinterested all at once.

"Yes?"

"Ed Ricketts sent me."

She held her breath before responding.

"You work for him? Catching cats?" The very thought of it made her want to laugh.

"Cats?" He frowned. "No."

"What does he want?"

"Just a moment of your time."

24

1998

HIS FINAL MESSAGE COMES TO HER FROM INSIDE A bottle.

The first sip is an arrival, especially after so many years of abstaining. The second sip, however, is nothing more than a false portal, so she caps it up and returns it to its hiding place in her desk drawer. It's night and the aquarium has closed hours ago, but she hasn't gone home. Instead, she's stayed here. The *Mola* problem persists, the anniversary of his death has come and gone without either resolution or recompense, and now she doesn't know what to do.

She looks outside the window. In the light of the crescent moon, she sees that the dead Humboldts are no longer on the beach. They've been taken away. They've been taken to a biological laboratory, no doubt, where they will be injected and preserved and sold for study, and the students who study them will learn certain things. They will learn that humans and squid share a common evolutionary history. They will learn that squid ink contains dopamine, the chemical responsible for sex and drug addiction. They will learn that squid blood is the same blue as a swimming pool.

What they won't learn, though, is how to keep them in a tank. She knows this because for a span of several years, she tried it. She tried to put live squid—the small ones native to Monterey Bay—on exhibit. The challenges seemed great but by no means insurmountable: a short life span, an extreme sensitivity to changes in pH, a penchant for cannibalism, a tendency to kill themselves by colliding with the tank walls. She put her best people on the job; she consulted experts of international renown. But after a string of spectacular failures, the truth became apparent. It wasn't worth the time or money or psychological strain. So, with a sigh of communal relief, the last crop of dead squid was returned to the sea, the tank was repurposed, the project was permanently abandoned, and, for the first and perhaps only time in her life, Margot accepted defeat with what an outsider would have certainly interpreted as grace.

The weird old clock on her desk, the same one that used to reside on her father's mantel, strikes eleven forty-five. The bay is alive with squid boats.

And she didn't get tired or sleepy, for the beauty burned in her like fire.

Good old Steinbeck. She smiles, rising from her chair. Always so much better with a modified pronoun or two.

By the time she arrives at the wharf, the squid boats are going out for their second set.

She finishes suiting up. In the window of the candy shop behind her, a hook works and reworks a giant pink tongue of saltwater taffy. In the water beneath her, rockfish hover and plot. Usually, the summers here are notoriously foggy, but this summer will be different. It will be wildly, inexplicably warm: the pinecones popping in the pine trees, their fat little grenade shapes bursting open under the shock of the unusual temperature. Crystal blue skies scarred with the thick, columnar evidence of forest fires. Algal blooms and acidic oceans, reports of extinction and collapse.

"Wait. Stop. *Stop.*"

The three-man crew of the nearest boat looks up at her in unison. She takes a step forward, her neoprene boots making low, muffled taps against the wharf. Feet on wooden planks? No: the fists of a giant on the skin of a huge tribal drum. She looks ridiculous in full scuba gear, even more ridiculous than that poor intern inside the otter costume. She doesn't *feel* ridiculous, though; that's the thing. She feels as though something is burning away her insides, something powerful and without precedent, something only an ocean can extinguish.

"Stop."

The vacuum is already on. She has to scream to be heard.

"What do you want?" one of them screams back.

And there are, she supposes, many ways to answer. The simplest, most honest answer, though, is that she wants to swim with the whale sharks again. Or at least Monterey's version of them.

"I'm Margot Fiske." She tightens her weight belt. "I'm coming aboard."

The crew's eyes grow wide. They nod in assent. She tries to make a respectable entrance, but she's far too old and far too eager, so she flings her torso over the side and lets the weight of the air tank do the rest. She staggers to the bow and stands there alone. Soon, the boat is moving again: past the moorings, past the breakwater and its resident sea lions, their shapes that of unbaked dough. For nearly an hour, nothing. Her legs shake, her courage wavers. Then, suddenly, light. Annihilating, brutal, shadowless, opaque, a false sun in a black sky. The boat heaves forward, cutting a sharp diagonal against the waves. The skiff races, the drum spins, the net slides, the floats skitter loudly off the gunwales and into the bay. A return to stillness, taut and total, the other boats drifting close and then drifting away, inspecting one another's territories with the careful aggression of diplomats. Some of the fishermen move to the edge alongside her, their eyes on the water, their bodies waxen beneath the halogen lamps overhead. She, too, looks down. At first, she thinks it's sickness; the ocean is sore and inflamed and lumpy with pus. But then there's an unexpected blast of vitality—reds and purples—which is when she knows it isn't sickness. It's squid. A huge, vibrant shoal of them, a kaleidoscopic swarm squirming and flashing, tentacles weaving as they rise toward the light.

She steps away from the edge. So many years of working and wanting, so many stabs at the metaphoric vein. It can all be put inside a tank. All of it. Except this. Except him. Anger is not new to her, but bewilderment is, and now all she wants is one simple courtesy: for everything to stop until she figures it out. The catch, however, proceeds. The door to the hold creaks open to expose the refrigerated blackness beneath. The crew rushes and shouts and shoves her out of their way as if they've forgotten who she is, what she's worth, how much she knows.

"If you're going to jump," one of them growls, "you've got to do it *now*."

The metal housing is inside the purse. The vacuum is on, sucking the squid belowdecks in greedy, globular drafts. The overhead lamps are fading, the bulb filaments glowing orange and squiggling in the darkness like neon worms. In the last of the light, she thinks she can see some larger bodies on the periphery of the shoal. Humboldts, dozens of them, arms reaching out not to embrace their tiny cousins, but to consume them.

Oh, Margot, she hears him whisper. *I always thought you were wonderful.*

And below the surface, she joins the riot. She's down there with the squid, just like the Chinese fisherwomen. Vast and noiseless, thousands, tens of thousands, joining and separating and rejoining, genderless to the naked eye, fused end to end, red arms flashing. A delicate, urgent process, one night only: mating, egg-laying, and dying, the decisive acts of a species' continuation. But they don't even notice her in their midst. They don't notice her big, clumsy intrusion. They simply carry on without disruption or pause, receiving her body as if she were yet another addition to the fray; as if, were they only able to relax certain physiological expectations, she would be fair game for anything they had gathered there to accomplish. Suggestions of terror but also of eternity, time both condensing and expanding, dizzy and happy, wishing the deepness were deeper. She's falling fast now—much too fast—into the grayness, but instead of fear, there's wonder. Why grayness? she wonders. Isn't it supposed to be blackness? But it's grayness, the clean grayness of the aquarium's Mozambique quartzite tiles, a beloved maze leading her in and up and around, up to the tops of tanks she has never imagined or seen, her own body replicated in the water below, the water above, her own body budded and cloned to produce the schools of endlessly circling fish, everyone she has ever cared for standing on the deck and looking down into the water, friends gazing on with fondness and confusion, parents alive with pride, lovers pointing at her and inventing reasons for wonder, wondering when she will do something interesting, wondering when she will be fed, wondering whether she will become placated or enraged once the things she's always wanted are finally between her jaws.

25

1948

THEIR TRIP DOWN THE HILL WAS FAST AND SILENT.

Along the way, sobriety appeared and disappeared like a mirage, the boy keeping several steps in front of her.

When they finally arrived on the Row, it was like being stabbed. There were still small groups of workers pacing the streets, still a pillar or two of exhaust wafting from the canneries' smokestacks, still a glowering cluster of packers standing outside the Del Mar building and gossiping over their cigarettes. Otherwise, it was empty.

And then they came within sight of the lab.

"What's happening?" she asked the boy.

Outside, at the base of the front steps, there was a crowd twice as large and loud as the ones that used to attend his parties, faces upturned, cameras snapping like claws.

"So many of them," he scoffed. "Ever since that damn book."

She tried to see above the heads but couldn't.

"Let's go," she said. "Let's get to the front."

For some reason, she tried to take the boy's hand, but he had already disappeared. So she moved forward on her own and then stopped. Ricketts was standing on the stairs, his back against the door, something huge and ugly in his hands.

A massive tentacle found his arm. A flashbulb popped. He peeled the tentacle away to reveal a stripe of bloody welts, some of them the size of silver dollars. The crowd murmured and flexed.

"What is it?" yelled one of the onlookers.

"Humboldt squid," he yelled back, his voice so familiar to her that it almost sounded fake. "*Dosidicus gigas.* Not usually found this far north."

"Where did you get it?"

"Came up in one of the nets last night alongside the smaller ones. Seemed to be eating them."

The tentacles writhed. The crowd surged. He lifted his chin and stared out into the masses, and that's when she saw him become fully revealed by the strobe of the flashing cameras. He was dressed exactly as she remembered—long apron, knee-high black rubber boots—but his face was different. The beard was gone, and in its absence his cheeks and jaw seemed sunken and creased, a downward slant to the corners of his mouth, a slackness in his lips, his skin bright white against the dark wall behind him. He looked both appreciative of his audience and dismayed by it, like an aging magician who had long since forgotten his best tricks but not the applause that used to accompany them.

Another flashbulb, another wince. His eyes found hers. She clenched her teeth. He appraised her for a moment and then extracted a damp hand from beneath the creature's mantle and beckoned her to his side. She began to push her way through the crowd again, but her progression seemed ten times as slow and laborious as before.

By the time she reached his side, the crowd was heckling her and she was breathing heavily.

"Thank you for coming," he said.

"You're welcome."

"You remember this fellow? From that very first bucket I sent up the hill?"

She nodded.

"We'll need to narcotize it before fixation." He was whispering now, his lips on her ear. "Decrease the salinity—slowly—and add a dash of ethanol if the arms are still moving after a couple minutes."

She nodded, ignoring the shouts at her back.

"And a formalin immersion won't work on this one." He smiled. "Find a syringe. We'll have to inject."

Later, she would remember the colors. Skin flashing devil red with the body's last angry pumpings. The chromatophores' final, dramatic assertions. A huge eye looking up at her from the bottom of the garbage barrel. The heart-stopping paleness of its sloppy weight as they hoisted it into the tallest glass display cylinder they could find.

When it was all finished, they put the cylinder in the corner because it was too big for the hutch, and then they went upstairs, Ricketts to the kitchen and Margot to the desk. She sat there and waited until he reappeared in the kitchen doorway with a beer in each hand. He put the beers on the bookshelf and ran both hands through his hair, which was sweat-heavy and unkempt, matted down around his temples and sticking up in the back like the plumage of a dark, flightless bird. He opened one of the beers and held it out to her, smiled a bit when she accepted it, and then settled himself into Steinbeck's old rocking chair. Her breath caught. Inside the lab, the squid safely bottled, he looked nothing like he had outside in front of the crowd. The weariness and pallor had disappeared, replaced by a handsomeness so potent, she could feel it taking up residence inside her.

"I don't suppose you have anything stronger," she said.

He raised an eyebrow and stood.

"I'm fresh out of formaldehyde, but let's see what else I can find."

He disappeared into the kitchen again and returned with a dusty ceramic jug.

"The boys gave this to me a month ago," he said. "I took a taste the other night. It cured my toothache, but I couldn't hear for a full minute afterward."

She took it from him, removed the cork, and sniffed its contents before putting her lips to the rim. When she drank, the effects were different from what he had described, but just as intense: her jaw went numb and her eyes started to water, almost as if she had begun to weep.

"Nothing has changed in here," she said, wiping her cheeks and trying not to cough.

"Really? I feel like it changes every time I blink. Sometimes I'll reach for a piece of paper or a book only to find that it no longer exists. That even the place where it stood was gone. But I suppose that happens to everyone."

He watched her take another sip, and the completeness of the inspection would have thrilled her were it not for its unimpeachable politeness. It was as if he were kicking the tires of a car he didn't intend to buy.

"You look just fine," he said.

She looked down at the span of skin between her wrists and

elbows. It was marked with welts from the squid's suction cups, just like his.

"Likewise," she replied.

"I heard about your father."

"Yes."

"You've been running the show on your own, then?" He sat down.

"No. I've been selling everything off."

"You must be very rich now."

"I am."

"And you dress like it, too. Although I must say I miss the days when you used to walk around here looking like an overgrown newspaper boy. Where's that funny little bag you always used to carry?"

To punctuate the ensuing silence, she drank again. As the liquid ran down the ladder of her ribs, she closed her eyes, hoping it would wash away everything her heart didn't need. For a moment, she actually *could* feel her body become cleaner, her mind lighter. When she opened her eyes, however, the sensation was immediately reversed. He was on his feet now and making his way in her direction.

"And you?" she asked.

"And me?"

"You've been well?"

His smile betrayed a lack of conviction that alarmed her.

"I suppose so. It's been interesting with the sardines or, rather, the lack thereof. We've got a top-notch population biologist on the case, woman by the name of Frances Clark. And a young chap from Long Beach has been making the trip up and back, advising on new technologies and the like. Works for the bureau of fisheries. Last name Casey. Don't remember the first."

"And the lab?"

"Oh, this old thing?" He waved a hand in a circle above his head. "Hard times, I'm afraid. During the war, I tried to keep it solvent by working up at the Presidio, running blood and urine tests for the army. Then a stint at Cal Pack as a chemist. And then a shred or two of hope regarding the Guggenheim, but that never came to pass."

"I'm sorry to hear it."

"Don't be. The money will come from somewhere. It always does."

There was the heat of a certain look, but then it subsided.

"And Wormy?"

His eyes narrowed, his arms beginning to fold themselves across his chest.

"Pardon?"

"The woman—"

"Ah yes. She finally came to her senses while the rest of us were away in Mexico, for which I don't blame her, although I must say it took me somewhat by surprise. As did the departure of our old friend Arthur. Here one day, gone the next. No explanations, no good-byes. Just picked up and went south. Last I heard, he was working in the canneries on Terminal Island."

He went over to his collection of record albums, selected one, and then put it back down.

"But I think it's John who's taken it the hardest of anyone," he continued. "After his book, things here took a bad turn and he started to feel responsible, so he hightailed it to New York."

"I was under the impression the book did quite well."

"It did. And perhaps that was the problem."

He glanced over at the window, at the faces that were now looking in on them, noses pressed to the glass, eyes leering without compassion or shame.

"You could close your curtains," she suggested.

"And become a prisoner in my own home? No. I'd rather have people look if that's what they want to do."

She turned away from him and met the gaze of the strangers outside. She thought of the huge squid eye, its exaggerated roundness like an artist's rendering of a shiny black sun, bright with the cruelty of never being able to set. She took another swig from the jug.

"Powerful stuff, isn't it?" he asked cautiously.

"Are you angry at him?"

"Who? John?"

She nodded. He shook his head.

"His only crime was remembering things a certain way," he said. "And I just happened to be in the middle of it."

She drank again.

"You might want to take it easy," he cautioned. "I only had one sip and it just about knocked me down."

"Then why don't you help me finish it?"

He let loose with a stilted laugh. And that's when he finally closed the distance between them, walking up to the desk and taking the jug from her hands.

"You know," he said, sipping and then wiping his mouth, "the worst part about getting older isn't the fear of death. It's the sadness of things that aren't anymore. All potential can't become reality. You've got to select. And it can make a person very sad."

"When I w-was a girl," she stammered, "on the night of the low tide, when you didn't come and you sent Arthur to—"

"I kept your original sketches," he said. "All of them."

She looked at the window again, at the faces that were still tracking her and Ricketts's every move despite the fact that they hadn't done anything worth watching. Not yet.

She gripped the edges of the desk.

"Are you all right?" he asked. "Do you need to lie down?"

"You're not—"

But then a sound at her back, and as she turned around she knew, somehow, exactly what she would find. A woman in the bedroom doorway, lovely and small, clothed in a child's white frock.

"Hello," the woman said.

"Hello," Margot replied.

There was the scent of perfumed soap as she walked past the desk and toward the phonograph. When the music started, Margot prayed for the fugue: for the baker's dozen of opening notes, measured and solitary. But it was chords instead, blaring and insistent. The woman fell into Ricketts's arms. Margot buried her chin and smelled herself. Cigars, menthol, moonshine.

"Hello, Wormy," he said, kissing the woman on the forehead and then slowly releasing her. "Will you be able to make it on time?"

"Just."

"Travel safely, then."

"I will."

When the woman was gone, Margot tilted back in her chair. Her entire body was brittle, illiquid, a net made of nails and hair and bones. She tried to speak, but her voice had turned to sand.

"That's Alice," Ricketts said, his words barely audible beneath the phonograph. "Music student up at Berkeley. We were married in January."

She looked down at her hands.

"And God, does she love her Mozart. She's probably transcribed *Don Giovanni* twenty times by now."

She squeezed her hands into fists, knowing it was useless to cry, but even more useless not to.

"Oh, Margot," he said. "I'm so sorry. I always thought you were wonderful."

She couldn't hear him, though, and she couldn't hear the music. All she could hear were the noises at the window. The people there weren't just watching anymore, she realized. They were tapping. One finger—tap, tap, tap. And then another. And then another, until five fingers became what sounded like five hundred and the sound was indistinguishable from drops of water against glass.

She looked up at him. His smile sprouted and grew.

"Your father once wondered if this town wanted an aquarium," he said, eyes twinkling. "And I think the answer is finally yes."

A shot of courage. A sudden change of plan.

"That's precisely why I'm here," she said. "To buy back his cannery from the Agnellis. To finish what he started."

"I'd be happy to assist. If you'll have me, that is."

"Looks like we'll need something else to drink," she replied, placing the empty jug on the desk.

He stared at her for a long, dangerous moment.

"All right," he said. "I'll go downstairs and start the Buick."

26

1998

WHEN SHE WAKES, SHE'S BACK ON THE HORSEHAIR sofa.

She's fifteen years old again and living in the small white house up the hill from Cannery Row.

Then she's back in the lab, back in his bed, the nearby canneries causing the walls to bend and shake.

But then she comes to her senses. She's lived in this house for well over two decades now—this modernist palace on Hurricane Point in Big Sur—and it's like this most days: the wind strong enough to make a weaker person question things, strong enough to make it sound as if the windows are popping free from their frames. *A fish tank on a cliff* is what the antidevelopment dopes once called it. But she didn't let it bother her, not then and not now. There was a similar peevishness directed at the aquarium once. And look how nicely that's turned out.

As for last night's bungled dive from the squid boat, she'd rather not consider it. So she pushes her blankets aside, takes care not to wake her boyfriend, and rises from her bed. From the windows in her bedroom she can see Bixby Bridge, its vaulted span the site of countless suicides and luxury car commercials. From the windows in the kitchen, she can see the road leading up to the house: a dynamite-blasted, switchbacked scar on the face of the gray-green hillside. The driveway is a Zen garden of glinting granite pebbles. The fog is thick, but the wind is doing its best to change that. By the time she washes, dresses, and leaves the house, her little territory will likely be bathed in sun, even if the rest of the coastline is still wet and gray.

Most days, she drives too fast. She takes great pleasure in carving the thirty-minute drive down to twenty, twenty-five tops. Today is different. She goes slowly and tries to pay attention. It's been years since the collapse of the benevolent hippie dictatorship of the yammering mystics at Esalen, but this stretch of Highway 1 continues to retain a modicum of its upscale stoner cachet nonetheless. As she crosses the bridge, she watches in the rearview mirror as a line of identical rental RVs falls into place behind her like the segments of a mechanical worm. At Monastery Beach, a motorcycle speeds past her on the left, the cyclist howling as he extends the middle fingers on both gloved hands.

When she reaches Cannery Row, she pulls the truck into the loading zone adjacent to the Hopkins Marine Station. She thinks of the Chinese fishing village that once stood on this spot, of the fire that consumed it: a fire her father didn't start. She closes her eyes and tries to see the flames. She tries to see herself reading the daily paper. She tries to see yesterday's squid beaching, but when she sees nothing, she presses on. Through the automatic gates and into the aquarium's employee parking lot. Through quarantine and straight to her least favorite exhibit: the one devoted to Ed Ricketts and his lab.

Or perhaps "exhibit" is putting it a bit too strongly. It's more like a display, small and unpopular, an enclosure barely four feet high and six feet wide, a preserved fetal dogfish or two arranged in their jars as if on a liquor store shelf, the only known snapshot of Ricketts and Steinbeck in a thick black frame. A wooden beer crate. A disembodied drawer from one of his file cabinets. Approximately twenty sheets of sketchbook paper on which one can see the shadows of someone else's doodles. The lighting here is strange—half-natural, half-incandescent—which makes everything look like an object in a bad still life, especially the Humboldt squid in the big glass cylinder. It's the one they anesthetized and preserved on their final night together, its body grown flaky and stiff from a half century of formaldehyde immersion, its actual length and girth so much more modest than memory always seems to insist.

Then the part that should trouble her the most but doesn't. No explanation of a life is complete without an explanation of the life's end, and in this regard, everyone did their level best. A carefully worded informational placard in the trademarked font, a photo of the immediate aftermath. The image is out of focus, the action framed at a slippery diagonal, a huge train engine looming in the background. There's the wreckage of an old black Buick, emergency personnel and onlookers, a body laid out on a stretcher. She remembers how slyly she stole one of the tourists' cameras, how expertly she lined it all up, how decisively she pressed the button even though her hands were shaking. It was not her fault, she recalls repeating to herself. It was not murder. She simply sent him out for more booze and he never came back. She had nothing to do with how the Buick stalled on the tracks. She had nothing to do with the train conductor: a weepy, tongue-tied fool who, having seen the obstruction, had neither the time nor the inclination to stop.

"So. You made it back alive."

Does Arthur understand? He must. He once suggested that, when Ricketts's body flew through the windshield, it probably looked like a fish-meal sack full of cats.

"Word traveled, then?" she asks.

He nods.

She cringes and closes her eyes. The crew of the squid boat will likely tell this story for years to come: how they noticed her buoyancy was incorrect the second she hit the water, how one of them was able to dive down and retrieve her before she got too deep. Usually, she doesn't feel like she's seventy-three years old;

not even close. But as they hoisted her back onto the deck of the boat, her body limp and brittle in their arms, her weight belt jammed with too many weights, her BCD underinflated, she felt like the smallest, most decrepit soul in existence. She was too embarrassed to let them take her to the hospital. Instead, she made them drive her home, and now, if she's thinking of her long-ago accident in the tide pools and the brief convalescence that followed, it's not in the spirit of forcing parallels. Not in the least.

"You know it's the same one, right? The train engine at the playground?"

She nods. Of course she knows. They've joked about it—darkly, nervously—for years. What he doesn't know is that she's never found it funny. She used to go there, not all that long ago, and watch the action in secret. She would watch the kids climb to the top of the same *Del Monte Express* engine that killed Ricketts. She would watch them laugh and fall and howl, and she knew that if she had ever had her own daughter, she wouldn't have been craven and she wouldn't have been foolish. She would have let her daughter climb all the way to the top and hit the big bell with the edge of a quarter. And when her daughter fell from the engine's tallest point, which she doubtlessly would have—because there is, after all, a symmetry to these things that makes them worth pondering in the first place—there would have been nothing in the way of hindsight or regret. They would have simply held each other and cried, shocked by their sudden reacquaintance with the type of thing that, as the old saying goes, should have only made them stronger.

"There are those who still think it was planned. That he did it on purpose."

"That's insane," she snaps. "He wasn't that kind of man."

"And you aren't that kind of woman."

"You're right. I'm even worse."

"Oh, Margot."

"I'm going home."

"You can't."

"Why not?"

"Because we've arranged a little something. In your honor."

"Right now?"

"No. Tonight. Just after closing."

"What is it?"

"The *Mola* release."

She stares at him. He shrugs and smiles.

"You told us to surprise you."

To pass the time until closing, she indulges in an old habit. She explores the town on foot.

First, she drives her truck to the head of the bike trail, to a little parking lot within spitting distance of the Naval Postgraduate School, the former site of the Hotel Del Monte. She gets out of the truck and inhales. There are eucalyptus trees here—planted long ago by a foreign-born boatbuilder who mistook them for teak—and it smells just like the menthol in Ricketts's lab.

Then she begins to walk down the bike trail in the direction of the Row, in the direction of the aquarium. Back in the late 1980s, when the aquarium was still brand-new, the bike trail was laid directly over the old railroad tracks, and she can almost feel the steel ribs beneath her feet. She walks past the dunes and the beach, joggers and in-line skaters swerving around her without pause or complaint. When she reaches the adobe plaza above the wharf, she makes a point of visiting the bocce courts. The elder Agnellis, who still control this part of town, play here every day, rain or shine, and they bid her a polite "Good morning" as she passes.

From the wharf, she climbs the hill. She sold the small white house shortly after deciding to stay in Monterey for the duration. She has, however, continued to keep tabs, spying on its residents through the window near the bougainvillea. For a while, aquarists lived here: aquarists who descended the hill much like the cannery workers before them. These days, however, it's a vacation rental property. Seashells and wicker, everything upholstered in sturdy, beachy pastels. On the walls, there are whitewashed pieces of driftwood painted with chatty, unambiguous demands: LIVE, LAUGH, LOVE.

Then, finally, she returns to the bike trail and visits the site of Ricketts's demise. Other than the aquarium, this is the only place in town that truly matters to her, so she lobbied hard to ensure a certain look. The railroad crossing sign still stands, even though the railroad itself is long gone. There is a commemorative bust of Ricketts himself, sculpted by a local artist of known mediocrity. The bust looks nothing like him, and she feels absolutely nothing when she looks at it. The same is true of the lab. Since Ricketts's passing, it has been meticulously preserved despite a number of functional incarnations. First, it was a boarded-up monument to Steinbeck's loss. Then it was a men's literary club founded on the principle that great poetry can be written and read only in the absence of wives. These days, it's owned by the city and is open to visitors only twice a year. She's never made the mistake of joining the tour groups and going inside. She's happy just to watch them as they enter and exit: young people with a penchant for polar fleece who have discovered his works and have become fanatic as a result, their faces alight with the eternal blood sport of disappointment versus rapture.

Back at the aquarium, there is still another hour to kill. So she reads a little Steinbeck. She has all of his books, except *Cannery Row*, hidden in the same desk drawer as the liquor bottle. She starts with her favorite: *The Grapes of Wrath.* A few pages here and there, just enough to get a taste of its angry beauty.

Then she moves on to the ones she hates: *Of Mice and Men*, *Tortilla Flat*, *Travels with Charley*. *East of Eden*, she's not surprised to discover, still offends and flatters her in a personal way: the succubus with the head wound, the photographs of the brothel, the corruption of the virtuous man. Finally, she peruses the book she's never known how to categorize: a retelling of the Arthurian legends, published eight years posthumously. It's a weird, childish, late-in-the-game offering, the players whittled-down archetypes who, despite their weaponry and armor and blustery shows of monarchical fealty, have no choice but to abandon themselves to love's predictable pitfalls. It's also, in her opinion, Steinbeck's most autobiographical work. There is no reason why this should be the case. The characters are not of his own invention, nor are the stories, but there it is regardless: a man writing about himself with the deluded, self-destructive certainty of an oil baron who's convinced the biggest payload is in his own backyard.

Then again, maybe it was. All these lofty motivations, but it's usually so much simpler than the creator will ever admit. Her father and the Chinese girl. Herself and Ricketts. Jean-Paul Sartre, she learned recently, became a philosopher for the sole purpose of seducing women.

"You know, I've never read any of that stuff. Not a single page."

Arthur, his hair a coppery white nest, is standing in the doorway and bouncing on his toes like a boy.

"Why not?" She closes the book and puts it away.

"I didn't like how he acted when Doc died. Breaking into the lab and burning everything controversial. It wasn't right."

She thinks of her old sketchbooks, the ones permanently lost to fire. Not right, but not wrong. The same could be said for Steinbeck's plans to improve Cannery Row after the canneries shut down. *Scatter it with fake sardine heads*, he had quipped. *Bring in some actresses to play hookers, pump in the smells of fish meal and sewage.* None of this happened, of course. Something hopeful and monumental and sincere happened instead. And this, finally, is how she knows she's won, because what is an aquarium except a gigantic heart? Fluid coming in and fluid going out, fluid passing through multiple chambers and then returning to the larger body with new offerings in tow?

"Is it time?" she asks.

"Sure is."

By the time they get to the top of the tank, the other aquarists have already arrived.

The volume of water is outrageous, the drones of the chilling and heating units unearthly. There are glaring halogen lights overhead, just like the ones the squid boats use to draw their catch to the surface. It's endless and shimmering and spooky, and she's hit with the urge to jump: an urge so strong, she has to remind herself she's too old to indulge in something so lamely symbolic. So she leans back from the railing. She cannot see what this water contains, and for a moment, there's a terrible suspicion. *Empty*, she tells herself, scanning the depths. *Completely empty.* But then she sees the familiar shape: a fish that doesn't resemble a fish so much as it does a massive severed head.

"I'm the *Mola. M-o-l-a, Mola*," Arthur sings happily. "You know. Like the banjo player's song."

She smiles at him and so do the other aquarists, who for the next minute or two do absolutely nothing. They just watch the fish's blunt circumnavigation, its rectangular dorsal and pelvic fins windshield-wiping through the water in awkward inverse. It moves behind the horizontal curtain of the water's surface very slowly, very carefully, an almost prehistoric stupidity in its eyes, an unshakable ignorance of its own place in the world and how that has or hasn't changed as a result of its captivity.

"All right," Arthur announces. "Let's go."

The aquarists spring into action. First, they usher the *Mola* out of the big tank and into a small outdoor holding tank via a gated underwater tunnel. Then, they drain the holding tank, a process that commands the better part of a half hour. When the water becomes too shallow for the *Mola* to remain vertical, one of the aquarists helps it flip onto its side and there is a brief murmur from the crowd, an expression of either recognition or sympathy. The body of the fish is a massive disk, a gigantic communion wafer, fins moving gently and without any visible signs of panic or displeasure. Its upturned eye is a ping-pong ball, its skin a crust of white, its forehead heavy and round and, from a certain angle, reminiscent of the top half of a human profile.

Then, with a sound that reverberates beneath their feet, the pipes are sealed shut. Two aquarists clad in wet suits descend a retractable ladder, step into the water, and position themselves on either side of the fish. One of them guides the sling—an expanse of blue tarp within a ring of PVC tubing—into the holding tank and the *Mola* immediately complies, situating itself calmly, voluntarily, in the exact center of the sling's perfect circle. A measurement is taken. Two hundred seventy-five kilograms. More than six hundred pounds.

And when the helicopter appears, she lets out an audible gasp because it is, in fact, a surprise.

"The fellows at the Naval Postgraduate School were happy to arrange things," Arthur explains. "Delighted, in fact."

The vehicle slides over the rooftops and into full view. All faces are upturned now, the sound growing, the column of air above the deck shuddering, the helicopter commencing its descent with the impassive self-assurance of a prehistoric bird, alarming and efficient. The *Mola*, however, remains indifferent. It simply rolls its eyes, flaps its pectorals. A cable drops from the helicopter's belly. The cable is secured to the sling. The last aquarist, a young woman who has cared for this fish since the beginning, makes her approach. She is holding a plastic bin in her hand. In the bin is a single prawn, a final offering that the *Mola* consumes with what seems like gratitude. When it is done eating, it spits some water from its lips: a sigh made visible in liquid form. Then it begins its labored, surreal ascent: a strange dot in a machine-loud sky, an insect in blue amber flying over the aquarium's roof and toward the mouth of the bay. Suddenly, some cold feet, some second thoughts, some of which she's certain the aquarists share. Say what you will about captivity—that it's involuntary and unnatural and inhumane—but at least it's cozy. Such awful things happening in the wild: sea lions approaching in a dark and swirling horde, tearing off fins and tossing them back and forth like Frisbees, not consuming what they remove but, rather, enjoying it on a level deeper and more necessary than food.

Either way, it's too late now. The sling hits the water. The *Mola* swims away. Tino rolls out a cooler full of beer, opens one, and hands it to her.

"To Margot," he says, lifting his bottle in stone-faced tribute.

"To Margot," the aquarists repeat.

She blushes and pretends to take a sip. How well she's taught them, she thinks, how much they've grown. Grown men and women, some of them with children of their own, children in the throes of familiar, formative tortures. Tonight, though, they just want a beer. A nice time. A chance to bid farewell to something they no longer have to care for. Tonight, the bay is vast and the sky is even vaster, and if they're lucky, they'll go home and dream. They'll dream of swimming in a warm, small space. Of being blind to everything save light and dark. Of hearing someone else's heartbeat. Of breathing through a pair of tiny, fleeting gills: the same ones that, as bean-sized creatures in the aquariums of our mothers' wombs, we all once had.

ACKNOWLEDGMENTS

Thanks to Julie Barer and The Book Group, for their vision and tirelessness; Ginny Smith and Penguin Press, for their faith and expertise; the Monterey Bay Aquarium, for letting me inside; Williams College and NYU, for not kicking me out; Joel Elmore, Matthew Flaming, and Abby Durden, for their talent; Jim Shepard, for his generosity; Allison Lorentzen, for opening doors; Heather Lazare, for her enthusiasm; Bill Priest, for convincing me I could get paid for this sort of thing; Christine Duncan and Fatima Chaves, for the time and space; the Benitez family, for their hospitality in the Philippines; George and Jacquie McClelland, for their patience and support; Brynn Hatton, for her artistry; Carol Hatton, for her immortal grace; Dave Hatton, for being the anti-Anders; Hazel and Agnes McClelland, for being my children; Geordie McClelland, for being my husband.

Small portions of this novel's text were adapted from or inspired by the following sources: *Renaissance Man of Cannery Row: The Life and Letters of Edward W. Ricketts*, edited by Katharine A. Rodger, The University of Alabama Press, 2002; *Breaking Through: Essays, Journals and Travelogues of Edward F. Ricketts*, edited by Katharine A. Rodger, University of California Press, 2006; *Cannery Row*, John Steinbeck, The Viking Press, 1945; *A Fascination for Fish: Adventures of an Underwater Pioneer*, David C. Powell, University of California Press, 2001.

These sources were also indispensable to my research efforts: *Between Pacific Tides*, Edward F. Ricketts, Jack Calvin, and Joel W. Hedgpeth, Stanford University Press, 1939; *The Log from the Sea of Cortez*, John Steinbeck, The Viking Press, 1941; *Beyond the Outer Shores: The Untold Odyssey of Ed Ricketts, the Pioneering Ecologist Who Inspired John Steinbeck and Joseph Campbell*, Eric Enno Tamm, Thunder's Mouth Press, 2004; *Shaping the Shoreline: Fisheries and Tourism on the Monterey Coast*, Connie Y. Chiang, University of Washington Press, 2008; *Working Days: The Journals of "The Grapes of Wrath,"* edited by Robert DeMott, Viking Penguin, 1989; *Beyond Cannery Row: Sicilian Women, Immigration, and Community in Monterey, California, 1915–99*, Carol Lynn McKibben, University of Illinois Press, 2006; *The Death and Life of Monterey Bay: A Story of Revival*, Stephen R. Palumbi and Carolyn Sotka, Island Press, 2011; *Storied Land: Community and Memory in Monterey*, John Walton, University of California Press, 2001; *Octopus and Squid: The Soft Intelligence*, Jacques-Yves Cousteau and Philippe Diolé, Doubleday, 1973.

A CONVERSATION WITH LINDSAY HATTON, AUTHOR OF *MONTEREY BAY*

You were born and raised in Monterey; you now live in Boston. Why did you choose to return to your hometown as the setting for your book?

It was mostly because of homesickness. Joan Didion puts it beautifully in *Where I Was From.* She admits to writing her first book with "the inchoate intent . . . to return me to a California I wished had been there to keep me." I feel the same way.

When writing, I was hugely aware of the burdens and potentials of place. Northern California is not only gorgeous and famous; it's also emotionally provocative. Whether they're occasional visitors or lifelong residents, people feel very strongly about that landscape, often in quite proprietary ways. I knew I'd be in for some criticism if my representation of the place didn't match readers' expectations. My treatment of the aquarium, in particular, was risky in this way, but I was willing to take that risk because it was true to what I've seen and how I feel.

Speaking of the Monterey Bay Aquarium, let's talk about your version of how it came to be. Is this a creation story or creation myth?

It's a creation myth, which is an outcome I wasn't expecting. For a long time, I thought I was writing a fictional treatment of the real-life founding legend. But the more I wrote, the more I realized I was more interested in exploring the imagined tale of heartbreak and ambition just below the factual surface: an alternate origin story that captured how it really felt to stand knee-deep in a tank full of hungry bat rays, to watch the morning fog roll in, to be alone on Cannery Row at midnight and hear the whispers of ghosts.

Still, I didn't abandon reality entirely. I was careful to stay almost completely true to certain realms of fact (the wheres/whats/whens/whos of John Steinbeck and Ed Ricketts, the marine biological detail, certain technicalities and logistics surrounding the aquarium's creation) and to allow myself wild, speculative freedom as far as Margot was concerned.

Let's talk about Margot. She's an incredibly spirited and resilient character, but also a somewhat difficult one for many readers. What was it like writing about a dark, complicated female protagonist? Were there any historical or fictional figures that inspired you?

Margot has definitely provoked some strong reactions in readers, which has been delightful—and sometimes challenging—for me to witness. As I was writing her, I enjoyed every second I spent in her presence. I loved creating someone with a multifaceted personality and complex passions and a big intellect. I loved setting her loose in the world to enact destruction and, eventually, creation.

There are two real-life women who shaped my perceptions of Margot. The first of these is Carol Steinbeck, John Steinbeck's first wife; the second is Julia Platt, a former mayor of Pacific Grove, California. Both women were ambitious, intellectual, and gleefully indifferent to the rules. I think they would have loved Margot and vice versa.

The fictional character with the most kinship to Margot is Cathy Ames (aka Kate Trask, Kate Albey, etc.), the villain in Steinbeck's *East of Eden.* Steinbeck presents a very two-dimensional, wholly evil version of this woman. It made me wonder what would happen if she was rounded out and given a soul. Would she turn out to be someone like Margot? Someone who is difficult by any measure, but also smart and sensitive and accomplished and interesting?

Unlike Margot, John Steinbeck and Ed Ricketts were both real people. How true to life did you intend their characters to be? Were you able to use any primary sources in your research of their lives?

I'm very confident in the accuracy of my portrayals of both Ricketts and Steinbeck, particularly during the years in which the novel takes place. Everything they do and say and think in the book can be linked back to primary sources like letters, journals, and essays. That being said, any attempt to confine a three-dimensional human to a two-dimensional page is bound to be incomplete. And when you add in an invented character like Margot, the prospect of achieving literal accuracy becomes even more difficult, if not impossible, but I like to think I did my best.

In part because of her unusual upbringing, Margot seems like a hybrid of an adult and a child. Did you view her time in Monterey as her coming-of-age?

I think all fifteen year-olds are child-adult hybrids, at least in their own minds. Margot is an unusual teenager in many ways, but she's also a very recognizable one, at least to me.

Maybe it's the story of a town's coming of age, not a person's. Monterey changes in the book more than Margot does, and largely by Margot's own devising. Is Margot Monterey's Ricketts? Do both relationships have that same uneasy combination of love and exploitation that takes years to manifest itself in evolution?

Margot's relationship with Ricketts is very age-inappropriate. Was there any indication that Ricketts, the real man, would have been on board with something like this?

How about if I let Steinbeck answer? Here is a quote from *About Ed Ricketts*, an essay Steinbeck wrote in eulogy to his friend:

"Sex . . . was by far [Ricketts's] greatest drive. His life was saturated with sex and he was to a very great extent preoccupied with it. . . . As far as women were concerned, he was completely without what is generally called honor."

The novel interweaves two stages in Margot's life: her young adulthood and her old age. What made you want to tell her story in this way?

I wanted the novel to showcase a curated selection of moments, not an entire life, much like an aquarium showcases specific habitats, not the entire ocean. 1940 and 1998 are when Margot experiences two of her life's most defining episodes, so it seemed both natural and intriguing to see what would happen if they were extracted from her overall biography and placed in juxtaposition. The interplay between the past and present is always a compelling notion, especially in a place like Monterey, and I think the book's structure speaks to that.

You worked at the aquarium throughout your high school years. What did you do there? What was the most interesting/surprising thing you learned?

I did a little bit of everything at the aquarium. I worked behind-the-scenes cleaning the tanks and feeding the fish. I went on collecting trips. I helped with exhibit fabrication. I also wrote and performed in some really goofy visitor programs. (The intern in the sea otter costume in chapter 8? That's me!)

One of the most surprising things I learned when I was working there had nothing to do with the animals on display; it had to do with the people who cared for them. As I mention in the novel, the aquarists are a particularly dedicated bunch. They believe wholeheartedly in the aquarium's mission and go about their work with incredible wisdom and precision. As a result, there's an almost devotional quality to the spaces behind the tanks, which was something I tried very hard to honor in my book.